A job remained to be done, a mission to be carried out

So John Kissinger and Jack Grimaldi went through the motions. But their hearts weren't in it. They'd fought side by side with Bolan for more years than they cared to remember, cheating death at every corner, yet resigned that one day, for each of them, the odds would go against them. But somehow they always thought that the Executioner was different, or at least that he would be the last of them to go.

Mack Bolan *was* Stony Man Farm; the notion of carrying on without him seemed absurd, a travesty. And yet, there was still an enemy out there to be fought, an enemy that would lose no sleep at the thought that one of their fiercest adversaries had been taken out of the game. With or without Bolan, the Kashmiri insurgents would have to be brought to justice or put out of operation.

DON PENDLETON's
MACK BOLAN.

SWORN ENEMIES

A GOLD EAGLE BOOK FROM
WORLDWIDE.

TORONTO • NEW YORK • LONDON
AMSTERDAM • PARIS • SYDNEY • HAMBURG
STOCKHOLM • ATHENS • TOKYO • MILAN
MADRID • WARSAW • BUDAPEST • AUCKLAND

First edition March 2002

ISBN 0-373-61483-7

Special thanks and acknowledgment to
Ron Renauld for his contribution to this work.

SWORN ENEMIES

Printed in U.S.A.

To be both religious and tolerant is a leader's
greatest asset. It is far easier and more effective
to win over one's enemies off the field of battle
than to have to defeat them in the course of war.
But if it comes to war, the time for tolerance
is past.

—attributed to Shavaji Bhonsole

I've seen more blood shed in the name of God,
by his various names, than any other cause. Spare
me the hypocrites who kneel one day and butcher
the next.

—Mack Bolan

CHAPTER ONE

Outskirts of Kottayam,
Kerala State, South India

"It happened very fast, apparently," Nhajsib Wal explained. "They were dragged from their car and stripped to their undershorts, then shot through the head and shoved into the ditch."

Mack Bolan stared out the rear window of the Colwyss-8A helicopter hovering fifty yards above where the bodies had been discovered. Below, the two dead men lay like discarded puppets, limbs splayed and twisted at unnatural angles. One had come to a rest facedown in the dirt, but the other stared lifelessly upward, past the knot of Indian authorities mingling around the crime scene. Bolan locked briefly on the man's vacant, unchanging gaze, then glanced away. Deep within the depths of his cold blue eyes sparked a blaze of fury. Bolan was no stranger to death—in his chosen work it was an almost everyday occurrence. Yet, unlike all the soldiers, paramedics, coroners and policemen who, of necessity, learned to view death's victims with clinical detachment, when it came to the butchered innocent, Bolan steadfastly refused to deny his sense of outrage. Savagery like this, he vowed with the same certainty with which he breathed the hot summer air around him, wouldn't go unpunished. If it were humanly possible on his part, the innocent would be avenged.

The Executioner's grim reverie was interrupted by a beeping at his waist. He unclipped the cell phone from his belt and took the call.

Meanwhile, up in the helicopter's front passenger seat, Nhajsib Wal, a deceptively youthful-looking member of India's Intelligence Bureau, pointed out the window.

"There's a clearing over there," he told the pilot, "just beyond that dike."

"On it." Jack Grimaldi, his ever-present ball cap tipped back on his head, shifted course away from the crime scene.

Like Bolan, Grimaldi had introduced himself to Nhajsib Wal under an assumed name back at the IB field office in Kottayam. He'd presented identification and credentials declaring he was part of a special U.S. Secret Service task force assigned to monitor security during the President's weeklong peacekeeping trip to South Asia. The deception was routine and not that far from the truth. Grimaldi's and Bolan's mission was indeed centered around protecting the President, whose itinerary would include stops in Maldives, Bombay, New Delhi, Islamabad and the Kashmiri capital of Srinagar, where heads of state would be meeting in hopes of defusing the latest escalation of hostilities between India, Pakistan and Kashmiri separatists. The aegis under which Grimaldi and Bolan operated, however, was not that of the Secret Service or even the CIA, but rather a smaller, elite core of operatives so covert their very existence was known by only a handful of men, one of them the President himself.

They were operatives for Stony Man Farm.

Also like Bolan, Grimaldi was particularly troubled by a certain aspect of the killings.

"They were priests?" the pilot murmured aloud. "As in Christian?"

"Yes," Wal replied. "Here in Kottayam, Christians outnumber Muslims and even Hindus. It goes back to the time of the Apostle Thomas. He roamed all along the Malabar coast, preaching the gospel. He found listeners."

"Well, somebody wasn't listening today," Grimaldi observed ruefully, leaving the bodies behind in favor of the clearing Wal had directed him toward. They were in the countryside outside Kottayam, a coastal Indian city barely a hundred miles from the southernmost tip of the subcontinent. Most of the surrounding rural expanse was given over to tea farms and rice paddies, but there were also a few scattered palm trees. Half a mile down the dirt road where the bodies had been discovered, a church spire marked where the priests had been driving from when they were ambushed.

"That was Cowboy," Bolan told Grimaldi as he clipped his phone back onto his belt. "Just got in from Sri Lanka. He's at the safehouse in Alleppey."

"Want me to swing back and pick him up?" Grimaldi asked.

Bolan nodded. "After you drop us off."

"No problem."

Wal looked puzzled. As the Colwyss-8A began to lower toward the clearing, he asked Grimaldi, "You have an agent called Cowboy? Or is that a code name?"

Bolan grinned faintly. "More of a nickname."

Before he could say more, there was a sharp, metallic clang outside the chopper. Almost immediately the aircraft began to pitch and wobble.

"Incoming!" Grimaldi jockeyed with the controls. There was another clang. "Somebody's using us for target practice!"

Grimaldi fought to keep the chopper aloft. Bolan and Nhajsib Wal focused on the terrain below, trying to trace the shot's trajectory. Some rice threshers in the nearby fields were looking up from their work, but their attention had been clearly drawn by the chopper's erratic flight rather than any activity on the ground.

"How we doing?" Bolan asked Grimaldi as he continued to scan the countryside.

"Got a handle on it, at least for now," Grimaldi called out. Already the chopper was stabilizing. "Must've nicked one of the rotors. Once we set down I'm gonna have to take a—"

"There!" Wal interrupted, indicating a bluff that overlooked the clearing. Half-hidden in the brush at the edge of the peak was a short man wearing a khaki tracksuit and a white skullcap. He was taking aim at the chopper with a high-powered rifle. Before Grimaldi could take evasive action, a bullet smashed through the side window and bored into a seat cushion inches from where Bolan was sitting.

"That does it!" Grimaldi banked the chopper sharply to the right, then switched course toward the bluff. "That bastard's toast!"

The Colwyss, an Indian-made helicopter modeled after the old Bell Model 47, was unarmed, so it was left to Wal and Bolan to provide some kind of firepower. The Indian drew a Walther PPK pistol, while Bolan unleathered his standard .44 Magnum Desert Eagle.

As the chopper swept toward him, the sniper stepped warily back from the bluff's edge. Rather than attempt another shot, he slung the rifle over his shoulder, leaped onto a dust-covered Suzuki dirt bike and kick-started the engine. Smoke spewed from the muffler as the bike lurched forward, front wheel springing briefly into the air. Moments later, leaning forward over the handlebars, the man was weaving through a ragged tangle of shoulder-high vegetation.

"Stay on him!" Bolan shouted.

"You bet your ass I will," Grimaldi said.

As the helicopter swept across the bluff, Bolan took aim through his shattered window. Below, the sniper slipped in and out of view amid the foliage. Bolan fired a few shots but quickly realized that between the chopper's vibration and the biker's varying course, he wasn't likely to take the man down from the air. Up front, Wal came to the same conclusion after squeezing off a round from his Walther.

The Indian turned to Grimaldi. "Can you pull ahead and drop down in front of him?"

"If we were on some kind of flatland, sure, no problem," Grimaldi said, "but this guy's like Brer Rabbit in the bramble down there. If I try to set down in that stuff, I'm gonna snag and wind up doing cartwheels."

"It thins out a little up ahead there," Bolan said, tracking the direction the biker was taking. "Stay with him and ease down as close as you can."

"That I can manage."

Once he'd put the chopper into a slight descent, Grimaldi glanced over his shoulder and saw Bolan unlatching his door. "Going somewhere?"

Bolan nodded. "House call."

"Are you nuts?"

Wal eyed Bolan warily. "Your partner is right. It's too dangerous!"

Bolan looked past Wal at the pilot. "Just do it!"

"Just do it," Grimaldi repeated sarcastically, shaking his head. "Like we're doing a Nike commercial or something."

With the sun behind them, Grimaldi found himself chasing the chopper's shadow, as well as the man on the bike. The sniper was quick to take advantage, altering his course to keep himself veiled by the ever-moving shadow. Frustrated, Wal let loose with a few more errant rounds from his Walther. Bolan, however, had already holstered his .44 and framed himself in the chopper's opened doorway. He eyed the man below as they swooped closer. Soon he could make out details of the rifle slung across the biker's back. It looked like a scope-mounted Weatherby bolt action; definitely sniper material. The man also had a handgun in the holster strapped to his right hip, but he was too intent on negotiating the terrain before him to concern himself with firing at his pursuers.

"A little lower," Bolan called out over his shoulder, "then ease ahead of him."

"Yeah, I've seen those old barnstorming movies, too," Grimaldi deadpanned, jockeying the controls. "Preparing to unload passenger..."

Bending to a crouch, Bolan drew in a breath and focused on the dirt bike, now directly below him. Once Grimaldi began to pull ahead, Bolan exhaled and flung himself from the helicopter. It was a fifteen-foot drop, and he timed it almost perfectly, coming down hard on the biker's right shoulder and knocking him from the bike. The Suzuki sped out from underneath him, bounding off a rock into a small tree before the engine finally died.

Back on the ground, Bolan and the sniper tumbled to a stop in a tangled heap near a clot of brush. Bolan had caught an elbow to the ribs that knocked the wind from his lungs. Sprawled on his back, he gasped for air, trying to blink away the sweep of stars flooding his vision. The sniper had lost his skullcap, and his long hair tumbled wildly about his head as he staggered to his feet. Silhouetted by the sun, the man loomed unsteadily over Bolan. He drew a 9 mm Tanarmi pistol and took aim at the Executioner's face. He was about to pull the trigger when Bolan lunged forward, knocking the gun free; it fell to the ground a few yards from the man's fallen rifle.

The sniper threw himself at Bolan, grabbing for the Executioner's holstered .44. Bolan's plan had been to take the biker alive for questioning, but at this point his only concern was survival. Still fighting for breath, he grappled his opponent back to the ground. Unable to grab hold of the Desert Eagle, the biker shifted his hands to Bolan's throat and began squeezing.

Bolan became instantly lightheaded. He knew he'd have to act quickly or the fight would be over as quickly as it had begun. He had one leg bent at the knee and instinctively brought the knee up, driving it into the other man's groin.

The sniper groaned, loosening his grip on Bolan's throat. The soldier remained on the offensive. He cocked his right arm, then shoved it forward, leading hard with the heel of his opened palm. He caught the sniper squarely just above the upper lip. With a wrenching crunch, the man's nose imploded in a shower of blood. Splinters of cartilage burst through inner sinus cavities into his brain.

As the man toppled to the ground, Bolan kicked away the fallen gun and unholstered his Desert Eagle. He wouldn't be needing it, however. The sniper lay still in the dirt. Bolan checked for a pulse to make sure he was dead, then regarded the man, whose olive-hued face was awash with blood, obscuring his features. Weaponless and stripped of his skullcap, there was little to suggest that he might be anything but a motocross enthusiast. Bolan knew better, however. He crouched over the man and was frisking him for identification when he heard sounds in the brush.

Someone was headed toward him.

Bolan raised his .44 and drew a bead on the section

of trail the sound was coming from. Soon he was able to discern the outline of a man advancing slowly through the brush toward him, gun in hand.

"All clear!" Bolan called out, relieved. It was Grimaldi. "Over here."

Grimaldi emerged from the brush, followed by Wal. The Stony Man pilot whistled low at the sight of the dead man.

"Nice job," he told Bolan.

"I'd rather've been able to get a few answers out of him," Bolan confessed.

Grimaldi leaned over the dead man's rifle and looked it over. "Nice condition," he observed. "Top-notch scope, too. We're lucky he didn't bring us down."

"We probably took him by surprise," Bolan ventured. "Just enough to throw his game off."

"Could be."

"How's the chopper?"

"Our friend here took a nice bite out of one of the blades, not to mention the window and back seat," the Stony Man pilot reported, "but I should be able to patch up things while I'm refueling."

Bolan quickly finished searching the dead man's pockets. "Nothing."

"Well, I figure he was in on the killings somehow," Grimaldi speculated. "You know, one of those dummies who gets their rocks off coming back to the crime scene."

"Maybe," Bolan said.

Wal picked up the dead man's gun, sniffed the barrel and said, "This wasn't used on the priests."

"Not fired?" Bolan asked.

Wal shook his head and came over to inspect the body. "I don't recognize him, either," he said.

"Maybe there's something with the bike," Bolan suggested.

"Already checked," Grimaldi said. "It was hotwired."

"We can probably figure where it was stolen from, but not much more," Bolan theorized. "If he's mujahideen, he wouldn't have stolen it anywhere near where they're staying."

"Mujahideen," Wal repeated. His features contorted with angry determination. "They must not be allowed to get away with this."

"I'll second that," Grimaldi said.

"It won't be easy," the Indian cautioned. "You don't know these people. This man here has probably already been replaced, and there are no doubt more waiting behind him."

"We know the type," Bolan said, "all too well."

The mujahideen were Kashmiri insurgents, self-proclaimed holy warriors for Islam determined to wrest free that part of their country under Indian control. Not content with mere rhetoric, for years the mujahideen had carried out acts of terrorism in their homeland, more than a thousand miles to the north. And in recent months they had begun to operate outside their borders, as well, perpetrating acts of sabotage throughout the subcontinent. More than sixty people had been killed in various incidents, most of them Indian, most of them innocent bystanders claimed by car bombs or other explosives detonated

near embassies, military installations and other sites
frequented by the mujahideen's avowed enemies.
Two Americans had been struck down as well, including a high-ranking envoy from the State Department dismembered the past weekend by a pipe bomb
planted under the seat of a taxi that had picked him
up after a formal dinner in the heart of New Delhi's
upscale restaurant district. The mujahideen were
quick to claim responsibility, stating that their next
target would be the American President, who had la-
beled the group as terrorists out to subvert the peace
process.

"Okay, let's take this from the top and see where
we stand. First," Bolan said, "IB intercepts reports
the mujahideen have sent men across the Ghats into
Kottayam, which makes it pretty clear they want to
take a crack at the President the minute he's out of
the starting gate here in India."

Wal nodded. "And our people in RAW passed
along the report directly to your Secret Service."

"RAW?" Grimaldi asked.

"Research and Analysis Wing," Wal explained.
"Right hand to the Intelligence Bureau."

"Okay, gotcha," Grimaldi said. "At any rate, once
the report came Stateside, we got thrown into the
mix."

"You were briefing us about the mujahideen when
the call came in about the priests," Bolan continued.
"You said something about their ringleader being
here with them."

The Indian nodded. "Dehri Neshah, yes. That is
not officially confirmed, but it is Neshah's mark to be

on hand at the front lines whenever there is an incident. He is not like most leaders, who stand back and let others take all the risks.''

Bolan and Grimaldi exchanged a look. While Bolan wasn't the de facto head of Stony Man Farm and its action teams, he had been as responsible for the group's founding every bit as Neshah was for his particular cell of the mujahideen. And, also like Neshah, when it came to battling the enemy in the theater of war, Bolan never gave any orders he wasn't willing to carry out himself. He was among that select breed that led as much by example as command. It was Bolan's hope that this shared trait would help him to get into the mind of Neshah and find a way to bring him down.

"Things start to get fuzzy for me with this priest thing," Bolan went on. "The mujahideen have grievances with a lot of people, but not the church. At least not that I know of.''

"As I was telling your friend," Wal conjectured, "Christianity here in India was introduced from abroad. And your President is a Christian, yes?''

"He campaigned as one, I know that much," Grimaldi interjected.

Bolan added, "I think he has plans to attend services tomorrow in Maldives.''

"There you have it, then," Wal said. "I say the mujahideen killed the priests to send a message to your President. They are Muslims, after all.''

"Being Muslims doesn't make them terrorists," Bolan was quick to assert.

"Of course not," the Indian responded. "But they

are extremists, and like all zealots, they recognize only one way of worship—their own. All others be damned.''

''If this was their doing, then wouldn't they have left behind some kind of statement?'' Grimaldi said. ''You know, something on paper, some kind of proclamation to make sure they got credit?''

''Perhaps our men have found something near the bodies,'' the Indian said. ''Or perhaps the mujahideen are waiting until the killings are made official to come forward. With the car bombing in New Delhi, they waited until it was on the news.''

''All right,'' Bolan said impatiently. ''For the sake of argument, let's say this was their doing. We can worry about their reasoning later. Right now we need to find them. That needs to be our focus.''

''Understood,'' Wal said. ''That is IB's top priority, as well.''

''If the mujahideen are behind the killings,'' Grimaldi reasoned, ''they had to have had a staging area somewhere around here. I say we get hold of topo maps, SAT-INTEL photos—anything that will help narrow down possible places where they could be holed up. Hopefully, by the time we do that, I'll have the bird back up and running and we can do some aerial recon.''

''Works for me,'' Bolan said. He looked out at the rolling terrain that stretched out in all directions from them. ''We'll have a lot of ground to cover, though.''

''Perhaps not as much as you think,'' Wal called out.

Bolan and Grimaldi glanced over and saw the Indian crouched over the dead man. He was holding the man's right hand, sniffing his fingers.

"What do you smell?" Grimaldi asked. "Cordite?"

"No, not cordite." Wal shook his head, lowering the hand. "Coconuts," he said. "I smell coconuts."

Slowly, the Indian shifted his gaze, staring out past the rice paddies to a gently sloping hillock several miles away. Tea was the primary crop in the higher elevations, and the hill was green with leaves fluttering in the hot summer breeze. But there was one plot of land that stood out from the rest, not only because of its groves of coconut palms—the only ones within five miles of where Nhajsib Wal was standing—but because of the series of scattered buildings whose high-ceilinged roofs protruded above the surrounding vegetation. They were *kalaris,* classrooms devoted to the study of *kathakali* and *kalaripayattu.* Before being recruited into the Intelligence Bureau, Nhajsib Wal had studied at the facility under the guidance of his uncle, Ziarat Wal, a master of the highly disciplined arts for which the Indian state of Kerala was famous.

Staring at the distant buildings, Wal felt a chill run down his spine. If, as he suspected, the dead man at his feet had come from the school, there was a chance the mujahideen had overtaken the grounds to use as its base of operations in Kottayam. Under his breath, he whispered a prayer for his uncle's safety, as well as that of the rest of those attending the school. In his heart, however, he feared that it was already too late.

CHAPTER TWO

Academy of Arts in the Ghats,
Outskirts of Kottayam

Ziarat Wal looked away from the short sticks being held out to him. Eyeing his tormentor, he solemnly shook his head. Enraged, the other man lashed out, striking Ziarat across the face. The sticks raised a fierce welt on the Indian's cheek and cracked the skin. A trickle of blood ran down his cheek.

"Fight!" Vargadrum Shili repeated. He held the sticks out before him again. Again Ziarat refused to take them.

"I am but a teacher," he explained. He spoke slowly in Urdu, the Kashmiri language he'd heard spoken most frequently by his captors. "You are clearly a warrior. It would be no contest."

"You are far too modest." Shili laughed. The Kashmiri pointed up at the brick walls of the *kalari*. "These pictures tell a different story."

Mounted above the rows of crossed swords and small metal shields mounted on the wall were many paintings and photographs. Several of them featured Ziarat. In one, a painting made several years ago, he sat on a bench, holding both sword and shield as he stared outward with a look of quiet dignity and pride. His young nephew, Nhajsib Wal, stood beside him. Barely twenty, Nhajsib was already a master in the martial art of *kalaripayattu*. Vargadrum Shili, however, was more intrigued in a framed photograph next to the painting. There, attired in military garb, his chest festooned with ribbons and medals, was Ziarat as a young army officer.

"That is you, yes?" Shili asked.

When Ziarat remained silent, the Kashmiri turned and looked at the handful of boys and young men who'd been corraled into a corner of the room. Dwarfed by the armed men on either side of them, the youths wore only white dhotis. Earlier this morning they had come with Ziarat to the *kalari* to begin their morning exercises, only to find the mujahideen had slipped onto the academy grounds during the night and taken over the building. Since then they had been held hostage, confined to this one small room. Rations—tea and boiled rice heaped on palm leaves— had been brought a few minutes ago, after which Vargadrum Shili had joined them for the first time, the sweet aroma of toddy on his breath. Shili was young, no more than thirty, but he seemed to be the one in charge, at least of the two men watching over Wal and his students. The power had clearly gone to his head as much as the toddy, and for several minutes now he had been trying to bait Wal into a fight. Wal's steadfast refusal was testing the Kashmiri's patience.

"Your 'teacher,' it seems, is quite the hero," Shili told the students. "Has he told you about the war and how he won all these commendations? I'm sure he must have. It's what all soldiers do."

None of the youths responded. Most of them spoke Malayaham and had no understanding of Urdu. Mistaking their silence for ignorance, Shili took the sticks over to the photograph and tapped at several of the medals on Wal's chest, medals unique to one particular conflict in India's brief history.

"Thirty years ago India invaded East Pakistan, the land you now know as Bangladesh. Like cowards, your teacher and his fellow soldiers waited until winter to attack, when the snow was so deep that China could not hope to cross the Himalayas to intervene. They beat down the forces West Pakistan had flown in to restore order in the land. They stole the land from Pakistan."

"West Pakistan flew in forces to terrorize those who wished for independence," Ziarat Wal countered calmly, again in Urdu. "They killed civilians, raped women, forced refugees to flee to India by the millions. We sought only to make it safe for them to return."

"So you say," Shili scoffed. He turned back to the youths. "India's only desire then was to weaken Pakistan. Today, all these years later, that is still their only desire."

"Lies," Wal said.

Shili ignored the Indian and continued to rail, "Only now, instead of in Bangladesh, India tries to beat back Pakistan to the north. They want to push back the Line of Control and seize all of Jumma and Kashmir! To seize it for themselves!"

"India seeks only to claim what is rightfully hers," Wal told Shili. "When our country first came into being, it was the wish of the Maharaja that Kashmir become one with India. Not Pakistan."

"But what of the people of Kashmir?" Shili countered. "Did we have a say in our fate? Have we ever been shown the same consideration as those in Bangladesh? Has anyone ever listened to *our* cries for independence?"

"If you have grievances, there are proper channels through which to address them," Wal said. "There is no need for you to come here, to a place of learning, and terrorize youngsters who have no part, no say in these matters."

"There's that word again," Vargadrum Shili said. "'Terrorize.' When your forefathers rallied for India's independence from Britain, did they call themselves terrorists? No, they called themselves freedom fighters. And that is what we, the men of Kashmir, are, as well. We are fighting for freedom from the oppression of India!"

"So *you* say," Wal countered echoing Shili's earlier argument. "And let us not forget that these Pakistanis you speak so nobly of would prefer to fly their own flag over Kashmir, not yours."

"Leave Pakistan out of this," Shili said. "We will deal with Pakistan once we have dealt with India."

"Then you are only pretending to be their ally, is that it?" Wal countered. "Are they aware of this? Do they know that the money they slip into your hands under the table will one day be used against them?"

Shili fell silent a moment, then quickly changed the

subject. "Since we set foot on these grounds, no one has been 'terrorized,'" he said. "No one has been hurt, of course, with the exception of my tapping you on the cheek for refusing to fight me man to man."

"What about the gunshots we heard earlier in the other buildings?" Wal asked. "How do we know you have not killed any of the others?"

Shili shrugged. "You have my word."

"Your word means nothing to me." Wal fairly spit the words at his captor.

Shili's face reddened. Once more he swung the small sticks, striking Wal again in the face. The cut on the Indian's face widened, deepening the flow of blood down his cheek. Wal struggled to blink away the involuntary tears the blow had brought to his eyes.

"Why are you here?" he asked calmly, his voice thick, hoarse. "What do you want from us?"

Shili smiled. "Fight me and perhaps I will tell you."

"Why is it so important to you that we fight?"

"Perhaps like you, I am not only a soldier, but also an educator." He pointed to the youths in the corner. "Perhaps I want to provide them a glimpse of the future."

"I do not understand," Wal said.

"You are India—I am Kashmir," Shili explained. "You are yesterday—I am tomorrow. Together, we can demonstrate how things will be."

"So now you are not just a 'freedom fighter,'" Wal surmised. "Now you want control of not only Kashmir but all of India."

"Perhaps I exaggerate," Shili said. "Let us take it

one battle at a time. For now, let us fight the battle for Kashmir.''

Wal regarded the Kashmiri. Vargadrum Shili wasn't only half his age, but a head taller and at least eighty pounds heavier. And yet Wal had every confidence that, were he to take the sticks—one form of weaponry in the practice of *kalaripayattu*—he could easily throttle the other man in a matter of seconds. After all, in the thirty years since he had first taken up the martial art, Ziarat Wal had come to be recognized as one of its greatest practitioners, rivaling even the vaunted Nairs, those of the Keralan warrior caste whose ancestors had first developed *kalaripayattu* centuries ago, when they were India's equivalent to the samurai of Japan. But what purpose, other than asserting his pride, would defeating the Kashmiri serve? There were another two thugs here in the room, each armed with a submachine gun, each clearly eager for an excuse to use it. Were he to humiliate their leader, there would likely be swift retaliation, and it would be directed not only against him. Looking past Shili, Wal saw the boys and young men of the academy trembling in the corner, their small, wiry bodies glistening as much with the sweat of fear as with the ceremonial oil they wore as part of their regimen. They were his students, their safety his responsibility. He wasn't about to incite a bloodbath.

Besides, though he had asked why the mujahideen had come, Wal already knew the reason; there was no need to fight for an explanation.

Kottayam was not only close to the coast, but it was also less than three hundred miles from the island

Republic of Maldives, where the U.S. President would be spending the first day of his trip to South Asia. The mujahideen despised America almost as much as they did India, so it only stood to reason that they would seize upon the President's visit as a call to action. And whatever their scheme, what better staging area in Kottayam than the academy? Isolated far off in the hills, the school, by design, had neither phone nor mail service. There wasn't another delivery scheduled until the middle of next week, and there would be no visitation by the youths' parents until the following weekend. Here, at least for the next few days, the mujahideen could go about their business, whatever it was, without anyone being the wiser.

What puzzled Wal most about this group wasn't its agenda, but rather its leadership. In talking with his nephew, Nhajsib Wal, it had seemed clear that the Intelligence Bureau expected any mujahideen terrorist activity in the area to be masterminded and carried out by their leader, Dehri Neshah. And yet, five hours into their captivity, Wal had yet to encounter anyone passing out orders save for the half-drunken lout in front of him. Could it be that Neshah had stationed himself elsewhere on the grounds? It didn't seem likely. From what Wal had read of the man, Neshah wasn't the sort of fool to delegate authority to a man who would drink while on duty. No, the likelier explanation was that something had happened to Neshah. If that was the case, it might bode well for the world in general, but Wal feared it could wind up meaning death for himself and those of the academy.

"Well?" Vargadrum Shili taunted. "Will you fight

me or would you have your disciples think you're a coward?''

''No!'' One of the younger boys—who apparently understood a smattering of Urdu—suddenly broke clear of the others, hands clutched into small fists. ''Ziaratashan is a hero, not a coward!''

The boy was about to leap into the air when one of Shili's cohorts stepped forward and swung hard with the stock of his submachine gun. Letting out a pained cry, the youth reeled to the floor, clutching his side where he'd been struck. Some of the other boys were about to come to his aid when their way was blocked by the other Kashmiri. Together the two soldiers fired several rounds into the dirt at the boys' feet, then raised their guns and aimed them threateningly. The youths shrank back, rejoining the others. Ziarat Wal was furious.

''You terrorize children and yet *I* am supposed to be the coward?'' Wal railed at Shili. ''Have you no decency? No shame? Were you raised by jackals?''

Again Shili's face reddened. His hand went to his holster. He drew a Coonan .357 Magnum pistol and aimed it at the instructor. Wal ignored the gun and glared defiantly at Shili. For several seconds the two men faced off, the Kashmiri's finger on the trigger of his automatic.

Suddenly, the door to the *kalari* opened. Another of the mujahideen strode in, carrying a pair of high-powered binoculars. Shili turned, lowering his gun. ''What is it, Shazad?''

''There is a problem,'' he said.

''Another problem?'' he shouted, venting his rage

on the man with the binoculars. "What is it this time?"

Shazad cautiously strode forward and murmured in Shili's ear. As he listened, the Kashmiri's features hardened. Once the news had been delivered, he stabbed his gun back in his holster and followed the other man out of the room without so much as acknowledging Wal or the other hostages.

Wal moved over to the injured boy and felt the youth's ribs. He could tell that several of them had been broken. He turned to the gunman who had struck the boy, telling him, "He needs medical attention."

The gunman reached to a ledge built out of the closest wall, where several folded, fresh-washed dhotis were neatly stacked. He took two of the cloth shorts and tossed them to Ziarat.

"Medical attention," Wal repeated. "He needs to see a doctor."

The gunman shook his head and pantomimed wrapping the cloth around the boy's chest. "Do it yourself," he said.

By now the boy was sobbing. Wal dabbed at his tears, then used one of the dhotis to bind the youth's chest. The boy grimaced.

"Be strong," Wal whispered to him.

The boy nodded tearfully. He took the other dhoti and wiped the blood trickling down the side of Wal's face. "Why did you not fight back, Ziaratashan?" he whispered back.

"The wise warrior chooses his battles," Wal told the boy. "When the right moment comes, *that* is when he fights...."

As HE FOLLOWED Shazad from the building, Varga-drum Shili drew in a deep breath, trying to settle his nerves. What he really wanted was another drink, but he'd already drained his flask and had yet to find the opportunity to refill it without the others seeing. Not that he cared what they thought, he assured himself.

There was another *kalari* situated higher up the hillside. Leading up to it was a winding path made of crushed stone that ground noisily under the men's feet. At one point Shili saw a serpent slither out of their way, vanishing into the brush.

"The monsoons have yet to come and already the snakes are taking to high ground," he said lightly, attempting a smile. "Maybe they know something we don't, hmm?"

Shazad, still bristling from Shili's earlier tongue-lashing, shrugged faintly. "Perhaps," he muttered. Taking advantage of a narrowing in the path, he lengthened his stride so that he could walk ahead of Shili instead of beside him. Shili was about to chastise Shazad yet again but thought better of it. As the path wound back on itself, he fumed silently and glanced downhill, past the buildings of the academy. In the days of the raj, schools for *kalarikath* and *kalaripay-attu* were funded by the crown and had no need to concern themselves with operating budgets. But times had changed, and now, where there had once been cricket fields and riding pastures, the lower grounds had been given over to tightly clustered tea bushes and row after row of stately coconut palms. The school was run by private hands these days and de-pended on crop sales to remain in operation. Hired families worked the land and lived in field barracks far from the academy; as such they weren't yet aware of the mujahideen's takeover, but Vargadrum was sure that would likely change soon enough, leaving him with yet another problem to contend with.

He licked his lips, aching for a drink. Everything was happening so fast. First it was the news that Dehri Neshah had been taken prisoner, forcing the mujahideen to raid the academy without him. Now, while Shili's brothers were off trying to free Neshah, he had been left in charge. He'd thought it would be an idle time, after which his brothers would return with Neshah. Instead, everything seemed to be coming apart. The toll of the arduous, months-long trek south from Kashmir was beginning to show itself. The men were restless, irritated by a lack of sleep, the oppressive heat and the insolence of their prisoners. And—given Neshah's capture before he could get his hands on a guidance system—there was still uncertainty as to whether they should attempt to use the missile launcher. If they *were* going to use it, then when? What if his brothers didn't return by the agreed-upon time to fire the weapon? Should he proceed without them? It was so hard to know.

The path finally brought Shili and Shazad to a courtyard outside the upper *kalari*. Near the front steps, the statue of a Bengal tiger loomed majestically at the head of a reflecting pool filled with koi fish and lily pads. Shili was staring into the carved eyes of the stone beast, mesmerized by the creature's lifelike gaze, when he suddenly became aware of a faint, putrid odor.

"What is that smell?"

Shazad sniffed the air. "The wisteria?" he said, indicating the flowering vine that drooped from a pergola extending across the far end of the courtyard.

"No, not the flowers." Shili tried breathing through his mouth, but the foul smell continued to assail him, growing stronger by the moment. He looked around the courtyard, his eyes wild.

"The woman," he snapped angrily. "What did they do with her?"

"They took her downhill and buried her, as you wished," Shazad responded.

"Did you see them do it?" Shili railed. "I tell you, I smell rotting flesh!"

Shazad sniffed the air again. "All I smell are flowers and the pond," he said. "No corpses. Besides, the woman was taken away right after she was shot. There was no time for her to have begun to rot."

"I'm telling you, I smell her! Where is she?" Shili paced around the reflecting pool, looking in all directions. "Where is she!"

Shazad watched Shili's manic pacing, more amused than concerned by the man's theatrics. "None of us have had the chance to bathe since coming down from the Ghats," he suggested, trying to keep a straight face. "Perhaps that would account for the smell."

Shili instinctively craned his neck and was about to sniff under his arm when he stopped himself and whirled, catching the half smile on Shazad's face.

"You find this amusing? Is that it?"

"No," Shazad claimed.

"Then what are you smiling at?" Shili demanded.

"I wasn't smiling," Shazad insisted.

"I'm not blind!" Shili snapped. "I know that look!"

"What look?" Shazad shouted back. He'd had enough of Shili's bullying. "First your nose. Now your eyes are betraying you, too. I wasn't smiling, and there is no smell of rotting bodies here. You must be imagining things."

"Oh, no, you don't." Shili went to his holster, pulling out his pistol. "I know this game, Shazad."

Shazad stared at the gun barrel pointed at his chest, then looked up. "Vargadrum, please…"

"You play tricks on my senses, then pretend you don't notice the same things I do," Shili ranted. "It's a plot. You want me to think I've lost my mind."

"No!" Shazad protested. "Why would I—?"

"If you can't convince me, you'll convince the others," Shili said. "Why? So you can take control! You're all plotting against me!"

"That's not—"

Shazad's voice was drowned out by the blast from Shili's weapon. The bullet ripped through the Kashmiri's heart, killing him instantly. Before he could fall to the ground, Shili rushed forward, jerking Shazad by the collar of his tracksuit so that he splashed headlong into the reflecting pool, scattering the koi fish. The body disappeared a moment, then bobbed to the surface, facedown, turning the water red.

The shot drew two gunmen running from the *kalari*. They stopped short at the sight of Shili standing over their floating comrade. Shili turned to them, still holding his gun. He aimed it away from them, however.

"We have a chain of command here," he told them, forcing himself to remain calm, in charge of his emotions. "It must be honored at all costs. Is that understood?"

The other men stood silently. They were both younger than Shili, and far younger than Shazad. There was no petulance in their gazes, no trace of mutiny. If anything, Shili saw that they were afraid, intimidated. He had them where he wanted them.

"Get rid of the body." He strode past, then paused in the doorway and glared back at them over his shoulder. "And do a better job than you did with the woman."

Without awaiting a response, Shili went inside and passed through an inner hall to the main chamber, used by the academy's *kathakali* troupe, a dramatic ensemble that employed some of the movements of *kalaripayattu*. Theatrical masks and costumes were piled in heaps on a row of benches, and along the far wall were makeup tables filled with wigs, jars of pigment and face paint. It took some looking, but on one of the tables Shili managed to find a ceramic cup half-filled with a creamy liquid that looked much like the coconut toddy he'd been drinking all day. Shili eagerly tipped the cup to his lips and took a sip. As he swallowed, however, he was suddenly overcome once more by the smell of carrion. He turned his head to one side and spit the liquid from his mouth. He threw the cup aside, then hacked several times, trying to rid himself of every drop he'd just ingested. But it was no use. Now he could not only smell death, but could taste it, as well.

"What is this?" Shili railed. "What did they do with her!"

The Kashmiri wiped his tongue on the sleeve of his tracksuit as he staggered about the chamber, tossing masks and costumes asunder in his search for the body. It was nowhere to be found, but off in the corner he saw the woman's sewing machine, still lying on the floor where he'd tipped it over this morning. A bolt of shiny red fabric trailed from the machine, snagged where the woman had been trying to sew a seam at the time she'd been shot. She had claimed to be the troupe's head seamstress, so Shili and his brothers had assumed she would be able to quickly turn a few existing costumes into something that could pass for the clerical garb worn by local priests. But the woman had kept trembling and jamming the machine, time and again, until Shili had finally lost patience and put a bullet through her head, forcing his brothers to look elsewhere for disguises to wear in hopes of freeing Dehri Neshah from the prison where he had been taken into custody.

Shili jerked at the bolt of red cloth. In the process he inadvertently tugged the sewing machine toward him, revealing a splotch of darkened blood marking where the woman had fallen. Trailing away from the spot was a crimson smear, no doubt left by the woman's body as it was dragged away. He dropped to his knees and crouched over the bloodstains. They were already dry to the touch, and didn't carry the smell of death that continued to gnaw at Shili.

"Enough!" the Kashmiri shrieked. "Enough, enough, enough!"

Shili leaped to his feet and fled the chamber. He bounded up the staircase leading to the observation tower, trying to put the smell behind him. It worked. By the time he reached the top step, the smell had dissipated. Pausing to catch his breath, Shili glanced out and saw another Kashmiri eyeing him strangely, a cell phone in one hand, binoculars in the other.

The other man quickly finished his call, then asked Shili, "Where is Shazad?"

Shili offered up a twisted smile. "He is in a conference," he replied, "with God."

"The commotion downstairs—"

"The commotion downstairs is none of your concern," Shili interrupted. He moved past the other man and stared southward. Stretching beyond the academy grounds in all directions were endless rice paddies interlaced by small canals. So much of the land was flat and muddy from irrigation that the academy, with its gentle hills and green-leaved crops, looked something like an emerald island rising up from a dull brown sea. A few miles away, however, there was another overgrown hillock, blocking Shili's view of the Catholic church save for a tip of the cross mounted atop its spire.

"That's where Shazad saw the helicopter?" Shili said, pointing to the top of the distant rise.

"Yes," the other man said. "Hafeez was there with his motorcycle. He was going to dispose of the priests' bodies as your brothers requested, but the authorities had already arrived. Before he could leave, the helicopter appeared. He fired at it, then got on his bike and tried to flee.''

''But he wasn't able to get away?''

The other man shook his head. ''As best we could see, a man dropped down on him from the helicopter, then killed him as they fought hand to hand.''

Shili cursed to himself. What else could go wrong?

''What about the helicopter?'' he wanted to know. ''Where is it now?''

''I tracked it while Shazad went to get you,'' the other man said. ''It passed over the city and was headed toward the coast, so I called our colleagues in Alleppey. They were able to sight it. Hopefully, they will see where it lands.''

''The way things have been going, I wouldn't count on it,'' Shili said. ''Has there been any other activity?''

The other man nodded. ''Two men stayed behind with Hafeez,'' he reported ''They were joined by others in an unmarked van. They loaded Hafeez into the van, then everyone drove off.''

''And since then?''

''Nothing.''

''What about these men?'' Shili wondered. ''Were you able to get a good look at them?''

''Not really. Most of them were Indian, I would say, though a couple were white, including the man who killed Hafeez.''

''Americans,'' Shili muttered. ''I should have known.''

''What should we do?''

''Stay here,'' Shili told the other man. ''Let me

know when you hear from Alleppey...or, of course, if you see anything suspicious.''

''Of course,'' the other man echoed. ''Where will you be?''

''I need to make preparations,'' Shili said gravely, ''in case we have unwanted guests.''

CHAPTER THREE

Alleppey, Malabar Coast

When looking for a coastal base of operations during the first leg of the President's trip, the Secret Service had selected Xerygon Tool & Die, a run-down, nondescript manufacturing complex on the outskirts of Alleppey. The Secret Service was sharing use of the facility with the CIA, who'd bought the property through one of its shadow companies back in the 1950s when the cold war was in full swing and Kerala had elected India's first Communist ministry. Like the CIA, the Secret Service was drawn to the site not only for its isolated anonymity but also because it was within close proximity to both the main highway and the largest of several waterways that made up Alleppey's vast canal system. In fact, when arriving in his bullet-riddled helicopter, Grimaldi's makeshift landing pad had been a wood-frame observation deck extending out over the river; he'd nearly wound up in the water when the deck had threatened to collapse under the chopper's weight. A resourceful crew had managed to haul the aircraft into an adjacent warehouse made of corrugated tin rust-eaten by twenty

years of monsoons. The whole structure rattled noisily
with the reverberations of a struggling, antiquated air-
conditioning system that lowered the inside temper-
ature, at best, a mere ten degrees. Grimaldi was already sweat drenched, even though he'd brought the
chopper in only a few minutes ago, having left Mack
Bolan and Nhajsib Wal to deal with the sniper Bolan
had killed near the site of the priest killings.

It didn't take long for the CIA's resident mechanic
to assess the damage to the helicopter.

"Be a couple hours before you're airborne again,"
he told Grimaldi as he stepped away from the chopper, wiping his grease-stained hands on a rag. "And
that's without patching up the window or back seat."

"That bad, huh?"

"Let me put it this way," the mechanic said.
"Your guardian angel must have pretty damn strong
wings, 'cause by all rights this bird should've dropped
like a stone back when you took that hit to the rotor
assembly."

Grimaldi grinned. "And here I thought it was my
keen flying ability."

"That, too, I suppose," the mechanic conceded. "I
take it you've done your share of combat flying."

"My share and then some," Grimaldi answered.
He wasn't about to go into detail about his flight ex-
perience, which—prior to his lengthy stint with the
Farm—dated back to Huey forays in Nam and some
regrettable freelancing for the Mob. During those
years, Grimaldi had piloted everything from mail-
order ultralights to a space shuttle, and he'd long ago
stopped counting the number of times he'd come un-

der fire while in the air. For him, it was just part of the job, a chance to continually test his mettle and make sure he was up to the demands of being the Farm's main go-to guy when it came to missions requiring aerial support.

"Go ahead and get cracking," Grimaldi told the mechanic. "I'm probably going to have to double back to Kottayam ASAP."

"I'll do my best." As he grabbed his toolbox, the mechanic added, "You guys must really rate."

"How's that?"

"I got a call from Washington saying to drop everything and give you top priority."

"Membership has its privileges," Grimaldi wisecracked.

"Membership to what is what I'd like to know," the mechanic said. "You're not with us, and I figure you're not SS, either. What's that leave? Rangers? Delta? NSA?"

Grimaldi shook his head and grinned. "Try NTK."

"'Need to know,'" the mechanic muttered, rolling his eyes. "You James Bond types are all alike. Everything's gotta be hush-hush. Hell, you're probably just gonna shuttle some high-ranks to that new golf course in Quilon."

"Right, and this here's my nine iron," Grimaldi said, patting the Mark I Grizzly .45 automatic pistol tucked in his shoulder holster. He glanced around the service bay. "Look, I'm supposed to hook up with somebody."

"Yeah, I know. Guy's even more tight-lipped than

you.'' The mechanic gestured to his right. ''Through the doorway, then hang a quick left.''

Grimaldi thanked the other man and crossed the work area. Off in one corner, two Secret Service agents, sleeves rolled up, collars unbuttoned, mulled over a corkboard bearing a map of India stuck with different colored pins. Both men wore cellular headsets and were talking through small condensor mikes as they referred to the map. Their focus was on the south edge of the Malabar coast between Mangalore and Trivandrum. Grimaldi figured they were beefing up security to account for a possible terrorist link to the priest killings in Kottayam. The air-conditioner made it hard to eavesdrop, but he overheard one of the men mention that the President would be landing soon on the northernmost of the Maldives atolls. After a day there acclimating and meeting with the island republic's trade minister, the President would fly to the mainland on his peacekeeping mission. And Grimaldi knew the President wasn't about to cancel his plans because of any purported terrorist threat. ''Our bite's worse than their bark'' was the way he always put it, referring to the number of times similar threats had been neutralized during previous state trips abroad, in many instances through the intervention of the covert warriors of Stony Man Farm. Grimaldi had a feeling that by the end of this latest trip, he and his colleagues would no doubt once again play a key role in making sure that ''Hail to the Chief'' wasn't a reference to an assassin's gunfire.

The mechanic's directions led Grimaldi to the complex's newest addition, a small, four-room building whose wood-and-adobe framework supported a tile roof that did a better job of reflecting the heat than the tin shell of the service bay. He found John "Cowboy" Kissinger in a tool room temporarily doubling as the Secret Service's armory. With its stockpiled munitions, workbench, lathe and assorted metal-working gear, the place reminded Grimaldi of Kissinger's workstation back in the States, where he served as the Farm's resident armorer and weaponsmith. The two men were roughly the same age, but Kissinger was taller and more sturdily built, a one-time Cleveland Brown wide receiver who still looked more than capable of shaking off a few tackles on his way to the end zone. Brown haired, brown eyed, dressed in combat fatigues, he was tinkering with something propped on the bench, so engrossed with his work that he didn't noticed Grimaldi until the pilot moved in front of the stream of cool air blowing through the air-conditioning vent.

"Leave it to Cowboy to find the coolest room in the house," Grimaldi teased.

"I hadn't noticed." Kissinger glanced up a moment, then turned back to his work. "You made good time getting back here."

"Wasn't about to dawdle on the scenic route." Grimaldi passed along the diagnosis on the helicopter, then quickly briefed Kissinger on the latest developments in Kottayam.

"Before we head back," he concluded, "this IB guy we're working with, Nhajsib Wal, wants us to pick up some fireworks from a warehouse down by the waterfront."

"Fireworks? What for?"

"He's concerned that if the mujahideen have taken over this academy it'll be tough to get close to them," Grimaldi explained. "He figures a diversion might help things, and this place on the waterfront supposedly has a stockpile left over from some spring festival they hold every year up in Trichur. Poobah, Poorboy...something like that."

"Pooram," Kissinger corrected. "It's kind of like their Mardi Gras."

"I'll put it on my calendar," Grimaldi said.

"Better brush up on your Hindi first."

"What you got there?" Grimaldi asked, eyeing the strange contraption Kissinger was working on. The size of a lunchbox and made primarily of plated steel and black plastic, it looked like an unlikely cross between a bazooka and a handheld vacuum cleaner.

"My DHL prototype," Kissinger said as he finished screwing a two-foot-long retractable nozzle onto one end of the apparatus.

"Dragon's Hairball Launcher?" Grimaldi laughed. "You're really going to name it that? I thought that was just an inside joke."

"It is. Once they go into production, I'll figure out something else for the initials to stand for."

Kissinger had been developing the DHL back at the Farm on and off for a few years now, coming up with the original idea while retroengineering a Russian air force ODAB-500 PM fuel-air mixture bomb. While the cluster-bomb-sized ODAB—an acronym for *obyomno-detoniruyschchaya aviatsionnay,* or volume-detonation aircraft bomb—released shock wave energy capable of immobilizing enemy forces within a range of one hundred yards, the smaller shells in Kissinger's miniaturized hybrid were more flammable. Like a well-thrown Molotov cocktail—or, as Kissinger had first described it when applying for funding, a well-spit dragon's hairball—on impact they would detonate into deadly, fast-spreading fireballs. The DHL had a number of advantages over conventional flamethrowers, perhaps the greatest being its ability to be fired from a greater distance without tipping off its position. There were still a few glitches in the weapon's design, and after flying to India with Grimaldi and Bolan, Kissinger had gone on to Sri Lanka, where he'd met with a Negombo weapons manufacturer specializing in incendiary devices. He had sent them specs for modifying a few parts of the DHL, including the retractable firing barrel, and it had been his hope to test the reconstructed prototype that morning at the firm's firing range. Instead, he'd gotten the call to head back to the mainland and help contend with the latest threat posed by the mujahideen. Now, though he'd just finished reassembling the weapon with the new parts, it looked as if testing it would once again have to wait.

After setting the DHL into its customized carrying case, Kissinger put the weapon in a locker the Secret Service had provided him with. "All right, enough high-tech," he said, heading for the door. "Let's go get some old-fashioned fireworks."

The quickest way to Alleppey's warehouse district was by water. The CIA normally had a small flotilla of boats gassed up and ready for use underneath the observation platform, but the officer leading Grimaldi and Kissinger down to the docks explained that the faster craft were already out in the field. Of the two boats available, the largest was a thatch-roofed country boat like those used by Keralan farmers to transport crops from farm to market. Lacking either sail or motor, the craft had to be propelled by prodding long wooden poles into the river bottom and pushing off. The other choice was a smaller, metal-framed, three-bench rowboat outfitted with a low-horsepower Evinrude engine.

"The tortoise and the snail," the agent said. "We use 'em mostly for undercover and surveillance. They fit in with most of the boats you see around these parts."

"I take it the other boats are out because they pack a little more wallop," Grimaldi said.

The agent nodded. "Sorry. Short notice and all…"

"Guess we'll take the tortoise."

The agent handed over the keys to the Evinrude, then, as Grimaldi and Kissinger boarded, he untethered the rowboat from its moorings. "Should be a clear run to town for you," he said. "Only watch out about a half mile downriver. There's a lagoon where they rent out Jet Skis, and some moron's always gonna wind up straying out of bounds trying to impress his girlfriend."

"Ah, tourists." Grimaldi chuckled. "Ya gotta love 'em."

Kissinger grabbed the oars and paddled out into midstream. Grimaldi started the motor and opened the throttle. With a faint lurch, the boat started downriver.

Kissinger drew in the oars and glanced at the river-banks, overgrown with thick-bladed shrubs. Several water buffalo stood shoulder high in the bushes, chewing cud as they watched the boat putter by.

"Hell, if they can swim we ought to yoke them and have them pull us," Grimaldi said, smacking the Evinrude with the flat of his hand. "Couldn't be much slower than this hamster cage."

Kissinger laughed, grabbing his bench with one hand while raising the other in the air above his head like a rodeo rider astride a bucking bronco. "Ride 'em, cowboy!"

Kissinger may have looked as if he belonged in the saddle, but his nickname had less to do with time spent on the open range than the kick-ass, no-holds-barred reputation he'd earned years ago busting drug dealers during a stint with the DEA. In recent years he'd found himself spending more and more time within the confines of the Stony Man armory, but whenever called into the field, the old juices invari-ably started flowing and Kissinger could be counted on to provide the kind of reckless daring sometimes needed to tilt the scales in a difficult mission.

"You should've seen Sarge take down that sniper this afternoon," Grimaldi yelled to Kissinger over the high-pitched whine of the Evinrude. "You'd've been proud!"

"Yeah?"

"Hell, yes," Grimaldi said. "It was crazy. This guy's high-tailing away from us on a dirt bike, so Sarge has me do a flyover low enough so he can hop out of the chopper and..."

Grimaldi's voice trailed off as he saw Kissinger bring a finger to his lips. The armorer was looking upriver past Grimaldi, his face etched with concern. The Stony Man pilot stole a glance over his shoulder and saw, less than a hundred yards away, another boat. It was difficult to make out any details, but the other craft was quickly gaining on them.

"Maybe it's our free upgrade," Grimaldi ventured.

"I wouldn't count on it." Kissinger slipped a hand to his shoulder holster, pulled out a modified Colt Government Model pistol and thumbed off the safety.

Grimaldi fished through a storage box near the rudder, reaching past a small hatchet and a three-gallon fuel canister for a pair of binoculars. He was trying to focus on the approaching boat when a gunshot whizzed past him.

"Not again!" Grimaldi tossed the field glasses aside and opened the engine's throttle. The boat crept forward, barely responding to the extra gas. Meanwhile, another shot buzzed near Grimaldi's ear.

"Are these guys sensitive or what?" he shouted over the engine. "I swear, all you've got to do is look at them and they start shooting!"

"Let me see if I can get them to back off." Kissinger braced himself and brought his Colt into firing position. The other boat kept coming, prow high in the water, blocking his view of the vessel's occupants. It looked like a cigarette boat, a sleek craft built essentially for speed. There was no way Grimaldi would be able to outrun it.

When a gunman rose into view, Kissinger fired a round from his Colt. The other man ducked, then quickly popped back up, unleashing another volley with his assault rifle. Most of the shots fell wide, but several clanged noisily off the rowboat's metal framework.

"We're like sitting ducks here," Grimaldi said. He yanked out his L.A.R. Grizzly and blasted away. The other boat took a hit to the hull but kept coming.

They were nearing a sharp bend where a tree grew out at an angle from the embankment, its lower branches dipping close to the waterline. The river narrowed, and there was no way around. Grimaldi was forced to slow down so they could pass underneath, limbo-style.

Halfway through the obstacle, the Stony Man pilot idled the engine and grabbed the hatchet from the storage box.

"Here!" he told Kissinger, handing him the tool. "See if you can get that big limb there to dip a little lower."

"Gotcha."

Grimaldi turned back and fired through the branches at the approaching boat, which was already slowing down. Kissinger, meanwhile, hacked fiercely at the largest of the tree branches. He stopped short of chopping all the way through, however. Once the limb began to give way, he let up, letting it creak lower to the waterline.

"Okay, let's scram!" he called out.

Grimaldi gave the Evinrude more gas, and they pulled away. There was no way the other boat could plow through the tree without capsizing, so he figured they had time to possibly move to shore and take cover on the embankment. As they rounded the bend, however, Kissinger glanced ahead and came up with a better idea.

"Get me over to that scooter," he called out.

They'd reached the lagoon the CIA agent had forewarned them about and, sure enough, a sunburned daredevil in floral swim trunks had hotdogged into the river on his Jet Ski and taken a turn too sharply, dumping himself into the water. He'd just swum back to his watercraft and was righting it when Grimaldi and Kissinger caught up with him. The man was blond-haired and blue-eyed, his handsome features seemingly stamped into the smug expression of someone used to getting his way without much effort.

"I need to borrow your toy there for a minute," Kissinger said, indicating the Jet Ski as he stood in the boat.

"Hey, no way, dude," the man on the ski said.

Kissinger pointed his .45 at the man. "Yes way, dude."

As if the man in the trunks needed more incentive, gunshots from the other boat began to shower around them. While the skier glanced toward the approaching boat with a look of annoyance, Kissinger grabbed him by the wrist and jerked him off the watercraft. Taken by surprise, the other man practically flew past Kissinger into the rowboat.

"Get down and stay down!" Kissinger shouted as he returned fire, then climbed onto the personal watercraft. The skier, no longer smirking, pressed himself against the bottom of the boat.

"Be careful, man," he called out, "I, like, passed on the insurance when I rented that thing."

"Not to worry," Grimaldi assured the man. "Cowboy here's as safe behind the wheel as they come."

"You're putting me on, right?" the skier said. "Guy's, like, practically psycho!"

Once astride the Jet Ski, Kissinger quickly familiarized himself with the controls. Fortunately, the ski was similar to ones he used back in Virginia at Lake Pena, a recreational facility an hour's drive north of Stony Man Farm.

"What's the game plan?" Grimaldi asked him.

"I don't know," Kissinger called out, "but I'm sure I'll think of something. Just cover my ass."

"Will do." Grimaldi checked his Grizzly. The skier glanced up at the gun and grimaced.

"Oh, man, you mean there's gonna be *more* shooting?"

"Afraid, so, dude," Grimaldi told him. "Bummer, huh?"

"Shit," the skier whined, "I *told* my girlfriend we should do Maui. But, no, she's gotta drag us to India... 'It's so spiritual,' she says. Yeah, right."

The man started to peer up over the side of the boat but ducked for cover when bullets zipped into the nearby water.

"If you don't keep your head down, you're gonna be as holey as they come," Grimaldi advised.

Back at the tree blocking the river, the other boat had been forced to come to a stop. Two men leaned out, firing through the branches draped across the top of their boat. Grimaldi countered with an autoburst and managed to nail one of them, toppling him into the river. The other gunman fired back with one hand while using the other to raise the branch Kissinger had weakened with the hatchet. Slowly, the speedboat inched its way under the obstacle.

"Here goes," Kissinger called out, opening up the throttle.

Once back in open water, the speedboat lunged forward. For the time being, though, its prow hung low in the water and Grimaldi was able to keep the gunman preoccupied, giving Kissinger some leeway.

At first the armorer jetted in a wide arc toward the far embankment. But as he gained speed, he guided the ski back to the middle of the river and straightened course.

"Oh, man!" the ski dude groaned, peeping once again over the side of the rowboat. "Dude's playing chicken! He's gonna wreck that ski for sure!"

Raising a fantail of spray in his wake, Kissinger bore down on the other boat, putting them on a collision course. He refused to let up on the throttle, and as their paths drew closer, he ignored the gunshots being fired his way and kept his eyes trained on the hands of the driver manning the speedboat. At the last possible second, the man's hands jerked the boat's steering wheel to the right. Kissinger simultaneously veered to his right, as well, and leaned away from the oncoming boat.

The two craft narrowly averted a collision. Kissinger, already leaning precariously to one side, was knocked off balance by the wake of the passing boat. Losing control of the Jet Ski, he leaped free and plunged into the river as it slid sideways and sputtered to a stop just short of the toppled tree.

Grimaldi, meanwhile, saw that the speedboat was now headed directly toward him. "Out!" he shouted to the man in the trunks. "Quick!"

Both men lunged into the water. The man at the controls of the speedboat tried to cut sharply to his left, but he still clipped Grimaldi's boat at an angle. The speedboat flew out of control almost instantly, flipping several times across the surface of the river before landing upside down in the water. A spark ignited spilled fuel and, with an earsplitting explosion, the boat disintegrated, spraying shrapnel in all directions.

Grimaldi swam back to the rowboat. The hull was bent but the craft was still intact and afloat. He pulled himself up, then turned and helped aboard the man in the shorts.

"What the hell's going on?" he wanted to know. His voice, like the rest of him, was trembling. "It's like a freaking war here!"

"Well, you're in luck," Grimaldi said, eyeing the strewed remains of the other boat. "I think there's a cease-fire, at least for the time being."

"That's like karma, right?"

Grimaldi shrugged. "You got me, pal."

As they doubled back to pick up Kissinger, the other man looked past the Armorer, his face brightening. "Looks like the ski's still in one piece! All right!" He stood in the boat. "Mind if I...?"

"Go for it, dude," Grimaldi said.

Grimaldi helped Kissinger aboard as the other man

dived back into the river and went to retrieve his Jet Ski.

"That was close," Kissinger said, shaking water from his body.

"You okay?"

Kissinger nodded. He drew his Colt and gestured toward what remained of the other boat. "Let's mop this up."

Heading back downriver, Grimaldi and Kissinger kept their eyes open for survivors. Two intact bodies floated facedown in the water near the smoldering debris, and amid the floating rubble were the scattered remains of at least one other man dismembered by the explosion.

"Mujahideen?" Kissinger said.

"Gotta be," Grimaldi said. "Must've somehow managed to track me when I was flying back. Dammit!"

"It's not like you had a lot of choices after you got clipped."

"Maybe not."

"I wonder if one of them was this Neshah guy," Cowboy said.

"Could be," Grimaldi mused, "but I wouldn't bet on it."

CHAPTER FOUR

Rahn-Maytt Detention Centre, Kottayam

His whitened hair glistening with sweat, Dehri Ne-shah stared through the barred window of his prison cell. As the late-day sun inched lower toward the distant hills, he watched long shadows stretch across the hot, teeming streets of downtown Kottayam. The already hectic cacophony—bleating car horns, braying pack animals, trishaw operators cursing in rapid-fire Malayalam—would become even more charged and oppressive once the workday ended and commuters found themselves thwarted in their rush home. Getting anywhere with any semblance of speed or ease would be next to impossible.

Neshah's callused fingers tightened around the bars. The heat and noise were giving him a headache. He cursed under his breath and pushed himself away from the window.

What was taking so long?

The approaching rush hour wasn't Neshah's only concern. This was his second day of incarceration. The longer he remained in custody, the greater the chance the authorities would see past his forged identification, as well as his meticulously dyed beard and scalp and realize his true identity. Once that happened, everything would change. There would be increased security. He would be placed in a different cell, one without a view, one where his every move would be monitored. There would be interrogations, beatings, torture. Some, no doubt, would clamor to ignore the legal process altogether and have him executed, on the spot or in a way that would insure that his death was slow and painful. Whatever the course, Neshah, on the verge of his greatest triumph, would find himself undone by his own grim reputation.

When pacing failed to ease either his nerves or his headache, Neshah returned to the window. His cell was three floors up, overlooking not only the business sector of Kottayam—extending for several blocks to where it merged with the city canals—but also the detention facility's parking lot. A handful of identical-looking patrol cars were parked in a neat row directly below, while an assortment of other sedans and trucks took up random spaces farther away from the building. Most of the vehicles were well kept and only a few years old, nothing like the barely operative, rust-eaten junk heaps that dotted the streets of Neshah's native Zalam.

His skull now throbbing, he closed his eyes and tried to blot out the heat and the sounds of the city. Stroking his temples, he mentally transported himself back home to Zalam, a sleepy Kashmiri village of farmers, tradesmen and artisans nestled at the base of the Himalayas. Though impoverished economically, Zalam was rich in far more important ways. This time of year, while summer heat tortured the rest of India, Zalam would remain temperate. Most nights there would even be a pleasant chill in the evening breezes.

Neshah imagined himself rising from his own bed after a restful night's sleep and pausing to admire his clean-shaved, dark-haired image in the mirror. Oh, how the women loved that face, so filled with charm and vigor, nothing like the ragged, bedraggled disguise that now gave him the look of a man twice his age. From his house, he would walk down a short hill and start the day with an invigorating dive into the cold, snow-fed waters of Lake Pajara. The icy chill would clear his head and leave his skin tingling. As he swam back to shore, he would find inspiration in the familiar sight of the mountains, peaked with frost above the tree line, where the mule deer and shaggy-maned tahr roamed amid the verdant pines. Once dry, he would walk to town, breathing in the rich fragrance of saffron being plucked from crocuses grown in neat rows in the surrounding hills. In Zalam, he would browse for fresh fruit and vegetables at the market bazaar. The Shili brothers would be performing acrobatic feats in the streets for spare change. His friends would be there and he would invite them all back to his estate for an afternoon of cricket, after which they would dine on the patio. Vikrab would have his flute with him, Andesh his battered sitar; they would play ragas as everyone else stared with idle contentment at the play of twilight on the treetops and in the meadows. Everyone would agree that Zalam, like all of Kashmir, was Paradise on Earth.

Neshah's meditation dulled his headache but also

filled him with longing. He'd been away for months, letting his hair and beard grow as he trekked circuitously southward, all the while furtively attending to the machinations that, God willing, would one day see Zalam—as well as all of Jammu and Kashmir—ushered into an era of sovereignty befitting a true paradise. For most of his adult life, Neshah had strived to help make his homeland become just such a gem—a jewel unto itself, not some bauble tugged at from either side by the covetous hands of India and Pakistan.

India and Pakistan. The mere thought of the interloping powers renewed Neshah's sense of rage.

Like other mujahideen cells, Neshah had initially sided with Pakistan on the issue of who should control Kashmir's destiny. After all, Pakistan was, like Kashmir, predominantly Muslim. And, of course, there was the matter of secret collusion—Pakistan steadily supplied the mujahideen with cash, munitions and other provisions for use in the ongoing battle against Indian forces stationed in Kashmir. It was only over the past year that Neshah had begun to think of swearing off his group's dependency on Pakistan and fighting instead for Kashmir's right to self-determination. What had changed his mind was one of those tranquil afternoons he'd just conjured up. He and the Shili brothers had been staring westward, hoping to enjoy the sunset. Instead, they'd witnessed—across the Vale of Kashmir—yet another in the endless barrage of shellings hammering the jagged peaks of Pir Panjal. Eerie tendrils of smoke rose up in the air, writhing slowly in the wind like restless ghosts of those just slain by the bombardment. The next day they'd learned that of the fifty-eight fatalities, only eleven had involved Indian troops. The rest of the dead had been Kashmiri mountain villagers, innocent men, women and children who wanted nothing more than to be able to go about their lives without fear that they might be claimed by the next errant volley. And this had been no isolated incident. The same ratio—five Kashmiris slain for every one Indian—had been maintained, more or less, for years, since the Line of Control had first been drawn up. It infuriated Neshah that Pakistan would routinely shrug off such fatalities—or justify them on the grounds that they suffered an equal proportion of civilian-to-military deaths due to Indian shellings across the Line of Control. Now, though his mujahideen still accepted Pakistani financing, they yearned for the day when the apron ties would be cut.

And that day was supposed to have been close at hand. Everything had seemed to be falling into place, and as recently as yesterday afternoon, all of his dreams had seemed within reach. Then, thanks to a small twist of Fate, everything had gone suddenly wrong and his dreams had been taken from him.

The Kashmiri felt a renewed sense of outrage when he recalled his capture. He'd been haunting an alley two blocks from Kyber-Vantz, a private computer firm specializing in tracking systems helpful in the recovery of stolen vehicles. Neshah had made queries and learned that the company was also a military subcontractor, providing many of the computerized guidance systems used in India's SHORAD missile defense program. He'd cased the facility most of the day and was waiting for it to close for the evening so that he could break in and get his hands on some replacement components needed to make operational a Sabre surface-to-air missile launcher that had recently come into the mujahideen's possession. Less than five minutes before Neshah was about to make his move, local police had stormed the alley and taken Neshah into custody along with five other men who shared his disheveled appearance. The others were part of a marauding band of street people who'd been responsible for a string of petty thefts in the area, targeting mostly clothing stores and food markets. Neshah had been mistaken for part of the gang, not only because of his appearance but also because he was carrying forged papers identifying him as a local resident. And what was he to have done? Claimed a case of mistaken identity? Asserted that the police had unwittingly captured, not some petty thief, but rather the mastermind of the dreaded mujahideen, the Kashmir Shredder himself? Ah, the wantonness of Fate.

South of Kottayam, Neshah could see the sun's reflection glittering, diamondlike, atop the choppy waters where the Laccadive and Arabian Seas merged with each other. A jet coursed over the waters, leaving in its wake a contrail of exhaust. Neshah wondered bitterly if it might be the plane they called *Air Force One,* bringing the U.S. President to Maldives. If so, how ironic. How cruel that his closest glimpse of the American infidel—the two-faced jackal who would simultaneously court both India and Pakistan while ignoring the cause of Kashmiri independence—

should wind up being through prison bars rather than the scope of a high-powered rifle or, even better, the range finder of an armed and operational missile launcher.

Unsettled, Neshah diverted his gaze to the entry gate. A police cruiser passed through, then a uniformed officer armed with a Kalashnikov assault rifle stepped forward to scrutinize a tan-colored sedan pulling up to the guard station. After exchanging a few words with those inside the vehicle, the officer stepped back and waved the car through. Sunlight glanced off the front windshield as the sedan backed into a parking space directly opposite the gateway. Once the car came to a stop, both front doors slowly swung open. Two men, their faces obscured by wide-brimmed crimson hats, stepped out onto the asphalt. Their matching ankle-length robes flapped slightly in the afternoon breeze as they strode toward the rear entrance to the jail, each carrying a small black satchel.

Up in his cell, Dehri Neshah's brooding scowl slowly gave way to a faint smile.

Raghubir and Penghat. They were here.

Neshah's headache dissipated, replaced by a renewed hope that his dream might yet still be alive.

"Yes," he muttered under his breath.

"WE'VE COME TO HEAR confessions and bring prisoners the Eucharist," Raghubir Shili, the taller of the two robed men, explained as he and his older brother, Penghat, were escorted into the detention centre. As at the front gate, the two men had been admitted with minimal questioning. Things changed, however, once they were turned over to the warden, a squat, avuncular man with bushy sideburns and eyebrows as thick as caterpillars. Although the man flashed an accommodating smile, both brothers remained on their guard, sensing a glimmer of shrewdness in the older man's eyes. Their concern was quickly borne out.

"Two other priests usually come by with the sacraments," the warden mentioned casually as he led the would-be priests through the next checkpoint. "Father Chaudhry and Father Rhamat."

Penghat wasn't sure if the warden was just making conversation or trying to trip them up. Fortunately, he and Raghubir had anticipated such questions.

"Yes, we were just at their parish," the shorter man was quick to explain. "They came down ill this morning with food poisoning. We spoke to an acolyte who thinks the heat spoiled some of their food."

"That wouldn't surprise me," the warden said.

"We were passing through, on our way from Cochin to Alleppey," Penghat went on, "so we volunteered to take their rounds."

Penghat spoke in flawless Malayalam, suppressing any trace of the Kashmiri accent that—given the countrywide paranoia in light of recent subversive activity by the mujahideen—might have prompted suspicion. Penghat was certain Dehri Neshah had restricted himself to Keralan dialect after his arrest, the better to pass himself off as some petty local criminal rather than one of the nation's most wanted men.

Raghubir finished embroidering his brother's cover story. "Father Chaudhry said he'd call later to make sure we did a good job,'' he interjected, ''so I hope you'll put in a good word for us.''

The warden smiled as he led the impostors down the hall. ''Well, if it's sinners you're looking for, you've come to the right place,'' he quipped, no longer as concerned with the priests' veracity as he was with the chance to trot out his homespun wit for a fresh audience. ''Never a shortage of them here.''

The shorter priest smiled indulgently, then tactfully inquired, ''Are there any prisoners we should be forewarned about?''

The warden shook his head. ''No one of consequence here,'' he explained. ''Street thieves, drunks, a burglar or two. The usual rabble.''

''All worthy of the Lord's forgiveness,'' Penghat replied, quickly adding, ''as long as they are truly repentant.''

''Repentant?'' The warden scoffed. ''They may confess to you, Father, but bring them before the magistrate and they'll all claim to be innocent.''

Both Penghat and Raghubir indulged the warden with faint smiles. Side by side, they bore little resemblance to either each other or their brother Vargadrum. Penghat, half a head shorter and every bit as stocky as Raghubir and Vargadrum were gaunt, was the oldest of the brothers, a member of Dehri Neshah's inner circle for more than a dozen years. Of the three, he was also the most savvy and outgoing, a wheeler-dealer whose wealth of personal connections made him indispensable to the mujahideen. It was Penghat who had made the necessary arrangements in the New Delhi bombing that had claimed the life of a U.S. envoy; Penghat whose contacts had made possible the acquisition of the two Sabre surface-to-air missile launchers that would be the mujahideen's trump cards in this, their most ambitious campaign ever to strike against those who would stand in the way of an independent Kashmir. And once it had become clear that Neshah had been taken into custody here at the Rahn-Maytt Detention Centre, it was Penghat who had made a few calls and learned the layout of the facility from an acquaintance who had been a former inmate. Now, having made it inside the building with far less difficulty than they had encountered getting their hands on their disguises, Penghat hoped they could free Neshah without any further obstacles and return to the academy in time to make arrangements for launching one of the Sabre missiles at the American President's plane.

As they passed a side hallway, Raghubir—whose disguise was supplemented by a light-gray beard and matching wig, as well as a pair of slightly tinted eyeglasses—glanced briefly down the other corridor, then shot a glance at his brother. Penghat, recognizing the layout from the description given him by the former inmate, nodded imperceptibly.

"Father Raghubir could start on the top floor," he said to the warden. "I need to use the facilities. Then I can begin with the prisoners down here."

"Of course." The warden indicated the hall they had just passed. "The first door on your right. When you're ready, just come down to the security gate. I'll see that you're cleared for admittance."

"Bless you."

Penghat watched the other two men round a corner, then backtracked to the side hallway. The first doorway was clearly marked as the men's rest room, but Penghat strode past it to a door farther down the hall. He gave the knob a turn, then frowned.

Locked.

Penghat checked his watch and drew in a breath, frustrated. He had a set of lock picks with him, but he lacked the skill to breach the tumblers as quickly as needed. Adding to his frustrations, he could see that both the door and its hinges were far too sturdy to be easily compromised. He would have to find another way in.

As he mulled his options, Penghat heard a faint squeaking at the far end of the hall. Moving away from the door, he crouched over a drinking fountain several feet away and rinsed his mouth with tepid, metallic-tasting water. As he did so, he glanced out the corner of his eye and saw a janitor approaching, pushing before him a three-wheeled mop bucket.

At the sight of Penghat's priestly robes, the janitor genuflected and made a sign of the Cross. "Good afternoon, Father."

"God be with you."

Penghat remained standing as he administered the blessing. He saw that the janitor was an older man, balding, with large, dark eyes that burned with religious fervor. A lamb of Christ, Penghat thought to himself. Heaven sent.

"Perhaps you could help me, my son," he told the janitor. Recalling what the former inmate had told him about the layout of the ground floor, he said,

"Some new equipment has been installed here recently, yes?"

The janitor seemed puzzled at first, but then he nodded and indicated the locked door. "The boiler. Yes, it was replaced just last month."

"Yes, the boiler," Penghat said, as if recalling some recent conversation. "That was it. The warden asked me to say a blessing over it. To assure its good running come winter, when it will be in more demand." With a smile, he added, "Not that he doesn't have faith in your ability to fix it should anything go wrong."

The janitor beamed, revealing gaps where he'd lost several teeth to bad hygiene. He reached to his side, producing a cluster of more than two dozen keys bound by a large, single ring. As he sorted through them for the one to the boiler room, Penghat casually set his satchel on the drinking fountain and reached into his own pockets, producing a rosary. To the eye, with its small wooden crucifix linked to evenly spaced prayer beads, the rosary looked much the same as any other. But there was one distinct difference; whereas the beads of most rosaries were connected by string or frail chain, here the linkage was comprised of thin but sturdy wire. In fact, the same wire was used by a Swiss firm in Bern for the making of garrotes, a weapon Penghat was far more trained in the use of than any religious object.

Looping the rosary around both hands, Penghat stood behind the janitor, watching him unlock the boiler room.

"There you are, Father," the older man said once he'd opened the door. "All you have to do is go—"

The janitor's voice was cut off as Penghat slipped the rosary around his throat and pulled tight. Though short, Penghat was a powerful man. Using his hip as a fulcrum, he pivoted the janitor off his feet even as he pulled the beaded wire tighter, muting his victim's attempted cries. The janitor struggled briefly, but he had been taken by surprise and was no match for Penghat's brute strength. In a matter of seconds he was dead in the would-be priest's arms.

Penghat leaned into the door, opening it and dragging the janitor inside. He eased the body onto the floor, then returned to the hallway for his satchel, as well as the mop and bucket. Once everything had been brought inside, he locked the door behind him and looked around. As he expected, the large room contained not only the new boiler, but also the furnace and the power box for the jail's circuit breakers. In a far corner was the main feed for the center's telephone lines.

Once he'd hauled the janitor's body behind the furnace, Penghat moved over to a lone, grimy window, which opened out to the parking lot. In fact, less than fifty yards away, he could see the tan sedan he and his brother had stolen from the priests whose robes they were now wearing.

Perfect.

Penghat unlocked the window and raised it slightly. It moved freely, with little sound. He raised it higher, leaving himself adequate room to squeeze through, then returned to the panel box. From his satchel he withdrew a bible. Its leather-bound cover was secured with a clasp, like a diary. Penghat sprang the lock, then opened the book, which was hollowed out. Rather than the word of God, the bible contained an assortment of tools. He chose a set of wire clippers and a screwdriver, then checked his watch.

He still had a minute to go before it would be time to cut off the prison from the rest of the world.

CHAPTER FIVE

Stony Man Farm, Virginia

When the National Security Agency came under fire for not foreseeing India's and Pakistan's initial nuclear weapons tests in the late 1990s, they quickly responded by launching an Orion spy satellite whose sole function was to monitor the activities of these two neighboring rivals. After more than three years in orbit, most of the intelligence gathered by the satellite continued to deal primarily with nuclear weapons developments, but other information—some classified, some not—was routinely pulled in from the Asian subcontinent, as well. Now, with the President about to embark on a tour of the region, NSA analysts were going over all incoming data with the cybernetic equivalent of a fine-tooth comb. They did so acting on the assumption that they alone were privy to whatever fell under Orion's vigilant gaze.

But they were wrong.

Deep in the underbelly of Virginia's Shenandoah Valley, an hour's flight from NSA headquarters, as well as the White House, Aaron Kurtzman sat pensively before his computer inside the Computer Room at Stony Man Farm. Along with colleagues Huntington Wethers, Carmen Delahunt and Akira Tokaido, all week Kurtzman had been paying close heed to pilfered signals from Orion and any number of other spy satellites circling the globe, including India's own UAVs. Along with helping orchestrate the covert operations of Mack Bolan, Able Team and Phoenix Force, Stony Man's cyberteam had occasion to glean vital intel that might otherwise slip through the fingers of their overworked and underfinanced counterparts in other, more official agencies.

Kurtzman had split his screen into four separate images so that he could simultaneously monitor feeds from both India's and Pakistan's leading news channels as well as random Orion SIG-INTEL and the steady flow of information being disseminated by every law-enforcement agency within a five-hundred-mile radius of the President's location at any given time. Predictably, each of the regional news channels offered slanted coverage of the President's visit, flashing sound bites from opposing heads of state righteously claiming they could settle their differences without America's meddling. Pakistan's minister of defense called the President a crass opportunist interested only in bolstering his reelection chances, while a noted Indian political analyst saw the visit as a veiled attempt to inflame global tensions so that Congress would be more inclined to pass upcoming legislation to fund the latest incarnation of the Star Wars defense system.

On the SIG-INTEL screen, Kurtzman took note of a classified report on speculation by Indian intelligence that sabotage may have had a part in a recent accident involving a military train transporting two Sabre missiles from the Vikram Sarabhai Space Centre in Trivandrum to an air force launch facility in Andhra Pradesh. Early indications had been that the train, while passing over the Western Ghats, had been mistakenly rerouted across a turn-of-the-century wooden bridge undergoing foundation repairs after being weakened by the previous year's monsoons. The weight of the convoy had been in excess of the revised limit and the bridge had apparently collapsed under the train's heavy load, dropping it into one of the deepest ravines on the subcontinent. Both the bridge's collapse and the explosion of fuel tanks had triggered a massive landslide that buried the train under several hundred thousand tons of rubble. Salvagers and investigators at the site had estimated that it would take a minimum of seven weeks just to clear away enough of the slide to gain access to what was left of the train, and even then it was thought that the remnants would be too charred by fire and mangled by the avalanche to offer much in the way of clues as to the fateful plunge.

In the immediate aftermath of the accident, it had been assumed that all twenty-four crew members had died in the accident, but search teams descending into the ravine had come across a lone survivor, one of the engineers, who'd apparently been thrown free of the train as it plummeted to its demise. The engineer, whose name was being withheld for security reasons, had lost his right arm to the landslide and had been in a coma when found. For the past two weeks he'd remained unresponsive, hooked up to a ventilator in a private ward at a military hospital in Munnar. That morning, however, the man had finally come out of his coma. Over objections from doctors, RAW and Intelligence Bureau investigators had been quick to move in for an interview. Their findings, disseminated under a cloak of secrecy to avoid a media feeding frenzy, had been disturbing.

"Uh-oh," Kurtzman murmured as he read over the transcript of the interview. "This isn't good."

"What's not good, Bear?"

Kurtzman, a paraplegic since taking a bullet to the spine during an ill-fated attack on the Farm, turned in his wheelchair. Standing behind him, glancing over his shoulder at the screen, was Hal Brognola, Stony Man's White House liaison. He'd just poured two cups of coffee from a machine near Kurtzman's desk.

As he took one of the cups of coffee, Kurtzman quickly briefed Brognola on the intel he'd just intercepted, concluding, "This engineer's saying the wreck wasn't an accident."

"How so?" Brognola asked. "Somebody deliberately rerouted the train there?"

"That's only part of it," Kurtzman reported. "This guy says the train stopped short of the bridge because there were some boulders on the tracks. When he got out to take a look, he heard gunshots and saw one of the guards fall from the train. He was going to check on the guy when somebody jumped him from behind. Next thing he knows he's lying in a military hospital being told the train went down the gorge with everyone aboard."

"Sounds like sabotage, all right," Brognola conceded. "In which case, you have to think mujahideen." He kept one eye on Kurtzman's computer as he sipped his coffee, waiting for more news to flash on the screen.

"That's exactly what I'm thinking," Kurtzman said. "And if we're right, I'm not so sure it was just sabotage."

Brognola nodded; he could see where Kurtzman was going with this. "Especially the way they stopped the train," he ventured. "I mean, if they were just looking to get rid of the convoy, they could've blown up the bridge while it was passing over."

Kurtzman looked away from his computer and called out across the room, a massive chamber in the Farm's recently built underground Annex. "Hey, Akira!" He waved to get the attention of a young man huddled over a nearby computer.

Akira Tokaido smacked his bubblegum as he glanced back to Kurtzman.

"You were following that train wreck with those Indian SAMs a couple weeks back, right?" Kurtzman said.

"Check," Tokaido said. "I take it you just found out about that engineer."

Kurtzman nodded. "Tell us about those missiles, would you?"

"No prob." As he started calling up a file on his computer, Tokaido told the other men, "Basically, it's a stripped-down version of the RAF's Rapier Field Standard."

"Same range?" Brognola asked. Already he was

moving toward the front of the room, where a central screen showed a detailed map of South Asia.

"Let's see..." Tokaido skimmed over the specs as they flashed on the screen. "Five hundred miles tops, it says. They're figuring on them to anchor their SHORAD system."

Brognola nodded. Over his shoulder, he asked Kurtzman, "Wanna throw up a radius around Maldives for me?"

"Already working on it." Kurtzman, operating the remote keyboard for the front wall map, toggled a few switches, and soon Brognola was looking at a computerized blowup of the southern tip of India and the surrounding waterways. A shaded circle fanned outward from the President's first scheduled stop. Most of the Indian state of Kerala fell within the circle, as did a portion of Tamil and the eastern half of Sri Lanka.

"Sabres are light enough to be hauled by a Hummer," Tokaido continued. "Weather-resistant antiaircraft cruise-snipe missile...highly resistant to electronic countermeasures."

"That's the same as with the Rapier," Kurtzman said. "Didn't they come up with some kind of modifications? Targeting, I think it was."

"Right," Tokaido said. "Says here they fiddled with the launch and target-engagement systems. They're still like the Rapier in that the launcher can heave two different missiles and have them head for the same target at different trajectories. You know, so if somebody gets lucky and takes out one, the other can sneak in from another direction."

"Got it," Brognola said, still musing over the map. "Go on."

Tokaido highlighted all pertinent launch information on the Sabre and read off key points. "Let's see... 'Missiles can be tracked manually by one or two gunners with option of optical sights or radar-screen tracking.' Wait, here we go.

"'The biggest breakthrough is the computer sighting mechanism, which in the Rapier is confined to timing firing sequence and correcting deviation between optical sightline and missile track. The Sabre, by contrast, is capable of assessing dimensions of an intended target and therefore less prone to targeting decoys. To an extent, the computer sensors can even detect a target's density, so that if a decoy has the same dimensions but different—''

"Hold it there," Brognola interrupted. He stepped back from the map and rejoined the other two men. Carmen Delahunt and Huntington Wethers were on break, so they had the cavernous enclosure to themselves. "Let's cut to the chase and spell things out in English.

"For the sake of argument," Brognola went on, "let's say the mujahideen had this train rerouted, then bushwhacked it, stole both Sabres, then sent the train down the ravine where it'd be buried under enough debris that no one would be able to figure out the Sabres were missing until it was too late."

"That's a reach," Tokaido murmured. "Or at least I'm hoping it is."

"Because...?"

"Because, if the mujahideen have a couple Sabres

and know how to use them," Tokaido said, voicing Brognola's and Kurtzman's worst fears, "they could program the targeting sensors to sniff out *Air Force One* once it's within range. Not only that—they could go after it with four SAMS at the same time."

"Each coming from a different trajectory," Kurtzman said.

"Yep," Tokaido said. "You're the President, anywhere you look, you've got an incoming warhead with your name on it."

Kurtzman whistled as he eyed the map on the wall. "If we're right about this, Kottayam's got to be on the short list for places the mujahideen would be firing from. They're right within range of Maldives."

"Which means Mack's on the right track with these priest killings," Tokaido said. "They've got to have something to do with the missiles. Beats me what it—"

"Wait," Brognola interrupted again. This time he was pointing at Kurtzman's computer screen. "What was that?"

Kurtzman glanced back at the corner of the screen flashing law-enforcement data. The quadrant was filled with an aerial map of what was obviously a coastal city.

"Bombay, I think," Kurtzman said. "Parade route the President's taking the day after—"

"No, not that," Brognola cut in. "What was showing on the screen before. Is there any way to bring it back up?"

Kurtzman grinned. "You have to ask?"

Racing his fingers across the keyboard, the burly

computer expert first eliminated the other screens so that the monitor was taken up entirely with images received from the law-enforcement feed. Then, by entering another set of commands, he was able to summon up the last string of images. To Brognola, it was much like seeing videotape play in reverse. As he looked at the whirring images, he was joined by Tokaido.

"There!" Brognola told Kurtzman, pointing at the screen. "Hold it right there!"

On the screen was what appeared to be a half-blacked-out profile photograph of a plain-faced, middle-aged man with a scraggly white beard and matching shoulder-length hair.

"Mug shot," Kurtzman said. "From a jail in Kerala somewhere...let's see." He typed in a command and read the response. "Rahn-Maytt Detention Centre."

"Kottayam," Tokaido whispered, reading the rest of the address.

"Why did the image black out like that?" Brognola wanted to know. "I thought you'd worked it out so these feeds never sent half images."

"I did," Kurtzman said, suddenly puzzled himself. He pulled down a menu and checked the receptor specifications. "Supposedly everything's working."

"Then why's this image cut off like that?"

Kurtzman shrugged. "Who knows? It's an output glitch, though, trust me. Brownout, freeze up, something like that."

Brognola leaned closer to the screen, squinting to better make out the obstructed image. His eyes narrowed, then he closed them a moment, as if trying to convince himself that when he reopened them he wouldn't recognize the man on the screen. No such luck.

"Neshah," he muttered, gazing at the man's features.

"What's that?" Kurtzman said.

"Dehri Neshah," Brognola said, pointing at the man's face.

"The Kashmir Shredder?" Tokaido said. "Are you sure?"

Brognola nodded. "He's dyed his hair and grown a beard, but it's him. I'd bet on it."

"Not according to the sheet they've got on him." Kurtzman backed up the images on the screen until they were looking at the Keralan equivalent of a rap sheet. Kurtzman highlighted the name. "Pervez Vajti. He's local."

"I don't buy it," Brognola said. "Call up your mujahideen files. Can you do that from here?"

"If you're looking for Neshah, let's skip the middleman," Kurtzman said, clicking away. He split the screen again and pulled up one of his self-created search engines, then logged in a specific request for a right profile shot of Dehri Neshah. Within seconds, the photo, culled from an archives on high-ranking terrorists, appeared, side-by-side with the prison shot from Kottayam. Although the file photo of Neshah showed a clean-shaved man with dark, close-cropped hair, there was no mistaking the other features.

"Nice call, boss," Kurtzman said.

Brognola was in no mind for flattery. "So what are

we dealing with here, Bear?'' he asked. ''Besides the fact that it ups the odds the mujahideen are in Kottayam gunning for the President...''

''It's one of those good-news, bad-news deals,'' Kurtzman said as he raced his fingers over the keyboard, trying to access the site that had dispatched the more recent photo of Neshah. ''The good news is that Neshah's in custody.''

''And the bad?''

''The bad news is whoever's got him doesn't know it.''

''Damn!''

''It gets worse,'' Kurtzman said as half the screen turned dark. ''This detention center's having some kind of blackout.''

CHAPTER SIX

Rahn-Maytt Detention Centre, Kottayam

Raghubir Shili was pretending to absolve Dehri Neshah of all his sins when his brother Penghat shut off the power to the entire detention centre. The lights and air-conditioning gave out simultaneously, and there was a fleeting, almost eerie moment of silence before the cell block erupted with howls and curses. Raghubir rose from Neshah's cot, taking off his wide-brimmed hat as he moved to the cell door. He peered out through a small, barred window. The closest guard was far down the corridor, barking into a wall phone. He sounded more annoyed than alarmed, testimony to the frequency of power outages during the summer months in Kottayam. Most of the other prisoners had moved to their doors, as well, clutching at the bars or clanging on them with bowls, cups and spoons, ranting for the air-conditioning to be turned back on before their cells turned into roasting ovens.

Raghubir turned from the door and called to Neshah in a whisper. "Quickly! We don't have long."

Neshah nodded, already stepping out of his dull, loose-fitting prison garb. He gave the clothes to Raghubir in exchange for the other man's robe. In silent haste the men dressed, Raghubir taking on the guise of a prisoner while Neshah turned himself into a man of the cloth.

"Here…" Raghubir took off his wire-rimmed glasses and handed them to Neshah. "With these, in the dim light and confusion they are sure to confuse you for me."

"You've done well, Raghubir."

Neshah donned the glasses, then reached into the black satchel Raghubir had smuggled into the detention centre. He pulled out a foot-long crucifix and gave it a sharp twist. The base separated from the crossbar, revealing a sheathed stiletto. Neshah grinned as he pulled the knife free and stared at its gleaming eight-inch blade. "Very well indeed."

The taller man smiled gratefully. "My way of making amends," he said modestly, "for what happened in New Delhi."

Raghubir was referring to a falling-out the two men had had back at the Indian capital. It was just prior to the bombing that had killed the American envoy. Raghubir had suggested they curtail their sabotage in hopes the authorities could be lulled by a false sense of security prior to the U.S. President's arrival. Neshah had disagreed, saying that continued attacks, especially over a widespread area, would keep their enemies distracted, their resources diluted. The men had argued their points vociferously, at one point almost coming to blows. Finally Raghubir had relented, apologizing for having questioned Neshah's authority. Neshah had been placated and the bombing had been carried out, but ever since there had been a gulf between them. Perhaps now, Raghubir reasoned, the gap could be closed and the matter put behind them once and for all.

"You will leave with Penghat," Raghubir said, spelling out the escape plan as he once more took a seat on Neshah's cot of straw. "I will explain that you overpowered me while I was hearing your confession and then took my place. Once they let me go, I will rendezvous with you at the academy and we can resume our plans. The missile launcher will be ready."

Neshah set the wide-brimmed hat atop his head, then adjusted the glasses on the bridge of his nose. Indeed, to an undiscriminating eye he could easily pass for Raghubir.

"You're forgetting," he reminded Raghubir, "I was taken in by the police before I could get my hands on the components for the guidance system."

"I realize that," Raghubir said, "but you yourself said that the missiles can be fired without the upgraded system. They will only be a little less effective, yes? Perhaps we will not disintegrate the jet in the air, but we can send it into the sea." With a grin, he added, "We can give the sharks a taste of democracy."

Neshah smiled briefly, but then his face took on a sad expression. "There is one problem with your plan, Raghubir," he said finally. "When you attempt to leave from here, don't you think it will seem suspicious that you can see just fine without your glasses?"

Raghubir shrugged as he finished buttoning his prison shirt. "I will squint a little, that's all. I'll pretend that without the glasses I am half-blind."

"And your beard?" Neshah inquired. "How will you pretend it's real if they give it a tug and it falls from your face?"

"That won't happen," Raghubir said, patting the costumed facial hair he'd taken from the wardrobe room back at the academy. "They will have no reason to pull it."

Neshah smiled sadly. "These men may be incompetent, but they are not complete fools. They will be looking for answers to what is about to happen. They will be asking questions."

"I'm no stranger to interrogations," Raghubir assured his leader. "They will get nothing from me."

Neshah looked Raghubir in the eyes. "I believe you, my friend, and I do not mean to question your integrity—"

Without warning, Neshah suddenly lashed out with the stiletto, thrusting it into the other man's chest, just below the breastbone. In almost the same motion, he gave the blade a sharp twist, tearing a gash through the heart it had just punctured.

Raghubir stared at Neshah, incredulous, his eyes already clouding with death. When he parted his lips to speak, blood spilled down his chin. No words came forth.

"Forgive me, Raghubir," Neshah intoned. "This is the way it must be."

Keeping the blade embedded in Raghubir's chest, he gently lowered the man, then laid him out facedown on the floor. He then withdrew the blade, wiping it clean on his robe as he strode to the door. Down the dimly lit hall, the guard had just hung up the phone and was shouting for the other prisoners to be quiet. Neshah raised his voice so that he could be heard above the others, doing his best to imitate Raghubir's higher-pitched voice.

"Something's wrong with my prisoner!" he called out. "Hurry! He's passed out on the floor!"

He had to repeat his cry twice before the guard finally heard and came to the cell door. Neshah stood back, lowering his head so that the hat's brim would shield his features. He pointed behind him, telling the guard, "I don't know what happened. I was listening to his confession when the power went out, and suddenly he collapsed."

"Just what I need," the guard muttered as he fumbled with his keys and unlocked the door.

"Perhaps it's the heat," Neshah offered. "He may have just fainted."

"If it's not one thing, it's another."

Still holding the keys, the guard strode past Neshah and crouched over Raghubir. When he saw blood seeping out from under the body, he frowned suspiciously. He was about to say something when Neshah attacked again with the stiletto, this time from behind. He swiped the razor-sharp blade across the guard's throat, severing both vocal cords and a carotid artery. For good measure, he then thrust the blade into the guard's back, just to the left of the spine. Again he gave the blade a sharp twist, ripping through several organs and taking a gouge out of the guard's spine.

The guard crumpled on top of Raghubir Shili, their blood mixing together on the floor.

Neshah wiped blood from his hands, then cleaned his blade once more and set it in a side pocket of the black satchel, leaving the handle exposed for easy access. He took note of which key the guard had been holding, then helped himself to the entire ring, as well as the gun in the man's holster. It was a standard police-issue .357 Magnum Smith & Wesson. Neshah had been hoping for a pistol with more rounds, but this would have to do. Pocketing the gun inside the folds of his clerical robe, he left the bodies behind and strode into the still-darkened hallway.

Instead of breaking into a run, he calmly went to the adjacent cell, using the master key to open the door. He told the prisoner, "I forgive you your trespasses."

The prisoner, a young man in his twenties, stared at Neshah, dumbfounded. "Forgive me?"

"You're a free man." Neshah swung the door open and pointed down the hallway toward a stairwell leading down to the main floor. "Go and sin no more," he told the man.

A grin broke across the prisoner's face as he stepped from his cell. As he started jogging for the staircase, the other prisoners let out a cry, wondering what was going on.

"Patience, patience," Neshah called out to them.

It took less than a minute for Neshah to release another twelve men. All of them were quick to abandon their cells and follow the first man to the stairwell. Neshah, meanwhile, went the other way, sorting through the keys for one that worked the door to a back staircase. He was bounding down the steps when he heard gunshots echoing in the other stairwell. Apparently the guards downstairs were taking exception to Neshah's release of the prisoners.

When he reached the ground floor, Neshah calmly stepped out into the hallway. There was pandemonium everywhere. Uniformed officers scrambled about in the shadows, guns in hand. Most of them were headed toward the commotion near the stairwell at the far end of the hall. One officer, however, heard Neshah behind him and whirled around, aiming his revolver at the would-be priest's chest.

"I was told to come down this way," Neshah explained calmly, keeping the Smith & Wesson secreted inside his robe. "For my own safety."

"Of course." The guard lowered his weapon. "Forgive me, Father. Follow me."

Striding behind the guard, Neshah was escorted to the same doorway through which the Shili brothers had been admitted to the building.

"I'd walk you to your car, but we have a situation here," the guard said as he held the door open for Neshah.

"I understand," Neshah said. "I'm sure the Lord will watch over me. And you."

The guard turned heel and charged back into the building. Neshah suppressed a grin as he strode across the parking lot. Penghat Shili sat behind the wheel of the tan sedan, engine running. Neshah circled around and let himself into the front seat.

"Did it all go well?" Penghat asked as he put the car into gear.

"Like clockwork," said Neshah.

"And my brother?"

"He was brilliant, as always," Neshah said. "He'll join us later at the academy. Now, let's go!"

Neshah held the stolen Smith & Wesson below the dashboard as they approached the front gate. The guards had taken cover and drawn their weapons, but they were less concerned with the would-be priest than the unseen furor being played out inside the building. Keeping their eyes trained on the complex, they quickly waved Neshah and Penghat out of the parking lot.

"There's another car waiting for us a mile from here," Penghat told Neshah as they merged into traffic. "We'll switch and leave this one for them to puzzle over."

"Good," Neshah said. "I knew I could count on you, Penghat."

Penghat flashed a grin, then, just as quickly, his face grew taut. Rounding the corner, he was forced to ease up on the accelerator. Traffic was backing up. By the time they'd reached the end of the next block, the sedan had been brought to a complete stop, hemmed in on all sides by other vehicles.

"Roadblock?" Neshah wondered.

"I don't think they're that fast," Penghat said, shaking his head. "It's just rush hour."

"Bad enough," Neshah said. "I was afraid this might happen." He closed his eyes, grimacing, his skull beginning to throb anew. The street noise that had tormented him up in his cell was nothing compared to the cacophony that now enveloped him. Every driver seemed to be either leaning on his horn or cursing loudly in Malalayam; some were doing both, raging at one another, as well as the trishaw operators and the small handful of men who'd chosen this, of all times, to herd their livestock through town.

Penghat could see Neshah was in pain. He was no stranger to the other man's migraines, and he knew that if they stayed here, stranded inside the car, Neshah would soon be incapacitated. They would be trapped. Something had to be done or all the effort put into Neshah's escape would prove to have been in vain.

Shifting the car into Neutral, Penghat stepped on the parking brake, then reached into the back seat, grabbing a pair of hiking shorts and a loose shirt. He handed the clothes to Neshah, then started to unbutton his own robe.

"Out of your disguise, Dehri," he said.

Quickly both men changed, ignoring the stares of those outside their car. Penghat then wadded their robes into a ball and stuffed them into a space between the two front seats. He grabbed the black satchel he'd brought with him into the detention center. Then, once he saw that Neshah was dressed, he took a cigarette lighter from his pocket and set fire to the robes.

"Out!" he told Neshah, shifting the transmission into gear. Even with the parking brake on, the sedan began to slowly inch forward. Neshah hesitated a moment, watching flames creep from the burning robes to the fabric of the seat covers. A foul-smelling smoke began to fill the car.

"Dehri!" Penghat shouted. "Now!"

Neshah blinked, as if snapping out of a trance, and nodded. Both men got out of either side of the car. Leaving his door open, Penghat reached in and released the parking brake. The sedan immediately picked up speed, crashing into the rear end of the idling minivan in front of it.

Out of the van sprang a tall, barrel-chested man, screaming with rage. He pointed out the damage to his vehicle, then shook a fist at Penghat, cursing. When Penghat tried to brush past him, the man blocked his way and gave him a sharp push. As Penghat staggered backward, Neshah fired his Smith & Wesson over the top of the sedan. The driver of the minivan took a bullet to the face and spun to one side before slumping over the hood of the burning sedan. A few cars away, a woman screamed.

Penghat quickly recovered his balance and broke into a run. Neshah followed close behind and they threaded their way through the congestion until they reached the end of the block, at which point they detoured through the alleyway between two buildings. Crossing a back parking lot, the men leaped a short fence and followed a side street that soon led them to a small city park. A gathered crowd paid them little heed, their attention drawn instead to a street performer goading his pet gibbon—dressed in a miniaturized white tuxedo—to dance in time with disco music blaring from a small boom box.

Running helped blunt the pain of Neshah's migraine, and he took heart that Penghat seemed to know where they were headed. Penghat, who'd carefully studied a street map of downtown Kottayam before leaving the academy four hours ago, next led Neshah across a narrow, arching bridge that spanned one of the city's canals. They climbed another fence, this one made of rusting chicken wire, then crossed a field strewed with weeds and litter. Both men were gasping for breath when they finally found themselves on an isolated dirt road a quarter mile from the highway leading out of town.

The only car in sight was an old brown Honda sedan parked on the shoulder. As the men approached the car, the front door opened and the driver stepped out. It was a woman. She was tall, red-haired, wearing jodhpurs, riding boots and a white silk blouse.

"I was beginning to worry," she called out as she opened the rear door. Her accent was American, East Coast. "Where's the other car?"

"There was a change of plans," Penghat said as he took the keys from the woman and climbed into the driver's seat.

Neshah smiled faintly at the woman, stroking her cheek as he moved past her into the back seat. The woman got into the car and sat next to him. As soon as the door was closed, Penghat pulled out onto the road and started for the highway.

Easing back in his seat, Dehri Neshah exhaled with relief. The woman beside him ran her fingers through his hair, then leaned close and kissed his forehead. At the same time, she took his hand and guided it between her legs, pressing them tightly together.

"Welcome back, Dehri," she whispered in his ear. "I missed you...."

CHAPTER SEVEN

Academy of Arts in the Ghats

Pressed into service, the thatch-roofed country boat that less than two hours ago had been moored at the CIA base in Alleppey now floated near the earthen dikes separating Kottayam's canals from the sprawl of tea plants and coconut palms being farmed on the lower grounds of the Academy of Arts. Nhajsib Wal stood in the bow of the craft, holding a long, round wooden pole that extended to the bottom of the shallow canal. The Intelligence Bureau agent's unruly mop of jet-black hair and boyish features gave him the look of an enterprising teenager, one of dozens who routinely ferried about these waterways looking to shuttle goods and passengers between the city and outlying areas. Wal glanced around casually. Once he felt certain no one was looking his way, he faintly shrugged his head to one side, as if working a kink out of his neck.

Inside the boat, Mack Bolan relayed the signal to John Kissinger, who was crouched between the stacked crates of sparklers and ceremonial fireworks he and Jack Grimaldi had picked up in Alleppey after

their altercation with the mujahideen downriver from
the CIA base. While a CIA powerboat had hauled
Kissinger and the country boat upstream to Kottayam
to rendezvous with Bolan and Wal, Grimaldi had returned to the base to await repairs on the helicopter.

Secret Service teams and a band of CIA field operatives based at the site, meanwhile, were presently
searching both sides of the river for any remaining
mujahideen forces in the area. In Kottayam, Nhajsib
Wal's IB cohorts were assembling a backup force to
stake out the academy's periphery. And a few miles
away, making their way across the choppy waters of
Vembanad Lake in massive powered barges, was India's Seventy-third Armoured Regiment. The closest
military force in the area—they'd been going through
maneuvers on the nearby coastal marshlands—the
regiment was coming prepared, if necessary, to use
its Soviet-made tanks to storm the academy. Such tactics, however, would be only a last resort, as there
was concern that if the mujahideen had indeed taken
over the academy armed with the missing Sabre
launchers, too strong a show of force might prompt
them to fire missiles, not only against the troops, but
also across the Laccadive Sea toward the President's
temporary quarters in Maldives. As a first court of
action, it was decided that Bolan and Kissinger, with
Wal's help, would first try to infiltrate the academy
and determine the extent—if any—of the threat posed
by Dehri Neshah's band of insurgents.

"Almost ready," Kissinger said, knotting the laces
of his calf-high boots. He'd turned his ankle while
being thrown from the Jet Ski back in Alleppey and

hoped the boots would minimize further injury. Like Bolan, he also now wore a Kevlar-lined flak vest over his combat fatigues.

When he saw that Kissinger was ready, Bolan stole from the boat's hold and scrambled up the embankment, taking cover behind a waist-high hedge that ran spinelike down the center of the dike, its roots anchoring the rich, loamy soil. Kissinger quickly slung on a backpack, then followed close on the Executioner's heels.

Looking the other way, Nhajsib Wal stabbed his pole into the water and eased his craft away from the dike. With a carefree smile, he waved to some of the threshers slogging their way through the nearby paddies. Much as he wanted to be in on the recon, Wal knew he was more valuable in this capacity, passing himself off as a local as he slowly encircled the academy grounds, keeping an eye open for suspicious activity. Once the other Intelligence Bureau agents arrived and took up their positions, he would await Bolan's signal. If an assault seemed possible without harming the residents of the academy, Wal would use the fireworks to help flush out the enemy. By then the Seventy-third Regiment would have crossed the lake and brought their tanks ashore. Of course, if he had to, Wal was prepared to abandon the boat and storm the academy single-handedly if he thought it would help keep the mujahideen from slaying his uncle and carrying out their agenda.

Up on the dike, Bolan and Kissinger watched Nhajsib Wal guide the boat away from them.

"I hope we can count on him," Kissinger whispered as the men further camouflaged themselves by streaking their arms and faces with soil from the embankment.

"I'd bet on it," Bolan said. Reaching beneath his flak vest, he drew his .44. "Ready?"

"Let's go." Kissinger thumbed off the safety on his Colt.

Dropping to the ground, the two men crawled from the dike to a tangle of thick brush growing wild alongside a dirt path that led past the tea plants and coconut palms. It was slow going, as they had to stop each time a low-hanging branch snagged on their clothing and threatened to snap. They were further impeded by swarms of large black flies drawn to their sweat as if it were some sort of nectar.

As he blew one of the flies from his face, Kissinger couldn't help thinking how less than twenty-four hours ago he was lolling at a beach cabana in Sri Lanka, discussing weapons designs over piña coladas with the R&D techies from Negombo who'd modified some of the components for his DHL prototype. Today he was supposed to be touring the firm's manufacturing plant, then attending a banquet featuring a pig roast and entertainment by the island's most captivating dancers, including a runner-up in last year's Miss Universe competition. Instead, here he was, pressed into last-minute field service, mud wrestling his way to a probable firefight in which most likely he and Bolan would find themselves, as usual, woefully outnumbered. This after he'd already put his life on the line playing water chicken with a boatful of gunmen back in Alleppey.

As they made their way across the lower grounds, Kissinger began to wonder if Nhajsib Wal had been mistaken about the mujahideen having seized the academy. There was no visible activity up near the *karalas,* and from all appearances, the farming operations down here on the flatlands seemed legitimate, the epitome of Keralan efficiency. Out in the fields, workers methodically made their way down the rows of shoulder-high tea plants, plucking at leaves with practiced rhythm. Near one of the storage buildings, meanwhile, men loaded freshly husked coconuts into the hold of a wide-bottomed boat tethered to a make-shift trailer. Once filled, it would be hauled down to the canals and eased into the water. Twenty yards to their right, in the shade of the surrounding palm trees, a team of women, oblivious to the heat, knelt amid the discarded husks, hammering them with wooden clubs. Up in the palm trees themselves, short, wiry young men made cuts in the bark with scythelike knives, drawing forth an oozing sap. To Kissinger it appeared that the men and women alike went about their business with single-minded focus and concentration, totally unconcerned with any activity except their own.

"I don't know," Kissinger murmured as he and Bolan watched the activity from their vantage point in the brush. "I don't think anyone here's any more mujahideen than we are."

"You might be right," Bolan said. "On the other hand, maybe they're just taking a page from our guys back home." He was referring to the blacksuits who worked the grounds at Stony Man Farm, which was laid out to pass for a bona fide agricultural enterprise, complete with crops, fruit orchards and timber harvested by an operational lumber mill.

"I don't think so," Kissinger murmured. "Our guys keep an eye on the perimeter no matter what they're doing. These people are all work."

"Could be the mujahideen have them working under gunpoint," Bolan suggested, continuing to scan the grounds.

As the wind shifted, Bolan detected a sweet, cloying aroma. He turned and traced the smell to the first rise leading up to the academy. Next to a small knoll overgrown with ferns was a mountainous pile of dried palm fronds, just beyond which a thin, barely visible cloud of smoke trailed up from what appeared to be some kind of ventilation pipe.

By now Kissinger had picked up the scent, as well. "A still?" he said.

"Could be," Bolan said. "Maybe that's what they do with the sap."

"White lightning."

"I'm sure they have another name for it," Bolan said. "Let's see if they've got something else brewing."

Hoping to circle behind the knoll, Bolan and Kissinger sprinted across a clearing toward another cluster of hedges. Before they could reach cover, gunfire suddenly hailed down on them from the nearby trees. Both men dived forward and tumbled into the brush. More shots rang out, chewing at the leaves and branches only a few inches from them.

Bolan rolled to one side and peered up through the

brush at the surrounding palms. High up, beneath the canopy of a nearby tree, a man leaned outward, having exchanged his knife for an assault rifle. He fired with one hand, gripping the tree with the other; it was enough to throw off his aim, and his shots scattered wide of their mark. Bolan calmly took aim with his Desert Eagle and squeezed the trigger. The sniper dropped his rifle, then followed it to the ground, arms flailing. Bones snapped as he landed headfirst, breaking his neck.

"Another one at three o'clock," Kissinger called out. He fired his weapon, but the other sniper had already taken cover.

"If they're all armed up there, we're in trouble," Kissinger muttered as he ducked more incoming fire. "Let's get some backup in here!"

Bolan was already keying his walkie-talkie to reach Nhajsib Wal back at the boat. Before he could transmit a message, however, a loud explosion sounded from the dikes, followed by a series of smaller blasts. Soon the air over the south end of the property was filled with multicolored pinwheels of smoke and flame.

"Wal must've touched the fireworks," Kissinger said.

"Trying to buy us some time," Bolan said. "Let's make the best of it."

While the gunmen in the trees were distracted, Bolan and Kissinger bolted from cover and advanced to a waist-high stone wall covered with ferns. They now had a clear view of the distillery.

"Check it out," Kissinger said.

The distillery was the size of a two-car garage, made of cinder block with a thatched roof. Two men were standing in the front doorway, looking in the direction of the fireworks. Both were armed with MP-5 submachine guns. One of them glanced over his shoulder and shouted back into the building. Someone called back to him, then both men went back inside, closing the door behind them. Moments later, a front window was raised partially open and one of the gunmen peered out from behind rustling curtains.

"I wonder how many are in there," Kissinger said.

"No telling," Bolan said. "But I don't think barging in's the way to go."

As they pondered their next move, Bolan and Kissinger listened to the steady popping sounds in the distance.

"I can't tell if there're any gunshots or it's all just fireworks," Kissinger said.

"Me, either."

Bolan licked his fingertip and checked the wind, then turned to Kissinger. "Maybe we can take the snipers out of the equation."

"How's that?"

Bolan gestured past them at the heap of dried palm fronds piled near the distillery. "You were saying how you wanted to test drive that DHL of yours, right?"

Kissinger was hesitant. True, he'd brought along his pet project, but this was a hell of a proving ground. Bolan was right, though; if it worked, the launcher was their best chance.

He took the DHL from its case and had it assembled in less than thirty seconds. Propping the weapon on his shoulder, he peered through its built-in scope, which used an integrated computer system to calculate firing distance and trajectory once he'd acquisitioned his target.

"One dragon's hairball coming up."

Kissinger pulled the trigger. The DHL bucked hard against his shoulder as it spit forth a six-inch-long projectile. The charge hissed through the air, detonating on impact when it landed a few yards in front of the stacked palm fronds. The fronds, dry as kindling, quickly ignited. Sparks flew outward and a thick column of black smoke took to the air.

"Nice shot, Cowboy," Bolan said.

"Thanks. Now comes the tricky part."

Kissinger ejected a shell from the DHL and quickly rearmed it with another cartridge. To date, the biggest flaw with the DHL had been the heat generated inside its retractable firing shafts during each launch; it was usually so intense that the tubes were thrown out of alignment, thwarting the accuracy of any follow-up shots by as much as forty percent. Kissinger was relieved his first shot had been on the mark, but as he took aim at the roof of the distillery, he could only hope the replacement tubes he'd picked up in Sri Lanka would be an improvement over the old ones.

"Come on, baby," Kissinger murmured. At the last second, he decided to factor in the weapon's tendency to fall short on its follow-up shots. Tilting the barrel, he aimed slightly higher than called for, then braced himself and fired the second round.

Whooooosh!

Straight and true, the incendiary charge beelined toward the building. Kissinger was stunned; the new firing shafts had held up so well there was virtually no change in trajectory from his first shot. In fact, it looked for a moment as if he'd overshot his mark. As the projectile hurtled over the distillery, however, it slammed headlong into the chimney pipe and disintegrated. Fiery shards hailed down on the roof, feasting on the dry thatch.

"I'll be damned," Kissinger whispered.

"Maybe so," Bolan said, "but let's get these bastards first!"

Kissinger ditched the DHL in favor of his Colt pistol. "I'll take the back."

Both men quickly vaulted the stone wall and split up. Kissinger circled around toward the rear of the distillery. Bolan went the opposite way, making sure to keep the blazing palm fronds between himself and the building. Once he reached the top of the knoll, he took cover between two fern-shrouded boulders. One boulder provided protection from any possible gunfire coming from the distillery, while the other shielded his back should anyone start firing at him from behind. So far, however, it didn't appear that he'd been spotted, either from the trees or the sentries inside the distillery.

Bolan could see flames devouring the building's thatch roof, and drifting smoke from both fires stung his eyes and burned in his throat and nostrils whenever he took a breath. It had to be even worse inside the building, he reasoned, and he was surprised that no one had yet been forced out into the open.

Seconds dragged on, and Bolan was still waiting for the Kashmiris to show themselves when his walkie-talkie squawked faintly on his hip. He kept the volume turned down low as he brought the transceiver to this mouth. "Striker here."

"You're not gonna believe this." It was Kissinger. He sounded angry. "I'm twenty feet down some freaking hole!"

"A trap?" Bolan wondered.

"No, I think it's an old well." Kissinger quickly explained how he'd been passing through a patch of high weeds behind the distillery when some rotting timbers snapped under his weight, dropping him down the shaft.

"You all right?" Bolan asked.

"Outside of my pride, yeah," Kissinger responded. "My ankle's smarting, but that's the least of my problems. I'm up to my armpits in water, and the walls are so slick with algae I can't climb out."

"Give me a second," Bolan said. "I'll head over and give you a hand—"

"Forget about it, man," Kissinger told him. "Stick with the program. I just wanted you to know why I'm a scratch."

Bolan glanced downhill, staring past the burning fronds. "Look," he told Kissinger, "I don't know why, but nobody's come out of the distillery yet, so I've got time to swing around and get you. If we're gonna have to go in after them, we'll have a better chance if there's two of us."

"You sure?"

"Tell me where you are," Bolan said.

Kissinger relayed his position as best he could remember it.

"I'm on my way," Bolan told him, then signed off. He was about to backtrack the way he'd come when he noticed someone peering out the front window of the distillery. Bolan couldn't break cover without being spotted. By the same token, he couldn't take out the sentry without tipping off his position.

Bolan grabbed his walkie-talkie again. He was about to check with Nhajsib Wal when a section of burning fronds suddenly tumbled free from the pyre. When it hit the ground, sparks scattered, igniting wisps of dry grass. The sentry's gaze shifted to the new fires. Bolan saw his chance and bolted from cover, crouching low as he passed through a cluster of wild tea plants.

Thirty yards behind the distillery, he came across the crumbling foundation of an older building being reclaimed by the elements. Kissinger had said he'd just spotted the ruins when he'd fallen into the shaft, so Bolan slowed and made his way cautiously. Finally, he spotted an opening in the tall weeds and headed toward it.

The well was barely five feet across. Kissinger had figured out that he could inch his way upward by bracing his shoulders against one side of the wall and extending his legs across for traction. It was slow going, but he was making progress.

Bolan called down to him. "How about a hand?"

"Wait till I get a little closer," Kissinger called

back. "Keep an eye open so we don't get bush-whacked."

"They're all still inside the building," Bolan reported. He grabbed his walkie-talkie and again keyed Nhajsib Wal back at the canals. No answer. He tried again, with the same results. So much for backup.

FROM HIS COVER in the brush, Nhajsib Wal watched the last of his fireworks erupt out over the canals. In their wake, a column of dark smoke rose up from the smoldering, half-sunken remains of his boat—this on top of the smoke coming from the foothills. Ash fell from the sky like snow. Though he'd yet to spot the Americans, Wal suspected they had started the second fire to deal with the snipers in the trees. He hoped the ploy had worked, but he was concerned that there was no more gunfire. Had the two Americans been taken out by ground troops? Wal wished he hadn't left his walkie-talkie back on the boat in his haste to get clear of the fireworks.

Of course, given his present position, Wal wouldn't have been able to communicate with anyone anyway. After leaving the boat, he'd managed to infiltrate as far as the trailer where coconuts were being loaded for shipment to Kottayam. On the way, he'd seen the teapickers flee—away from the academy rather than toward it. Wal was glad for their sake; away from the property, they lessened their risk of being taken hostage. Unfortunately, the same couldn't be said for some of the other workers. Across the driveway from where he was hiding, Wal saw two armed gunmen scanning the grounds while a third led the fear-struck women away from the battered husks and herded them into a nearby storage building.

Much as he wanted to intervene, Wal was forced to stay put; behind him, he could hear the men who'd gone to investigate the fireworks. They were on their way back. Walther in hand, he crouched lower in his hiding place, shielding himself in shade cast by nearby palm trees. Soon the men were passing within a few yards of him. They were mujahideen, all right; Wal could see it in their dress and appearance, hear it in the Kashmiri dialect with which they cursed themselves for having been duped by the fireworks. Wal knew only a smattering of Urdu, but it was clear to him that they were assuring themselves that if they got their hands on whoever had broached the grounds, their lives would be as worthless as cocktail umbrellas in a monsoon.

Wal wished he'd been more insistent on waiting for backup before making any move. Bolan had overruled him, concerned that if they waited, a sentry might spot the backup force and alert the mujahideen, making their recon even more difficult. In any event, that was all in the past. Wal had his hands full dealing with the present.

Eleven men, all armed, assembled briefly in front of the building where the women had been taken. The one in charge, a man wearing a white skullcap and a blue-green paratrooper's outfit, split the others into groups of two and sent them off in separate directions. No one was headed directly toward Nhajsib Wal, but he could see that he would be quickly hemmed in from either side. If they found him, they wouldn't kill him—not if they could help it. He would be more valuable to them alive, not only as a hostage, but as a source of information. They would want to find out how their compound had been discovered. They would want to know how much the authorities knew of their plans and activities. If he refused to cooperate, they would no doubt resort to torture. He was prepared for that; he knew he could endure any measure of pain without giving in. But the mujahideen would know that. They wouldn't waste their energies torturing him, not when they had women they could drag before him, threatening them with the worst kind of abuses if he didn't tell them what they wanted to know. Wal couldn't let things come to that.

He slowly raised his Walther and drew a bead on the man in the skullcap. He would kill their leader first, then charge from the brush, making himself an open target. With any luck, he would be able to take out a few others before the return fire ripped through him.

Before he could pull the trigger, Wal was startled by a rustling overhead. He glanced up just as a Kashmiri sniper leaped from his place of concealment beneath the drooping fronds of the nearest palm tree. Before Wal could react, the man was on top of him. As he was hauled to the ground, the Indian tried to fight back, but at such close quarters the martial arts taught to him by his uncle were of little use. He managed an off-balance swipe with his left hand, but it merely glanced off the other man's shoulder. More irritated than immobilized, the mujahideen shrugged off the blow and slammed the butt of his rifle against Wal's skull, turning his world dark.

THREE HUNDRED YARDS uphill, Nhajsib Wal's capture was witnessed by the two terrorists standing guard over his uncle, Ziarat Wal, and his young charges in the academy's *kalaripayattu* hall. The two Kashmiris had gone to the window at the first outbreak of gunfire several minutes ago, and there they remained, dividing their attention between their prisoners and the drama unfolding on the grounds below.

Listening intently to the men from across the room, Ziarat was able to get some sense of what was going on. He at first welcomed the news that someone was attempting to reclaim the academy from the mujahideen, but when he heard that one of the liberators had been captured, Ziarat's blood ran cold. The man they described sounded like his nephew. Ziarat didn't want to believe it, but he knew all too well that if there was a raid on the academy, Nhajsib would more than likely be in on it.

As he strained to hear more details, Ziarat was interrupted by the youth with the bandaged ribs. The boy, who crouched nearby, had tears in his eyes.

"I smell smoke, Ziaratashan," he whimpered. "Are they going to burn the school down?"

"Shh." Ziarat hushed the boy and whispered back to him. "No, this school will not burn down."

"You'll stop them?"

Ziarat slowly nodded, trying to reassure the boy. "Yes, they will be stopped."

"When?"

"Soon," Ziarat said, his gaze trailing to the wall, where weapons hung next to the painting of him and his nephew. The guards hadn't concerned themselves with the weapons, figuring they were hanging too high on the wall for anyone to reach. Ziarat knew better, however. He leaned close to the youth. "Listen to me carefully," he whispered. "When the time *does* come, here is what you must do...."

CHAPTER EIGHT

Alleppey, Malabar Coast

Jack Grimaldi stood at the railing of the wooden deck where he'd earlier landed the Colwyss-8A at the CIA river base in Alleppey. The pylons seemed to have recovered from the strain of supporting the chopper's weight; they wavered only faintly under the gentle force of the river's current. Famished, Grimaldi chewed on a protein bar with the consistency of hardtack, washing each bite down with swills of canned water. Both rations were compliments of the CIA, whose senior communications officer was presently inside trying to patch through a satellite call to the States so Grimaldi could apprise Stony Man Farm of his and Kissinger's skirmish upriver with the mujahideen. A report had just come in that search teams had captured a handful of men suspected of abetting the terrorists, but security at the base remained heightened on the chance that other insurgents were still on the loose. Grimaldi had been advised not to stand out on the deck, where he posed an ideal target for snipers, but the Stony Man pilot had had his fill of sweating inside the service bay. Out here it was hot, as well, but there was some measure of relief in the breeze blowing off the river.

Presently, Grimaldi heard, carried in that same breeze, the now familiar deep roar of the Agency's Mark V Special Operations Craft. The SOC's pilot had radioed ahead, announcing their approach, but no one at the outpost was about to let down his guard. Directly below the observation deck, a heavily armed four-man crew—two each from the CIA and Secret Service—pulled away from the docks in a Combat Rubber Raiding Raft propelled by twice the horsepower of the motorized rowboat Grimaldi and Kissinger had been stuck with earlier. Behind Grimaldi, armed sentries atop the service bay assumed firing positions with M-4 A 1 carbines. The men had Grimaldi's sympathies; even with insulated foam mats to crouch on, he was sure they could still feel the heat radiating up from the metallic roof.

One of the sentries signaled for Grimaldi to take cover. He pitched aside his rations and crouched behind the deck railing, drawing his Grizzly automatic. Moments later, a long, sleek gray boat rounded the bend, prow high above the waterline. It was the same Mark V that had earlier hauled John Kissinger and the boatload of fireworks up to Kottayam. Acquired from the Navy SEALs after years of service in the Pacific, the SOC had twin aft gunnery posts flanking a slanted back ramp that dipped low enough in the water to allow direct boarding by powered CRRRs. Two of the latter craft were tethered to the ramp, and the officers who had used them in the search for the mujahideen could be seen standing nearby, guns trained on a handful of swarthy-skinned men wearing tan tracksuits and white puggarees. As the boat eased its way into a mooring slip beneath the observation deck, an officer on board called up to Grimaldi, reporting that the prisoners were not likely mujahideen, but rather local accomplices rousted from a squalid encampment half a mile upriver. There had been tire tracks leading to the river's edge, and the men had been in possession of a pickup truck hitched to a trailer large enough to have carried the speedboat that had stalked Grimaldi and Kissinger on their way to Alleppey.

Grimaldi called down to the officer, "What about binoculars and some type of radio transmitter? Did you find anything like that?"

"Both, as a matter of fact," the man on the deck called back. "Why?"

Grimaldi started to explain how he'd apparently been tracked when he'd flown back from Kottayam earlier. Before he could finish, the base's communications officer—a lanky blond Californian whose nose was slathered white with zinc oxide—strode out onto the deck carrying a Motorola LST-5C satellite radio. Trailing from the radio was an antenna cable that snaked all the way back inside the building.

"You're on," he informed Grimaldi, holding out the radio and its amplified two-way headset. "You can take it out here if you want."

"Thanks." Grimaldi took the equipment and fed out more of the antenna cable until he'd reached the far end of the deck. The headset alone would probably have been adequate for keeping the conversation private, but Grimaldi wasn't taking any chances.

"Flyboy One here," he spoke lowly into the headset's microphone.

"You've been busy, Flyboy." On the other end of the line was Barbara Price, mission controller at Stony Man Farm. She'd been a part of the program for nearly as long as Grimaldi, stepping in to fill the shoes of April Rose, who'd been killed in the same assault on the Farm that had put Aaron Kurtzman in a wheelchair. Though she reported to Hal Brognola, Price had earned a high level of autonomy when it came to managing the Farm's field teams.

Grimaldi quickly apprised her of the recent events in Alleppey, including the capture of the alleged mujahideen accomplices. He concluded, "I'm sure they have translators here. I was thinking I'd take first crack at interrogating them."

"Only if you can't get airborne pronto," Price told him.

"They need me in Kottayam," Grimaldi guessed.

"I think so. We've lost ground communication with Striker and Cowboy, but they're somewhere on the grounds of the academy. Aaron just tapped into an Orion satellite view of Kottayam, and there are two fires downhill from the school buildings. The bigger one's throwing up so much smoke we can't see past it."

"What about the tank troops?" Grimaldi asked. "And these IB guys who are supposed to be there for backup?"

"The Seventy-third is halfway across Vembanad

Lake,'' Price reported, ''and the IB's chopper is just taking on fuel now.''

''In other words,'' Grimaldi said, ''Striker and Cowboy are up shit creek without any paddles.''

''That's one way of putting it.''

''I'm on my way,'' Grimaldi said.

''Don't take that helicopter up until it's ready,'' Price warned. ''Do you hear me, Flyboy?''

Grimaldi reached into his pocket for the wrapper to his protein bar. He held the headset out at arm's length and crinkled the wrapper close to the microphone while calling out, ''What's that? You're breaking up....''

''I know what you're doing, and I don't—''

Grimaldi clicked off the radio and took it back inside the service bay, handing it to the communications officer. Without breaking stride, he hurried across the floor to the helicopter. The mechanic was kneeling on the roof of the chopper, tightening down the replacement rotor assembly.

''Hey, perfect timing!'' he called out to Grimaldi. ''I just—''

''Is this sucker fueled up?'' Grimaldi interrupted.

''Yes, but—''

''Off!'' Grimaldi shouted, gesturing for the mechanic to get down from the chopper. The two men crossed paths as the pilot was strapping himself into his seat.

''Listen, until the new assembly wears in you've got to take things slow and easy, got it?''

''Slow and easy.'' Grimaldi grinned savagely at the

other man as he started up the engines. "Yeah, right."

"What are you doing?" the mechanic cried, leaping away from the aircraft. "You can't take off in here! You need to wait for a tow out to—"

"I'm in a hurry!" Grimaldi shouted over the engines. "Clear the runway!"

The mechanic continued to protest, as did several of the agents who suddenly found their paperwork swirling about the enclosure thanks to the chopper's rotor wash. The service bay had a raised ceiling, but Grimaldi still had barely enough clearance to get the chopper aloft without clipping the exposed ductwork for the air-conditioner.

The mechanic rushed in front of the opened bay doors leading out to the observation deck and tried to block the way, but Grimaldi throttled the bird forward and sent the man diving to the floor. He swooped out through the opening and quickly pitched upward, narrowly avoiding the deck railing and the nearest treetops.

As he took the chopper higher, Grimaldi saw funnels of black smoke rising in the distance like idling tornadoes. Kottayam was less than ten miles away. If he pushed the chopper for all it was worth, he could reach the academy ahead of the others and hopefully find out what kind of trouble Bolan and Kissinger had gotten themselves into.

"Slow and easy's gonna have to wait for another day."

Grimaldi opened the throttle. Forward he sped, toward the billowing smoke.

Krula Pass, Western Ghats

THE SIGHT OF SMOKE rising from the grounds of the
academy filled Dehri Neshah with a sense of urgency.

"The base has been discovered," he said. "This is
a problem."

He was still seated in the back seat of the Honda
Accord, which Penghat Shili had parked on the shoul-
der of a two-lane mountain road leading up through
Krula Pass.

Briley, as the woman was known by, was outside
the car, standing on the far side of the guard railing,
staring through binoculars out at the valley floor below. Even from their perspective, Neshah and Shili
could see the winding dirt road the mujahideen had
used the previous night when they had come down
from the mountains to take over the academy. Shili
had hoped to take the same road back, but, as Neshah
had just suggested, that plan no longer seemed viable.

Up in the front seat, Shili cursed and slammed his
handheld AN/PRC-119 radio against the dashboard,
then tried—again without success—to establish communication with his brother Vargadrum at the academy.

"Perhaps we're beyond range," Neshah speculated.

"No!" Shili insisted. "We should be close
enough! And I know the battery still has power."

"Then maybe it's broken," Neshah said pointedly.
"From rough handling."

Shili glanced over his shoulder at Neshah. "I've
seen you try to fix radios the same way, Dehri."

"With the same results."

Before Shili could respond, they heard the sound of another car heading downhill toward them. Both men fell silent and drew their weapons as they dropped low in their seats. They could hear the other car slowing to a stop, less than a dozen yards away.

"Can I be of assistance?" the driver called out to Briley. It was a man, his voice friendly, solicitous. He spoke in English, but with a local accent.

"Just admiring the view," Neshah heard Briley answer.

"It *is* quite a view," the driver said.

Shili and Neshah tensed. If the man pulled over and got out of his car to engage Briley in further conversation, he would be likely to spot them, in which case he would have to be killed. Neither man wanted it to come to that; this high up in the mountains, the sound of gunshots—or even a struggle, however brief—would likely echo through the pass, drawing suspicion their way.

Briley had to have had the same concern, because the men heard her step over the railing and stride past the Honda to the other car. She lowered her voice and neither Neshah or Shili could hear what was being said between her and the other driver. Finally, Neshah heard the sound of laughter—Briley's—and then the other car shifted back into gear and headed past, continuing downhill toward Kottayam. Only then did the two Kashmiris relax their grips on their automatics.

Briley came over and let herself into the back seat.

"A tour pilot," she told them. "He has a plane at that private airfield we passed a few minutes ago."

"How did you get rid of him?" Neshah said, watching the woman refasten the top buttons of her blouse. "As if I didn't know."

"He said if I liked the view from here I'd love it more from the air," Briley said with a sly smile. "He's getting the plane ready."

"He'll be disappointed when you don't show up," Shili mused.

"When I don't show up, he'll find himself another passenger," Briley predicted. "I know his type."

"And he yours, too, I'm sure," Shili said.

Briley shot Shili an angry glance, then set the binoculars aside and told Neshah, "There're two fires on the grounds. A small one by the dikes and a larger one near a building just uphill from the farmland."

"The distillery," Neshah murmured. He and Shili exchanged a look. If the academy had been raided, the distillery was the last place the mujahideen wanted to have targeted. This wasn't a good sign.

"Could you see any forces on the ground?" Neshah asked. "Ours or theirs?"

"No," Briley reported, "but with all the smoke it was hard to see much of anything."

"It has to be a raid," Shili said. "There's no other explanation."

"I did see something else," the woman said. "A few miles beyond the academy. A large lake."

"Vembanad," Penghat said. "What about it?"

"There were some kind of boats on it, heading this way, in formation."

"How many?" Neshah asked.

"Ten? A dozen?" Briley said. "They're low boats,

almost like barges, and they're carrying vehicles of some sort. Maybe tanks.''

Shili leaned over the seat and grabbed the binoculars. ''I need to see.''

''We agreed it was safer for her to be the one who—''

Shili cut off Neshah. ''I know what we said, but I need to see for myself!''

Shili got out of the car and went to the railing. Neshah stared at him coldly.

''Insolent,'' he muttered. ''Just like his brother.''

''It's just stress, Dehri,'' Briley told him. ''Don't take it personally.''

''He's lucky he's more useful to me than Raghubir,'' Neshah said.

Briley reached out and ran her fingers through Neshah's hair. ''You still have your migraine,'' she guessed.

''I'm fine,'' Neshah said.

Briley smiled. ''Then it must be you're jealous. Of the pilot.''

Neshah shook his head. ''Men will stop wanting you the day Ganesh grows wings. I have accepted that.''

''Dehri the philosopher.'' Briley kissed Neshah lightly, then glanced out the window at the other Kashmiri. ''Penghat is the jealous one. I think he would like it if you shared me with him.''

''Penghat does not understand how valuable you are to us, that is all,'' Neshah said. ''That, plus he is upset by all that has gone wrong since we came to Kottayam. For that I can't blame him.''

"Things *have* been going wrong," Briley conceded, watching Penghat Shili head back toward the car. "Not like at our other stops."

Shili got back in the front seat and tossed the binoculars angrily onto the seat beside him.

"They are tanks, all right," he said, grabbing the radio. "A whole regiment. There are also helicopters, at least two of them. One is a transport, Boeing or Sikorsky."

"A special-forces team, no doubt," Neshah said.

Shili tried once more to make contact with the academy, but again he couldn't raise a signal on the radio. His frustration was rising. "Vargadrum," he shouted, "answer me!"

Neshah ignored Shili's tantrum and stared out the window. He didn't need to hear from Vargadrum to know that returning to the academy was no longer advisable. True, they could take the dirt road down and help the others make a stand, but to what end? His followers might draw inspiration from his return, but given the force massing against them, there was no way they could make a stand and survive. It would be suicide. And though martyrdom had its merits, Neshah felt he could better serve the mujahideen cause alive. And the cause came first.

"Penghat," Neshah called out patiently, "there is nothing we can do here. We must leave things in Vargadrum's hands and move on."

"Vargadrum is not equipped to lead," Penghat Shili countered. "We both know that."

"Maybe he will prove us wrong." Neshah pointed

northward, toward the higher reaches of Krula Pass. "Let's go. We'll see to the other launcher."

Shili stared back out the window at the columns of smoke. He weighed Neshah's words, then closed his eyes briefly and moved his lips; whether he was praying or saying farewell to his brother, Neshah couldn't be sure. Then, opening his eyes, Shili started up the Honda and pulled back onto the road.

"It is more than seven hundred miles to Maharashtra," he said, swerving to avoid a chuckhole. "On these roads that could take days. Too long if we want to reach the other launcher in time."

"There is a train in Munnar," Neshah suggested.

"If it's like any of the others, it stops in every town," Shili countered. "It could wind up even longer than driving."

"What if we flew?" Briley asked.

Shili stared coldly at the woman in the rearview mirror. "Our arms would be quite tired, I should think," he said dryly.

"Penghat," Neshah said warningly.

Briley smiled stiffly back at the other man. "My friend the pilot," she told him. "I'd bet you anything his plane seats four."

CHAPTER NINE

Academy of Arts in the Ghats

Standing in front of the building where the women farm workers were being held captive, Vargadrum Shili stared down at the man who'd been hauled out of the nearby brush. Nhajsib Wal, still unconscious, lay sprawled in the dirt, blood trickling from his scalp into the dirt.

"He looks like one of the boys up in the *kalari-payattu* hall," Shili snorted derisively. "Am I supposed to believe he's the one responsible for all these fires?"

"He was lurking in the brush with a gun," said Babu Sukha, the sniper who'd leaped down on Wal from the coconut palm. There was an edge in his voice. "He must have had *something* to do with it."

"You're saying we're under attack by children? Is that it?"

"He's at least as old as you," Sukha said evenly. "And he was about to shoot you when I stopped him."

The men faced off, Shili glaring at the other's impertinence, Sukha refusing to look away. Their stand-off was interrupted by some of the other men who were venturing back from the brush, having heard of the prisoner's capture. Shili looked away from Sukha.

"What are you doing?" he railed at the men, waving angrily. "Get back out there and find the rest of them!"

"What about the fire?" one of the men said, indicating the cloud of smoke billowing up near the distillery.

"What about it?" Shili shouted.

"It'll draw attention here," the man responded. "Shouldn't we try to put it out?"

"Attention has already been drawn here! Can't you see that? What do you think we're dealing with, tourists who like to play with matches?"

Shili took out his exasperation on Nhajsib Wal, kicking him. Though still unconscious, the Indian instinctively recoiled from the blow. Looking up, Shili saw the others eyeing him warily. He took a deep breath and tried to collect himself. He needed to be a leader, he told himself. He needed to be decisive, in control. Think! What would Dehri do? Raghubir? Penghat?

While Shili contemplated, Babu Sukha was quick to offer an opinion. "I think we should reinforce security around the perimeter," he suggested.

"Once we have taken out *all* the enemies on the grounds," Shili snapped irritably, "*then* we can worry about any others who might be on their way!" In hopes of appearing decisive, he smacked a fist into his open palm, the way Neshah often did. "*Then* we can put out the fires. Not before! Now, go!"

After a moment's hesitation, the other men began to disperse. Sukha stayed put.

"What about him?" he asked, gesturing at Nhajsib Wal.

"Tie him up with the women," Shili ordered. "I'll question him when he comes to."

Shili took hold of Wal's ankles while Sukha grabbed him under the arms. Raising him off the ground, they were guiding him through the doorway when Shili's radio transceiver bleeped.

"Again?" Shili let go of the prisoner, and Sukha hauled him the rest of the way across the floor. Stepping back outside, Shili yanked the radio from his waist. He was about to switch on the receive button when he stopped himself. Several times in the past few minutes he'd been signaled about an incoming call, and in each instance he'd been quick to respond, hoping it would be Penghat or Raghubir saying they'd freed Neshah and were on their way back. Each time, however, he'd been unable to hear anything but static. Now he was concerned that it wasn't his brothers but rather someone connected with the intruders; perhaps they were cueing on his frequency and using it to pinpoint his position. Could they do that? He didn't know. But if that's what was happening, then continuing to activate the radio would be like putting a target on his chest.

He heard the signal again. His heart raced as he stared at the transceiver. The signal seemed to be coming in clearer now. Or was it? Was it only clearer because he was holding it in front of his face? No, no, he decided. It was definitely clearer. It had to be

Neshah and his brothers. It *had* to be. Fumbling with the controls, Shili quickly identified himself and waited to hear familiar voices.

It turned out he'd been mistaken on both counts. The call was from the sentry in the observation tower. He had important news, he said.

As Shili listened, both the anger and color drained from his face. He signed off and slowly lowered the radio, almost letting it drop from his hand. This couldn't be happening. It couldn't.

"What is it?" Sukha asked as he rejoined Shili.

"A tank regiment is on its way," Shili said numbly as he lowered the walkie-talkie. "A tank regiment, along with foot soldiers and helicopters. They will be here any minute."

"We need to take the offensive," Sukha insisted. "We have missiles, a launcher...I say we use them!"

Shili shook his head with resignation. "The missiles are for limited targets," he said. "Planes, bunkers. We could maybe take out a few tanks or one of the helicopters with them. But a whole regiment?"

"Strike them with a few missiles and we might be able to turn them back," Sukha asserted. "Then we can reload and strike again!"

"If we strike them with a few missiles, they won't turn back," Shili countered. "They'll retaliate. And maybe their missiles aren't as powerful as ours, but they have far more of them. If a full regiment of tanks fires at us, it will be like a monsoon. There will be no hiding...."

Shili's voice trailed off. He glanced past Sukha, staring into the building at Nhajsib Wal and the captive women. A plan was beginning to formulate in his mind. Sukha, meanwhile, continued his calls for stronger action.

"Hide?" he exclaimed. "We have not come this far to hide from our enemies!"

"Sukha, wait, I have a plan," Shili said. "What if we just show them that we have missiles? What if we show them and threaten to use them unless they back away?"

The sniper stared sullenly at Shili.

"Threats? We went to all the trouble of acquiring missiles and launchers so we could make threats?"

"What do you suggest?"

"We can aim them at Kottayam," Sukha said. "The heart of the city. It's still rush hour. There will be tens of thousands of people in the streets…"

"No!" Shili said. "We will not give them reason to annihilate us!"

"This is a time to be strong!" Sukha snapped angrily. "Not to be cautious. If Dehri was here, he would say—"

"Dehri is *not* here!" Vargadrum Shili retorted. "*I* am in charge! *I* make the decisions! Is that understood?"

Sukha was about to say something but held himself in check. He took a deep breath, then stiffened, standing at attention. He snapped a salute. "Forgive me, Vargadrum," he said, the anger gone from his voice. "Tell me what you would have me do."

Though suspicious of Sukha's sudden change of heart, Shili felt there was nothing to be gained by further argument. "We need to haul the launcher out into the open, where they will see it. The same with the women and children. Let them know we have hostages, as well as the missiles and we can negotiate from a position of strength. We can demand free passage back to Kashmir.''

''An excellent plan,'' the sniper said. ''But some of the hostages should be taken to the launcher so no one will be tempted to fire at—''

''I've already thought of that,'' Shili interjected. He handed Sukha his walkie-talkie. ''Have the launcher brought out into the open. I will bring down some of the children. We'll strap them to the framework.''

Sukha held the walkie-talkie and watched Shili head for the winding path that led uphill to the academy *karalas*. Behind him, one of the men standing watch over Nhajsib Wal and the captive women ventured to the doorway and asked, ''Where is Vargadrum going?''

''He wants us to hide behind children and barter for a chance to whimper back to Kashmir with our tails between our legs,'' Sukha scoffed. ''That, rather than fight!''

''Fight who?'' the guard wanted to know.

''Our enemies,'' the sniper said. ''I think we need to teach them respect, and to do that we need to show them what we are capable of.'' Drawing the walkie-talkie to his lips, he made contact with the building where the Sabre launcher was being kept. When he received no answer, Sukha identified himself and said that he had orders from Vargadrum Shili.

''Prepare the missile for firing,'' he said. ''I'll give you the signal.''

ALL OF THE HOLDING vats, beakers, pipes, tubes and burners used to make toddy from the academy's coconut sap took up less than a quarter of the large building in which the still was housed. Normally, the rest of the distillery was used for storing the liquor in large kegs for sale to distributors who would bottle the drink at their own expense before peddling it in Kottayam and other cities throughout the southern half of Kerala. Some might have considered the distillery an ignoble enterprise, particularly for an academy so well-known for promoting enrichment through the arts, but—as the absentee proprietors of the school were often fond of saying—fund-raising, like politics, sometimes made for strange bedfellows. And when one considered that toddy sales brought the academy more revenue than charitable donations and all other crop sales combined, it wasn't surprising that a relatively blind eye was turned to the undertaking, not to mention the often unsavory clientele known to pull up to the back gate in the dead of night. Bribes would exchange hands and the vehicles would be waved through, usually pulling directly into the distillery so that they could load their cargo more discreetly.

That afternoon, however, the guards at the rear gate were dead at their posts—throats slit, bloated corpses clenched in rigor mortis after lying unattended all day—and the distillery was the domain, not of bootleggers, but the mujahideen. Several kegs of toddy had found their way down the insurgents' thirsty gullets, but the building had been taken over for more tactical reasons: it was ideally suited for the concealment of their trump card, the weapon they hoped would elevate them from the ranks of what India's prime minister had termed "bothersome gnats in need of a good swatting." Parked inside the distillery, next to a makeshift loading dock, was one of two Sabre short-range missile launchers recently hijacked from a military train convoy in the Western Ghats. Still hitched to the primer-gray Hummer that had hauled it down from the mountains, the Sabre featured a droidlike, swivel-mounted control console and streamlined firing racks cradling finned missiles that gleamed like so many flying fish about to leap from their tank. Unlike fish, however, these projectiles took to the air packed with modified WGU-12B/B guidance control units and twenty-five-pound Mk 84 warheads.

Seven men were gathered around the launcher. Three, armed with Russian-made DshK 108 mm machine guns, were posted at each window and doorway of the building, peering out in hopes of glimpsing the enemy that had set fire, first to the palm fronds in front of the distillery—where the bodies of the toddy bottlers had been heaved after their summary executions—then to the distillery roof itself. Another two Kashmiris scrambled about frantically with brooms and foam-spewing extinguishers, attacking the fiery bits of thatch that dropped from the roof like a steady rainfall. They looked almost comical, like clowns performing a skit. However, given that an unchecked fire could very well ignite the stored liquor or, worse yet, one of the large wooden crates containing still more of the surface-to-air missiles, the men went about their task with grave, humorless determination.

The remaining two men were huddled over the control console, doing their best to carry out the orders just handed down to them by Babu Sukha. The youngest, Kadas Rodvikode, meticulously carried out a prelaunch check, following instructions jotted down by the other man, Govankrishna Vanat, who squinted through his bifocals at the inner workings of the Sabre's computer guidance system. The system had sustained damage during the hijacking, and since Neshah hadn't been able to get his hands on the necessary replacement parts, it was Vanat's thankless task to repair the motherboard and other components as best he could in hopes the launcher could be made operational.

If there was one member of the mujahideen closer to the breaking point than Vargadrum Shili, it was Govankrishna Vanat. A balding, soft-spoken man in his late fifties, Vanat had been employed up until earlier this year at British Aerospace, makers of the Rapier missile, after which the Sabre was modeled. Three months ago, one of Penghat Shili's London contacts had overheard Vanat grousing in a corner pub about how he'd resigned from his job to protest the number of times he'd been passed over for promotions because, he claimed, of his ethnicity. Penghat, who, with Dehri Neshah, was just then beginning to concoct plans to hijack a military train carrying warheads and launchers, had authorized his contact to spare no expense in recruiting Vanat to the mujahideen cause. As it had turned out, Vanat had come cheaply enough, agreeing to lend his missile expertise in exchange for a vintage Aston Martin convertible and the sexual favors of a high-priced call girl working out of a penthouse suite two blocks from Trafalgar Square. The sports car was presently garaged back in London, but for Vanat the woman was still part of the bargain, scrupulously following the mujahideen's itinerary, albeit once removed. The woman, a statuesque redhead, was being put up in first-class hotels rather than the string of derelict safehouses Dehri Neshah invariably preferred his men to stay at. Vanat was infatuated with the woman; she made him feel young and virile. Though he knew there were undoubtedly other men in her life, when she was with him, it was as if there were no one on Earth but the two of them. Whatever his problems, they would be left at the foot of the bed along with his clothes and the woman would take him to another place, where he was like a god and she worshiped him.

Her name was Briley.

Much as he knew the importance of his assignment and the dangers he faced now that the launch compound was under siege, Vanat found it difficult to focus on the matter at hand. One would have thought that his distracted state was due to fear or a sense of urgency, but the truth had more to do with his carnal appetite; specifically, the mujahideen allowed him only one rendezvous with Briley for each city they traveled through, and, as far as their stay in Kottayam was concerned, this was supposed to be his appointed night. The mere thought of being alone with Briley was both maddening and consuming. Vanat couldn't so much as brush his fingers against a circuit board without fantasizing what it would be like to stroke Briley's soft, smooth skin and drink in the heady aroma of her perfume. And, despite all the loud commotion taking place around him, all Vanat could hear in his mind was the way Briley always teased him when she reached between his legs to take hold of him. "Remember, Vanat, the countdown must reach zero before blastoff." A slow count to ten? He could never hold out that long, not the way she handled him. God, he couldn't wait to see her.

"Vanat?"

The older man turned and saw Rodvikode eyeing him with concern.

"Yes?" Vanat said.

"The countdown," the younger man said. "Are we ready?"

Despite the gravity of the situation, Vanat couldn't help but smile. "One can never be fully ready for the countdown," he murmured.

"I don't understand."

"Someday you will," Vanat assured him. Just then a glowing ember fell down from the ceiling, glancing off his arm to the floor. As Vanat stared at the charcoallike smear on his shirtsleeve, it was as if, for the first time, the reality of his situation had finally dawned on him: he wouldn't be seeing Briley again. Not tonight, not ever. They were under attack, trapped in this oversize box like fish in a barrel. How soon before another incendiary charge came hurtling into their midst? And this time there would be no roof to take the brunt of the detonation; the fireball would erupt inside the distillery and it would be all over, just like that. Flames, explosion, gunfire... One way or another he realized he was about to die, here, within these cinder-block walls, and soon. And yet here he was, making jokes only he could understand, obsessed with his craving to rut a whore like some animal in heat. Had he lost his mind completely?

"Is the guidance system fixed?" the younger man wanted to know.

"No," Vanat confessed after a moment's hesitation. True, they hadn't tested it, but he knew in his heart that his repairs to the system were inadequate. "There was too much damage," he explained. "If Dehri had been able to return with a new motherboard, with more equipment, then maybe—"

"There is no time for speculation!" Rodvikode interrupted. "We have our orders! When the call comes, we must fire at least one of the missiles. I need to know if we can pick out a target and have any chances of hitting it."

Vanat shook his head. He felt himself smiling again. Words spilled from his lips, almost as if he had no control over them. He found himself trying to recall a nursery rhyme from his childhood in the English boarding schools. "'I shot an arrow into the air. Where it lands I do not care.' No, that can't be right." He chuckled and tried again. "'I shot an arrow in the air. Where it lands I know not where.' No, that's not it, either."

Rodvikode grabbed Vanat by the shirt and began to shake him furiously. 'What is the matter with you?'' he shouted in the man's face. "Why can't you give me a simple answer?''

"A simple answer?'' Vanat shouted back. He took hold of the younger man's hands and pried them away. "If the guidance system is not working, the missile will go up, then come down. Where? Who can say? Maybe in the sea, maybe on land. If we're lucky, it will strike a city and kill many Indians and we can pretend we meant that to be our target so that our enemies will be afraid. You and I will be heroes to the mujahideen! Our enemies will speak of us with awe, the same way they speak of the Kashmir Shredder! Bollywood will turn out a movie where you and I will be played by handsome movie stars. There! Is that simple enough for you?''

By now several of the other terrorists had stopped what they were doing and were staring at Vanat. He stared back at them, tears streaming from his eyes. He began to laugh. "Butchers!'' he cried out. "With his little knife, Dehri is the Shredder! He stabs deep, then shreds his victims organs to insure death. But us? We have missiles! Ha ha! Missiles! We stab our targets and shrapnel does the shredding for us! Chop, chop, chop. We'll cut up our enemies, just like butchers. How glorious!''

"Enough!'' One of the men fighting the flames inside the distillery lashed out with his fire extinguisher, striking Vanat in the back of the head. The older man pitched over the console he'd been working on, then toppled to the concrete floor. There were flecks of foam at the corners of his mouth.

"He's like a mad dog,'' muttered the man who'd

felled Vanat. He cast aside his fire extinguisher and drew a 9 mm Makarov semiautomatic pistol from his holster. He pointed the gun at the old man's head. "He needs to be put out of his misery."

"No!" Rodvikode grabbed the other man by the wrist, turning the gun away from Vanat. "He has been overworked, that's all. He will be okay."

"Overworked?" The man with the Makarov grinned and thrust his pelvis back and forth a few times. "Oversexed is more like it."

Another one of the men called out, "It's that American whore. She fucked his brains out and now there is nothing left between his ears!"

There was a burst of laughter inside the building, but it was uneasy, forced, and when the last few embers wafted down from what was left from the roof, the men were startled into silence. Looking up through the charred hole, they could see the sky, boiling over with dark smoke. It looked apocalyptic, like the end of the world.

They were still staring when a walkie-talkie near the missile launcher bleated. Rodvikode reached for it.

It was Babu Sukha.

Rodvikode quietly listened for his orders, then switched off the communicator and set it aside. All eyes were on him now, grim, resigned.

"It is time," he told them. "Make ready to fire the missiles."

CHAPTER TEN

Krula Pass Airfield, Western Ghats

While his vintage Balsa Twin Ghurka warmed up at the edge of the tarmac, Daeon Murawd hurried about the cabin, making certain everything was presentable. It was a quick task. He'd painstakingly restored the plane over the past thirteen months after inheriting it as an unflyable junk heap bequeathed by a distant uncle in Bhopal. The craft was now nearly as immaculate as it had been when it first rolled off the production line more than thirty years ago. Murawd had been faithful with the restoration, too, scouring salvage yards and Web sites on the Internet for original replacement parts or their equivalent from other planes of the era. In the rare cases when he couldn't find the part he was looking for, he'd had a machinist friend make it for him according to the manufacturer's specifications. He'd also cannibalized parts from an older Ghurka Thresher, a smaller, single-prop aircraft he'd bought at auction and kept in running condition as his backup plane.

A notable exception to Murawd's desire for authenticity in the Twin Balsa was the rear seating arrangement. The original Ghurka had seated six, with two pairs of bucket seats located in rows directly behind the cockpit. Murawd had taken out the seats and replaced them with a wet bar, minifridge and a single, well-padded bench seat, the back of which could be lowered a full ninety degrees, creating, in effect, a bed well suited for overnight layovers...or, as was more often the case, idyllic lovemaking trysts in remote pastures or atop isolated plateaus.

Though he had business cards vouching that he was owner of Krula Pass Air Tours, Murawd was independently wealthy thanks to the same uncle from whom he'd inherited the Ghurka. As such, he rarely bothered to advertise his services, and the only clientele he actively sought out were attractive single women deemed a worthy challenge for the self-proclaimed Casanova of Kottayam. The redhead Murawd had chanced upon while driving to the airfield was just such a prospect, and Murawd hummed gaily to himself with anticipation as he readied the rear compartment of the plane. It was months since he'd had an American woman. And he was sure he'd have her. After all, hadn't she looked him in the eye and told him that she'd come to India to work on her Kama Sutra? Well, he would show her a position or two, all right.

Another way Murawd had strayed from authenticity while refurbishing the plane was installing a sound system. He'd rewired the cabin to accommodate six speakers as part of a seven-thousand-dollar stereo system, complete with a digitalized remote control that could quickly cue up any of fifty different long-playing musical compilations he'd put together to suit a range of musical tastes. He took this woman, the American, for a jazz lover. He hoped she would want to do it to some Charlie Parker or Miles Davis, but, if need be, he was prepared as well to ply her with anything from Kenny G to John McLaughlin and the Mahuvishnu Orchestra.

Ah, and there she was! Murawd was puzzled to see her walking through the main gateway instead of driving, but the important thing was that she'd come. Murawd clambered down from his plane and walked past the older Ghurka parked outside his hangar. He caught up with the woman on the tarmac.

"Where is your car?"

"Back up the road," Briley lied. "I got back in to drive it here and the engine was dead."

"Strange," Murawd said.

"I'll deal with it later," Briley told him as he led her toward his prized Ghurka.

"I'm glad you decided to come," Murawd told her.

"I'm so excited!" Briley squeezed the man's hand. "Thank you so much for inviting me."

"Not at all," Murawd said. "It's a perfect time of day, too. One hasn't lived until they've seen the sun set on the Laccadive Sea!"

He helped the woman up into the plane, gauging her reaction when she eyed the rear cabin. "This looks wonderful!" she said. "It's like you have your own little suite on wings!"

"Quite," Murawd said. "In fact, I happen to have some provisions in the fridge. Some champagne, cheeses, fresh fruit. There is a plateau I know near the coast. If you'd like, we could set down there and take our time enjoying the sunset.''

"I'd love it!'' the woman told him as she fastened herself into the passenger seat. "Oh, I knew this was going to be my lucky day! I just knew it!''

"I feel the same,'' Murawd assured her. This was one of those times he wished he'd partnered up with another pilot, so that he could turn the controls over and focus himself entirely on "hospitality.'' Here, after all, was a woman who, if she hadn't already done so, would definitely jump at the opportunity to join the mile-high club. Alas, such pleasures would have to wait.

"Now, then,'' Murawd told the woman as he gave the controls a quick once-over in preparation for take-off. "On the way to our plateau, I can take several routes, depending on which sites most interest you. First, of course, there are the old churches that date back to medieval times....''

The pilot's voice trailed off. Out of the corner of his eye he'd seen the woman reach into her purse and assumed she was taking out a compact. When he turned to her, however, he saw that she was holding a derringer.

"Our first stop will be just off to the right,'' Briley told him, gesturing with the gun. "You can stay on the tarmac, but get as close as you can to the trees.''

"I don't understand,'' Murawd said.

"We have some friends to pick up,'' Briley explained, "and they aren't particularly patient, so I suggest you quit stalling and get a move on.''

It took Murawd a moment to regain his composure,

then he eased the Ghurka along the runway. This late in the day there were only a couple other planes still out on the field, and both were untended, parked before a larger, shared-use hangar on the far side of the runway. The hangar had windows facing the runway, but Murawd doubted anyone was looking out. For all intents and purposes, he and the woman might as well have been alone. Only a few moments ago he would have relished such an arrangement; now he was filled with fear and uncertainty. What had he gotten himself into?

As they neared the trees—a grove of hardy, close-grown acacias—Murawd saw two men crouched behind the one with the widest trunk. Their faces were obscured in shadow, but he had a feeling that neither of them was American. One thing he could see for certain; like the woman, they were armed.

"Closer," the woman advised him. As if he needed any incentive, she added, "If someone spots them and there is trouble, you will be the first to die. Do you understand?"

Murawd nodded. Rather than veer sharply off the runway, he took a wide turn and eased off the tarmac into the hard-packed earth of the airfield, which had been chiseled out of the side of a gently sloping range. He left the engine running. The other two men dashed from cover and quickly climbed up onto the wing of the Ghurka. The woman motioned for Murawd to stay put while she opened the door.

"Gentlemen, meet my good friend Daeon," she told Neshah and Penghat Shili as they climbed into the cabin.

Murawd shuddered and glanced away from the men. It was already too late, however. They knew he had gotten a good look at them, and the fact that the woman made a point of making introductions only underscored the grim realization he had to face: these were wanted men and he had seen their faces. Once he had fulfilled his usefulness to them, they would kill him. He knew it as surely as he was breathing.

"You have a nice plane here," the older of the two men called out as he slumped leisurely into the bench seat. The other man had already opened the mini-fridge and taken out a bottle of carbonated mineral water. When he opened it, water spritzed out of the bottle and onto the floor. Normally, Murawd would have been frantic about the likelihood of stains on the restored carpet. His perspective had changed, however. If the carpet was going to be ruined, he feared the stains that did it would be blood. His.

"Take us up," Dehri Neshah told the playboy. "I see from the controls that you have a full tank of gas. That should be enough to get us to Maharashtra, yes?"

Academy of Arts in the Ghats

WHEN HE HEARD the guards say that Vargadrum Shili was on his way up the hill, Ziarat Wal figured the time had come. All he needed was an opportunity. Unfortunately, Providence didn't appear to be in an accommodating mood: with Shili headed their way, the guards stepped back from the window, not wanting it to appear as if they were being derelict in their duties. Before they could assume their positions on either side of their prisoners, however, they heard a droning sound in the air outside the hall. Together they returned to the window and stared out through the drifting smoke. One of them pointed, shouting to the other that helicopters were headed toward the academy.

The moment the guards turned their backs to him again, Wal rose to a crouch, took a deep breath, then bolted forward. After two running steps, he leaped to the top of the stone staircase leading up to the main doorway. He knew that the door was locked from the inside, but he wasn't thinking about escape. Instead, the moment he landed upon the top step he coiled his legs again, then once more sprang upward and outward. High, sustained vertical leaps—much akin to what American basketball players referred to as hang time—were a trademark for practitioners of *kalaripayattu* and Wal was no exception. While suspended in midair, he reached to the wall and, in one swift motion, unmounted both a half sword and shield. When he landed, he was ready to use both.

Detecting motion behind them, both guards turned from the window. One of them immediately staggered backward, screaming in pain, hands going to his face. With deadly accuracy, Wal had thrown the shield, discus style, striking the guard across the bridge of the nose with so much force that it almost embedded itself. Blinded by his own blood, the man reeled to one side and fell howling to the ground.

The other guard was raising his assault rifle into firing position when Wal let fly again, this time with the half sword. End over end, the weapon whistled through the air. With deadly accuracy, it buried itself to the hilt in the second man's chest. The guard stared down in shock and grabbed at the weapon. The moment he tried to pull it free, his legs gave out underneath him and he pitched forward, dead.

Several of the younger boys were about to cry out when the older youths, prompted by the boy with the bandaged ribs, covered their mouths, then whispered for them to be quiet. Trembling, the students watched Wal pull the sword from the second guard's chest and, without hesitation, plunge its blade through the heart of the man who'd been blinded by the hurled shield.

Once he'd reclaimed his keys and the bloodied shield, Wal motioned for the two older youths to pick up the assault rifles. "Do you know how to use them?"

Each of the youths nodded solemnly.

"Good." Wal led the youths to the top of the stairs, then unlocked the door. "You are to stay here and watch over your fellow students," he instructed. "If someone comes through that door without identifying themselves first, you know what you must do."

Rifles clenched tightly in their small hands, again the youths nodded.

Before heading out the door, Wal picked up the sets of small sticks Vargadrum Shili had attempted to lure him into a contest with earlier. He tucked them inside the waistband of his dhoti, then stared out at his youthful charges.

"For a time I must ask you all to be men, not

boys," he told them. "Always remember—fear, however strong, can always be tamed by valor."

With that, he turned and left the room.

IT TOOK TWO ATTEMPTS and nearly twenty agonizing minutes for John Kissinger to muscle his way up the slime-lined walls of the well, but finally he made it to a point where Mack Bolan—lying flat on the ground, one hand clinging to a sapling for support—could reach down and help pull him up the rest of the way. The armorer was a mess. The two separate falls had left him splattered with foul-smelling, stagnant well water, and at least half a dozen finger-sized leeches had attached themselves to his hands, arms and face. He pried one off his cheek, leaving a trail of blood.

"I think I'll pass on the thank-you hug," Bolan told him.

While Kissinger caught his breath, Bolan surveyed the nearby distillery. The fire on the roof had burned itself out, but the palm fronds on the other side of the building were still ablaze. The smoke that continued to fill the air was every bit as dense as before, but now it began to carry a foul, pervasive stench nothing like the earlier scent of brewing toddy. Both men cringed, recognizing the smell.

"Flesh," Kissinger muttered. "Somebody's on fire."

"I'll circle around and check," Bolan said.

"Careful," Kissinger advised him. "You ask me, the only reason those bastards are still inside the building is because they figure help's on the way. Those snipers have got to be out of the trees by now.''

"I'll be looking for them, don't worry," Bolan assured Kissinger. "If it's all clear once I'm back out front, I say we flush these guys out of the building."

"Fine by me," Kissinger said, "but I wouldn't count on the DHL." He unslung his waterlogged backpack and pulled out the incendiary launcher. Water dripped from the casing, and leeches were crawling into the firing tubes.

"I'll handle that end," Bolan said, patting his own backpack. He checked his watch. "Give me two minutes, then be ready to fire."

Kissinger nodded and grabbed his Colt, which he'd managed to drop in the grass, along with his walkie-talkie, before plunging into the well.

Bolan crept into the tea plants and began circling his way back to the knoll. He stopped briefly once he was able to see the front of the distillery. At the base of the bonfire he saw the charred outlines of two bodies being consumed by flame. They were already burned beyond recognition, but Bolan doubted any of the mujahideen would have rushed out of the distillery only to throw themselves into the bonfire. More likely the fire victims were innocent bystanders killed when the terrorists had stormed the grounds.

Bolan was about to move on when he suddenly froze, then slowly dropped to a crouch. Less than twenty yards away, he saw steady movement in the brush. Someone—or maybe it was more than one— was headed his way. Bolan switched his gun to his left hand. With his right, he reached down and gently unsheathed a Russell Backwoods knife strapped to his boot. As the name implied, the Russell was an all-purpose backpacker's knife with a thick, serrated blade strong enough to be used as anything from a saw to a crowbar. At the moment, all Bolan cared about was its efficiency as a weapon of self-defense.

The density of the tea plants worked for and against the Executioner, giving him good cover but also making it difficult for him to get a good look at who he was up against. All he could do was, like the mujahideen inside the distillery, stay put and wait for the enemy to come to him.

Soon his patience was rewarded. A figure slowly materialized before him, taking shape with each step forward, each branch of tea leaves brushed aside. Bolan finally saw that it was a short Kashmiri, wearing a toddy tapper's weathered dhoti but carrying a submachine gun. After each step he took, the man stopped and looked about, occasionally leaning forward to take a closer look at one of the tea plants. He was clearly following the path, however faint, Bolan had forged while circling to the rear of the distillery. Since the Executioner had been following the same path back, he knew it would likely be only a matter of seconds before the two men came face-to-face.

Once he'd determined that the other man was alone, Bolan tightened his grip on the knife and held it out before him, then crouched still lower in the brush. As the other man drew closer, the soldier could make out his features—hardened, attentive, eyes filled with concentration. Now he was only ten yards away.

Nine...

Eight...

The man took one more step forward, then stopped. He glanced away from Bolan, but the Executioner knew it was only a ploy; he was sure he'd been spotted and that the other man was just trying to catch him off guard. It wasn't to be. The moment the terrorist began to whirl, sweeping the submachine gun before him, finger on the trigger, Bolan dived forward as if being shot from a cannon. Tea leaves slapped at his face, forcing him to involuntarily close his eyes. He'd timed his move perfectly, however. Not only did he knock the submachine gun from the other man's hand, but he also plunged the knife blade deep into the man's chest with so much force that the Kashmiri staggered, losing his balance. He fell backward, Bolan on top of him.

The Executioner let go of the knife—which had already done its job—and cupped his hand over the Kashmiri's mouth, muffling his cry for help. Blood seeped through Bolan's fingers. Even with his dying breath, the man's expression was less one of surprise than driven malice.

The kill had been quiet enough, but Bolan stayed put a few moments nonetheless, senses alert for signs of any other Kashmiris in the brush. Above the fiery snapping of the palm fronds he could hear activity inside the distillery and, far off in the distance, the faint drone of at least one approaching helicopter. Grimaldi, Bolan figured. The only other sound was the nearby buzzing of insects.

Bolan proceeded with slow caution, taking the dead man's MP-5 with him. He made it back to the knoll without encountering any other enemy forces, but he knew they had to be around somewhere, closing in. He and Kissinger couldn't afford to wait any longer to make their move.

Keeping one eye on the distillery, Bolan quickly unslung his backpack. Along with more ammunition for his Desert Eagle, he had packed an Ingram MAC-10 and three Ben/Berg-327 stun grenades. He slipped his gun back in his shoulder holster and carefully removed the grenades, setting them side by side in the grass, pins facing upward.

Bolan was no more than fifty yards from the distillery, well within lobbing range. In quick succession, he rose from a crouch and heaved the first two grenades. The first detonated just to the right of the bonfire, doing little more than jostling the bodies. His second toss just missed the front window of the distillery and wasted itself on the cinder block exterior of the building.

Bolan grabbed the third grenade, intent on tossing it as far as the distillery roof in hopes it would drop through one of the openings made by the DHL. Before he could make his lob, however, the Colwyss-8A suddenly swooped into view, dropping below the smoke screen. Grimaldi banked the chopper sharply to his right, then rose up and hovered directly above the distillery. Gunfire erupted inside the building and bullets began to plow into the chopper. Grimaldi stayed put, however. Moments later, he was on the transceiver to Bolan.

"Don't throw that grenade!" Grimaldi shouted. "Repeat, do *not* throw your grenade!"

"Why not?" Bolan asked once he'd grabbed the transceiver from his hip.

"They've got a launcher in there!" came Grimaldi's reply. "Sucker's loaded, too! Four missiles, ready to fire! That's four! Lob a grenade in there, and this place turns into a jigsaw puzzle!"

"Damn!" Bolan cursed.

"My sentiments exactly," Grimaldi said. "I'm blocking their line of fire right now, but I don't know how long I can keep it up. They're chewing the hell out of my chassis."

Bolan stared out and saw bullets spark off the helicopter's landing skids. He didn't even want to think what it would look like if, instead of 9 mm slugs, a surface-to-air missile were to come charging out at the chopper.

He was pondering their next move when Grimaldi came back on the squawk box. "Hey, I just heard from Kissinger," he reported. "He thinks if I pull up a little higher, my rotor wash will push down enough smoke to foul up their game plan. What do you think?"

Like a chess player, Bolan thought through the possible consequences of such a move, looking for a way to throw the advantage back in their favor. An idea came to him.

"Look, I don't know how well you can jockey that smoke around," he told Grimaldi, "but if you can put a lid over the distillery and still have some left over to spread out our way for cover, Cowboy and I can rush the place and try to shut them down."

"Sounds risky."

"I'll take risky over sitting by and waiting on their lead," Bolan said. "And, like you say, you can't hang up there much longer."

"Good point," Grimaldi said. "What the hell, let's go for it!"

Moments after Grimaldi signed off, the helicopter again pitched to one side, then lifted up, disappearing a moment inside the overhead smoke. Within seconds, the smoke began to drift downward like some biblical plague cloud, enveloping the distillery, as well as the building's perimeter. Bolan knew the effect was only temporary, however, as the same rotor wash directing the smoke's flow would eventually help dissipate it. He quickly keyed Kissinger's frequency.

"On five," he said quickly.

"Ready when you are," Kissinger responded.

Bolan tossed the transceiver aside and snatched up the Ingram MAC-10. It was lighter than the Kashmiri's MP-5, and he knew its 32-round magazine was full. Along with his Desert Eagle, that gave him more than forty rounds. Add that to the dozen Kissinger would be bringing to the dance—provided he'd reloaded—and it seemed they stood a good chance of pulling this off. At any rate, they were about to find out.

"...four, three, two, one!"

Bolan broke from cover and charged into the low-hanging cloud of smoke. As he passed the burning fronds and the charred bodies, the air grew thick with the smell of death. It was as if the Grim Reaper himself were close at hand, breathing down Bolan's neck, ready to tap him on the shoulder and tell him that at long last his time had come.

CHAPTER ELEVEN

Academy of Arts in the Ghats

As he stormed the rear of the distillery, John Kissinger had to make a quick decision. Obviously, the fastest way inside the building was through the back door. Even if it was locked, he felt he could jar it open with one of the full-force shoulder slams he'd perfected years ago during drug raids with the DEA. Such a slam was likely to throw him briefly off balance, however, and if, as he suspected, there were gunmen poised on the other side of the door, even a split second of vulnerability could prove fatal.

That left one other option.

Propped against the back wall of the distillery were stacks of wooden skids, three layers high, holding empty kegs and barrels. When he reached them, Kissinger began climbing upward, choking on the smoke as he sought out foot- and handholds as if scaling a mountain peak. This mountain was far from stable, however. Stacked unevenly, the skids groaned and wobbled each time Kissinger moved, threatening to collapse any second and take him down with them.

Fortunately, the noise was drowned out by the drone of the helicopter.

He continued upward, shifting his weight to stabilize the load beneath him. Finally, he was within reach of the eaves. He drew in a breath, held it, then grabbed hold with both hands and pulled himself up onto the roof.

Sections of thatch continued to smolder from Kissinger's earlier incendiary round, but enough of the roof was intact to allow him to cautiously inch his way toward one of the openings. Once he reached it, the Stony Man armorer clasped his pistol in both hands and slowly rose to a crouch. As Grimaldi had forewarned him, he found himself staring down through the smoke at one of the stolen Sabre launch systems. None of the Kashmiris gathered around the weapon had yet spotted him; most of them were either contending with the foul-smelling smoke that engulfed them or else blasting away at the helicopter with their MP-5s. Much as Kissinger wanted to take out the gunmen first, he was more concerned with the youngest member of the group, who stood over the launcher's control console, clearly preparing to fire the first of the missiles.

"Not so fast," Kissinger murmured. He took quick aim and fired a single shot.

A bullet tore through Kadas Rodvikode's neck. As his knees buckled, pulling him to the ground, he clawed at the console, trying to hold himself up and complete the launch. Kissinger fired again. Rodvikode, half his head obliterated, let go and slumped to the ground. The console blinked and buzzed, but the proper sequence of commands hadn't been completed. The launch was aborted.

Kissinger had little time for self-congratulation. His shots had drawn attention, and several men down in the distillery were quick to shift aim and fire at him. He ducked as the volleys whistled past, then popped back into view and returned fire, managing to drop one of the sentries.

There were other gunmen shielded from Kissinger's view. One, crouched behind the far side of the launcher, slowly raised his MP-5 and lined up his adversary in his sights. He thumbed the firing selector and was about to let loose on full automatic when the window behind him suddenly imploded, showering him with glass. It was Bolan, diving headfirst into the building, forearms crossed in front of him to deflect the shards. He landed on Kissinger's would-be executioner, throwing off the man's aim. Still, the man managed to send a burst of autofire ripping up through the roof. He'd been trying to hit Kissinger in the head, but the rounds instead stitched their way across the armorer's chest.

His Kevlar vest kept the bullets from piercing flesh, but the staccato thumps threw him backward and nearly took the wind out of him. As he staggered to one side, Kissinger stepped on a weakened section of roof. With a loud snap, the thatch gave way beneath him, and, as with the well only a few minutes before, he found himself in a free fall. He landed hard on the concrete floor of the distillery, grimacing at the additional abuse heaped on his already throbbing ankles. He stayed on his feet, however, and, more importantly, he still had his Colt. He put it to quick use, gunning down the man closest to him and sending another ducking for cover behind the launcher. All the while, smoke swirled around him, making it difficult to breathe and giving everything the eerie feel of a dream.

Several yards away, Bolan fired a kill shot into the face of the gunman he'd dived onto, then scrambled away from the body. Once he joined Kissinger, the two men turned their backs to each other, maximizing their view of the perimeter around them. Overhead, the helicopter pulled away. Almost immediately, the smoke inside the distillery, like a theatrical curtain, began to rise. Bolan and Kissinger spotted two men attempting to flee through the building's front and rear doorways. A hail of gunfire dropped them in their tracks.

Now, with the helicopter gone and a lull in the gunfire, the distillery became deathly quiet. As Kissinger quickly reloaded, Bolan kept an eye open for enemy activity.

"I think that's it," the Executioner whispered.

"Let's check to make sure."

Fanning out, the two men slowly circled the launcher in opposite directions. Six Kashmiris lay on the ground, none of them moving. Kissinger was stubbing out a burning scrap of thatch when he thought he noticed movement underneath the launcher itself. Dropping to a crouch, he spotted Vanat curled up in a near fetal position, staring out, his eyes wild with fear.

"Come out," Kissinger told the old man. "The party's over."

LYING ON his side, legs bent at the knees, hands bound behind his back, Nhajsib Wal slowly opened one eye just enough to allow him to glance across the floor of the farm building where he was being held captive with the women workers. Two mujahideen guards milled about impatiently, smoking cigarettes and occasionally glancing out the windows. Wal had overheard enough of their mutterings to realize that his fellow Intelligence Bureau officers were on the way, backed up by a tank regiment crossing the lake on powered barges. Already one helicopter had passed overhead; to Wal it sounded like the Colwyss he'd flown in earlier. So perhaps the Americans had brought in reinforcements, as well. Much as he welcomed the news, the Indian intelligence officer had no intention of waiting helplessly to be rescued.

While his captors assumed he was still unconscious, Wal had, in fact, come to shortly after being kicked by Vargadrum Shili outside the building. He'd played possum while Babu Sukha had dragged him inside, and when tied up, Wal had put to use his hard-earned mastery of *kathakali* hand gestures, folding his thumbs inward on his palms to exaggerate the thickness of his hands and wrists. Though Sukha felt he had bound Wal's hands tightly behind his back, when Wal later relaxed his thumbs, there was a faint slack to his binds.

Now, after fifteen minutes of patient, unseen wriggling, the Indian's hands were free. Slowly extending his arms, he next reached down to his feet. He'd taken care not to strain the knots securing his ankles, and they remained loose enough to work at without any excess movement. In less than a minute, he'd untied himself completely without the mujahideen being any the wiser.

What remained was timing his next move. The guards had also spoken of parading him and the women out into view long enough to make it clear they had hostages. Now that the helicopter had arrived on the scene, it seemed as if the time was at hand. Sure enough, a few moments later Sukha appeared in the doorway, exclaiming that something had gone awry with his plans to have missiles launched at the enemy. The guards were told to get Wal and the women on their feet; Sukha said he would round up the other men and disappeared from the doorway.

Wal closed his eyes and remained still. He could hear the guards drawing closer. As they leaned over to grab hold of him, he sprang into motion. Kicking his legs outward, he caught one of the guards in the shins, tripping him. In the same motion, he brought his hands up, grabbing the other man by the wrist and jerking him to the ground. An MP-5 submachine dropped to the ground beside him. He swiftly picked it up and clubbed the man closer to him, knocking him unconscious. The other man, startled, fought to bring his gun into play, but Wal was a step ahead of him, already bounding to his feet. He lashed out with another kick, jarring the second gun free, then brought the stock of the gun he was holding down hard on the other man's skull, dropping him alongside his fellow guard.

The women were equally surprised by Wal's sudden outburst. They eyed him uncertainly as he approached them, carrying a knife he'd taken off one of the guards.

"It will be all right," he whispered as he began cutting at their binds. Once he'd freed three of the women, he asked one to continue untying the others, then handed the guards' MP-5s to the other two, instructing them to keep an eye on the front doorway and gun down Sukha should he reappear.

"What about you?" one of the women asked.

"I have another matter to attend to."

Unarmed, Wal jogged to a back doorway and let himself out of the building. He spotted the path Vargadrum Shili had taken up to the academy and headed for it, hoping he would be in time to save his uncle.

"OVER HERE!" Sukha shouted.

Following his directions, two of the mujahideen took up positions near the trailer holding the country boat. The other twelve men he'd managed to round up had already spread out, taking cover at various points offering a clear view of the trailer. Sukha figured he would have the captive women form a human chain around the trailer. When the enemy forces drew close, he would bluff and say that beneath the coconuts piled inside the boat were several of the Sabre's surface-to-air missiles, rigged to plastic explosives that Sukha would detonate if his demands were not met. Now that his plans to launch missiles from the distillery had been thwarted, he would grudgingly resort to Vargadrum Shili's ploy of using hostages to barter for free passage from Kottayam so that the mujahideen might live to fight another day.

They didn't have much time. The sentry in the observation tower had just reported that the tank regiment was still several miles away, but another helicopter was already in view, hovering low over the nearby rows of tea plants, its rotors turning the field into an undulating sea of green. Soldiers—at least twelve of them—were climbing down a sectioned rope ladder dangling from the chopper, then dropping the last few feet to the ground. If they stayed low to the ground, they would be able to advance undetected, even from the tower.

Sukha turned back to the trailer and nodded to one of the men who carried, along with his MP-5 submachine gun, a powered megaphone.

"Now!" Sukha commanded.

Raising the amplifier to his mouth, the other man cried out for the enemy soldiers to keep their distance. Sukha, meanwhile, strode quickly back toward the farm building, angrily wondering why the women hadn't been dragged out yet. He got his answer when he passed through the doorway and found himself staring down the barrel of an MP-5 clutched in the capable hands of one of the women. Before he could react, a burst of 9 mm Parabellum rounds burrowed into his chest, killing him instantly.

The woman charged past Sukha, followed by the other would-be hostages. One of them paused to grab Sukha's handgun, giving them three weapons, which they promptly turned on the men crouched around the trailer. Taken by surprise, the men went down quickly.

Other mujahideen in the surrounding brush fired at the women, felling two of them. But the others took cover near the trailer, picking up the MP-5s of the men already gunned down. They returned fire fearlessly, holding the mujahideen at bay until the helicopter forces arrived on the scene. Caught in a cross fire, half the terrorists quickly threw down their weapons in surrender. The others continued to shoot and were quickly dropped by return fire. In less than two minutes, the skirmish was over.

VARGADRUM SHILI couldn't believe what was happening.

Halfway up the hill path to the academy, he'd seen the approaching Colwyss-8A and had taken cover inside a pagoda set off the path at the edge of a lookout. Though nowhere near as high up as the observation tower, the pagoda still gave him a clear view of the grounds below. He'd witnessed, through patches of drifting smoke, the siege of the distillery building and seizure of the missile launcher. And now he could see Babu Sukha and the others being routed back near the husking area. It was all but over. Given a chance to lead, he'd failed Dehri Neshah and his brothers.

Unless...

Shili turned and started back up the hill. Perhaps he could no longer take the boys of the academy down to the launcher, but they could still be used as hostages. There had been perhaps a dozen mujahideen stationed uphill from where the battle was now taking place; if enough of the men refrained from joining the fight, he could marshal them together around the *kalaripayattu* hall. They could still barter for their freedom.

Formulating a revised plan, Shili rounded a bend in the path. There was a sudden rustling in the brush to his right. As he whirled, the flat edge of a sword blade came crashing down on his wrist. Wincing in pain, he dropped his MP-5 and staggered back.

Ziarat Wal stepped out of the brush and kicked the man's weapon off the path, then stepped forward, striking him in the side of the face with the short sticks he'd taken with him from the martial-arts hall. Shili's cheek began to bleed, just as Ziarat's had earlier.

"That makes us even." Ziarat tossed two of the sticks at Shili's feet, then assumed a fighting stance. "Now, pick them up and let us complete our history lesson. But understand this—you do not represent all of Kashmir. Only the lawless mujahideen."

"There are no children here to instruct," Shili said uneasily.

"My students are young men, not children," Ziarat said. "And it is you who need to learn this lesson, not them."

His pride stung, Shili snatched up the sticks and glared at Ziarat. "As you wish, old man."

Ziarat quickly took the offensive. Shili, though inexperienced with stick fighting, was agile enough to parry the older man's first few blows. He even managed to get in a few thrusts of his own, though they, too, were blocked by his opponent. The sticks clattered against one another like castanets as the men circled around each other in the confined space, neither paying heed to the larger battle taking place downhill from them. As far as they were concerned, for the moment theirs was the only fight that mattered.

To Shili, it seemed as if he wasn't only holding his own, but slowly taking the upper hand and wearing down the Indian. Ziarat, however, was merely conserving his strength and lulling the Kashmiri into a false sense of confidence. All the while he patiently evaluated Shili's fighting style, detecting weaknesses to capitalize on. Once he had his enemy figured out, Ziarat stepped up his own offensive, adroitly avoiding blows with the same frequency with which his own slashes and thrusts began to connect. The tide of the battle quickly turned. Welts sprouted along Shili's arms, chest and face as he absorbed more and more punishment, each stinging blow taking more out of him. Soon he was forced to abandon his offensive strategy and concentrate solely on fending off Ziarat's relentless onslaught.

Finally, the Kashmiri sank to his knees and tossed his sticks aside, covering his head and face with his forearms.

"No more!" he cried out. "No more!"

Ziarat loomed over Shili. "Tell me," he said. "If things had gone the other way, would you have shown mercy?"

When Shili said nothing, Ziarat prodded him hard with the sticks, forcing him onto his back.

"And is that why you were on your way up to our

kalari?'' Ziarat demanded. "To show compassion to the youths you tormented?"

"Yes," Shili lied, "I was coming to free them."

"You lie the way you fight," Ziarat told him. "You give yourself away too easily. Now, on your feet. I'll take you down to—"

"Uncle!"

Ziarat turned and glanced over his shoulder. Nhajsib Wal had just rounded the turn near the pagoda. His face beamed with relief at the sight of his uncle.

"I was concerned," he called out. "I thought maybe— Watch out!"

Nhajsib lunged forward, but it was too late. Vargadrum Shili had rolled to one side on the path and snatched up his fallen MP-5. He managed to get off a shot before Nhajsib was upon him, grabbing at the submachine gun. The two men struggled briefly, then Nhajsib grabbed the gun by the barrel and yanked it away from Shili. Using it as a club, he struck Shili on the side of the head. The Kashmiri slumped to the ground.

Still holding the MP-5, Nhajsib rose to his feet and turned to his uncle.

"No!"

Ziarat was kneeling on the ground, hands pressed to his midsection. Blood seeped through his fingers as he looked up at his nephew.

"I will be fine," he said, smiling weakly. His eyes glazed over and he began to swoon. Nhajsib dropped to his knees and slowly eased his uncle to the ground. Ziarat stared up at him, his eyes unfocused.

"I did this to you!" Nhajsib shouted, grabbing at

Ziarat and holding him tight. "Please, you can't die on me!"

But Death had come to claim Ziarat Wal. Allowed a few last words, he hoarsely told his nephew, "You have made me proud...."

As Ziarat died in his nephew's arms, Nhajsib noticed Shili stirring a few yards away. Enraged, his eyes welling with tears, Nhajsib grabbed the man's MP-5 and turned it on the Kashmiri. Vargadrum Shili's body twitched as round after round slammed into him. It was only when the gun was empty that Nhajsib slowly turned it away and set it on the ground. Perhaps there would come a time when he would feel he had avenged his uncle's death, but for now, Nhajsib could feel only emptiness.

CHAPTER TWELVE

Academy of Arts in the Ghats

Less than thirty minutes after the last gunshot had been fired, India's politicos were already hard at work milking the skirmish with the mujahideen for all it was worth. Their take on things entailed a little distortion of facts, but, they reasoned, such sacrifices were sometimes necessary in the name of the greater good—which in this case involved bolstering the prime minister's credentials as a man prepared to step forward and decisively stem the recent tide of terrorist attacks on Indian soil.

The prime minister was presently airborne from New Delhi in the fastest military jet available, hoping to reach Kottayam before sundown so that he could indulge in photo opportunities at the academy. While they waited on his arrival, the press—or at least those members who could be counted on to provide favorable coverage—had been escorted to the pagoda near where Ziarat Wal and Vargadrum Shili had both died after their symbolic duel. A high-ranking party speechwriter vacationing in Alleppey had been brought in and passed off as a military spokesperson, and he put the necessary spin on certain details as he briefed reporters on the events of the past three hours.

Cameramen, meanwhile, busily clicked away, making the best of what little time they had before night fell on Kottayam. Some had earlier managed a photo or two of officials tending to the bodies of the duelists or the sight of several academy youths trying to console a grief-stricken Nhajsib Wal, but these would be incidental shots, buried in the back pages of the newspapers and magazines that would put forth the initial account of what the media was already peddling as the Comeuppance In Kottayam. On the front pages of those newspapers and the covers of those magazines, the Indian public would be treated to impressive wide-angle shots now being taken of the stalwart-looking Seventy-third Regiment, visible downhill in every direction, encircling the academy grounds with their tanks meticulously spaced apart at regular intervals, cannons pointed toward the now vanquished enemy as if their mere presence had been instrumental in bringing about the mujahideen's surrender; all this against the backdrop of a stunning Keralan sunset made all the more breathtaking by ribbons of smoke still rising from the heap of burning palm fronds. Adjoining news stories would pay lip service to contributions made by the American Secret Service and CIA, but the bulk of the credit for rescuing hostages and preventing the terrorist launch of surface-to-air missiles would go to the tank regiment, RAW and the Intelligence Bureau, and to the hostages themselves, particularly Nhajsib Wal and the women huskers who'd given the terrorists a taste of their own

MP-5s. And, of course, there would be special side-bars devoted to the heroic martyrdom of Ziarat Wal, playing up the irony that his stand against the terrorists came almost thirty years to the day after he had been decorated for his part in the liberation of Bangladesh from the mujahideen's alleged sponsor, Pakistan.

Conspicuously absent in all these accounts would be any mention of those truly most responsible for saving the day, not only for the untold thousands who would have likely perished had the terrorists succeeded in getting even one missile into the air, but also for their American President. But then, the covert warriors from Stony Man Farm could never be acknowledged. They operated from the shadows, didn't, in fact, exist.

Mack Bolan, John Kissinger and Jack Grimaldi had yet to leave the grounds of the academy. Along with the other Americans who had been part of the force dropped by helicopter into the tea fields, the Stony Man trio was uphill from the press and tank troops, cloistered in one of the rooms usually used as a dormitory for the youths of the academy. After being filmed by the press corps, all of the students had been whisked from the facility to a downtown Kottayam hospital, where, over the next two days, they would undergo testing and counseling for the trauma they'd been forced to endure at the hands of the mujahideen. In their absence, the main gathering hall had been turned into both a command post and interrogation room. Besides Govankrishna Vanat, five other surviving terrorists, all cuffed around the wrists and ankles, were being questioned. Another six, critically injured during the siege, had been flown to a military hospital in Munnar and would have their turn before the inquisitors once their wounds had been tended to.

Not surprisingly, the terrorists were being uncooperative. Their identification papers, including Vanat's, were obviously forged, but no one was willing to admit it, much less come forward with their real names. Photos had been taken and they had been fingerprinted, however, and it was hoped that once the information was disseminated to the appropriate sources, results would come back and the pieces of the puzzle would start to fall into place. In the meantime, the authorities had to contend with their prisoners' silence or, equally frustrating, their rote recitation of mujahideen propaganda.

"They're like those play dolls with pull strings," Grimaldi complained to Kissinger as he stepped away from one of the interrogations. "They talk all right, but it's the same three or four things over and over again. And I'm not talking name, rank and serial number. With them, it's 'We are instruments of God' and 'Mujahideen is the lifeblood of Kashmir.'"

"We all have our slogans, I guess," Kissinger reflected. He was sitting in a corner, bare feet propped on a desk, ankles packed in ice. Also on the desk was a laptop Grimaldi had taken from the helicopter. The computer came with a sophisticated built-in scanner and SAT-COM link—both innovations courtesy of Aaron Kurtzman and his cybercrew—and Kissinger had already been in touch with the Farm, detailing what had just gone down and sending along photos taken of the mujahideen, both dead and alive. As he waited for a response, he picked away at a mound of food heaped on a plate in his lap. He concentrated on a bed of seasoned rice, ignoring large chunks of something that looked like chopped artichoke hearts the color of raw steak.

"What are they feeding us?" Grimaldi asked, pointing at the plate.

"Jackfruit," Kissinger said. "A fruit that tastes like meat. Or at least that's how they peddled it to me."

"Sounds interesting." Grimaldi plucked one of the pieces of fruit and bit into it. He grimaced and turned to one side, spitting it into the trash. "Mmm, just the way Mom used to make it," he deadpanned, grabbing a bottle of mineral water so he could try to wash away the taste.

Kissinger was shifting the ice pack on his ankle when there was a sudden disturbance across the room. Cursing epithets, Nhajsib Wal had charged one of the mujahideen, shoving him so hard the Kashmiri fell backward off his chair. Wal was quick to grab the man and haul him back to his feet, then shove him into the nearest wall.

"Answers!" he bellowed, grabbing the other man by the lapels of his tracksuit and shaking him. "I want answers!"

The Kashmiri, clearly in pain, blood trickling from a gash to his chin, gazed sullenly at Wal and repeated his self-chosen mantra for the interrogators. "My righteous cause will prevail. My righteous cause will—"

Wal's hands went for the mujahideen's neck, choking the words in his throat. Several other men—two IB, one CIA—rushed over and grabbed Wal from behind. He fought against them, but they powered him away from the Kashmiri, who rubbed his neck as he calmly hobbled back to his chair.

"I knew they should've taken him out of the loop, at least for now," Grimaldi observed, watching Nhajsib Wal argue heatedly with his peers.

"You can't really blame him," Kissinger said. "Here he goes to help his uncle, only to have the guy die in his arms in a way that makes him think he's responsible. I'd hate to have to drag a load like that around."

"Which is exactly why they should put him on leave," Grimaldi argued.

"I hear you," Kissinger said. "But tell me something. Suppose Hal took one to the head right in front of you. Or Striker. Do you really think you'd let anybody put you on the sidelines when it came time for payback?"

Grimaldi didn't need long to answer. "Touché," he said. "And, since you win, I'll be the one who goes and finds us something more edible for dinner."

Grimaldi was about to make his way to the mess area when Mack Bolan came in from an adjoining room and signaled for him to stay put.

"Any progress?" Kissinger asked once the Executioner joined them.

Bolan shook his head. He'd been conferring with the joint team that had taken charge of investigating the mujahideen's presence in Kottayam. "They're still mostly bickering about turf," he reported. "Everybody wants to be in charge and nobody wants to take orders.''

''Where have I heard that one before?'' Grimaldi said dryly.

''They *have* pretty much swept the grounds for evidence,'' Bolan went on. ''Not much to go on, though.''

''Meaning we've still got this Dehri Neshah guy on the loose somewhere with a second missile launcher.''

Bolan nodded. ''It's pretty clear the priest killings are tied into his escape and that they used disguises to pull it off, but beyond that there's not much.''

''What about Kottayam?'' Grimaldi asked. ''Haven't they turned up anything about the prison break?''

''Neshah and one other man ditched their getaway rig in a traffic jam and disappeared after killing some guy they rear-ended. IB has the local cops putting out APBs and trying to lay a dragnet, but my guess is Neshah's already long gone.''

''You know those cockroaches,'' Grimaldi agreed. ''Give them a chance, they'll slip through the first crack they come to.''

''So where does that lead us?'' Kissinger wondered.

''In a holding pattern for the moment,'' Bolan confessed. ''You heard back from the Farm?''

''Nope, not y— Hold on...'' Kissinger swung his feet off the table and sat upright in front of the laptop, viewing the screen. ''Even as we speak...''

Grimaldi and Bolan huddled behind Kissinger so

they could all see what Kurtzman and the others had come up with back in the States. So far, photo pro- filing had come up with two matches. The man Ziarat Wal had killed before being gunned down was Var- gadrum Shili, one of three Kashmiri brothers with close, long-standing ties to Dehri Neshah. Since nei- ther of the other brothers had matched up with the head shots taken on the grounds, it seemed likely they'd played a part in Neshah's escape.

"Should be easy enough to confirm that," Gri- maldi said. "Just show mug shots to the clowns that let Neshah get away and see if they recognize any- body."

"That still doesn't leave us with much in the way of leads," Bolan said.

"Maybe this'll help," Kissinger replied, indicating a photo next to an icon indicating a file being trans- mitted from the Farm. "It's the old guy we found curled up under the launcher. Looks like they've got a dossier on him."

"Now, that's promising," Grimaldi said. "He's the one guy who's not spouting any rhetoric."

"Of course, he's also acting like he's ready for the rubber room," Kissinger observed, glancing across the room at Vanat. The engineer sat in a chair with his legs bent upward and his arms wrapped around his knees, allowing him to softly rock back and forth, ignoring the CIA and IB agents trying to question him. The agents both seemed frustrated, perhaps con- templating the use of Nhajsib Wal's tactics as a way to get the man to snap out of his delerium.

Bolan continued to stare at the screen as Vanat's

dossier came up. As he reviewed the engineer's background, particularly with regards to the last few months before Vanat quit his job at British Aerospace, Bolan tried to formulate a strategy for getting the engineer to be more cooperative. Though he'd never so much as cracked open a textbook on psychology, Bolan had had his share of dealings with disturbed individuals over the years; he felt they had nothing to lose by his trying to get the man to open up. What he needed was some psychological ammunition.

Finally, as he skimmed through a series of short letters Vanat had written to his employer's personnel office before his resignation, Bolan felt that he was onto something. Kissinger could see it, too, just from the look in Bolan's eye.

"I think I just saw a light bulb go on," Kissinger said.

Bolan nodded, glancing first at Vanat, then at Nhajsib Wal, who had walked away from his fellow officers and was now staring out the window at the fading twilight. "I think I've got a way to kill two birds with one stone."

"YES," NHAJSIB WAL told Mack Bolan, "I think it can work."

"Bloody well worth a try," wisecracked Les Marris, a Cleveland-born CIA agent who'd worked enough foreign assignments with British intelligence to have mastered the passable accent of a native Londoner.

"Okay, then," Bolan said, indicating the door leading from the command center back to the hall being used for interrogations. "Shall we?"

Marris led the way, with Wal and Bolan close behind.

"Before we go in," Wal told Bolan, "I want to thank you. You helped put things back in the right perspective."

Prior to conferring with Marris, Bolan had taken Nhajsib Wal aside to offer condolences on the death of the IB agent's uncle. He'd empathized with the Indian's grief, recalling how consumed he'd been with a sense of helpless rage years ago, immediately following the deaths of his own family. The circumstances had been far different, but there was some common ground, particularly in terms of all the deaths having come about directly as a result of tainted contact with forces of evil—in Bolan's case the Mafia. Bolan had sided with Wal's outburst, saying it wasn't only acceptable, but vital that he feel rage toward those who were ultimately responsible for his uncle's death. By the same token, he'd suggested to Wal that there were times when vengeance could be best achieved circuitously, through means other than brute force, such as in their dealings with Vanat.

Wal still knew it would take time to work through his grief and sense of guilt, but as he followed Bolan and Marris into the interrogation room, he was determined not to be consumed by those crippling emotions. Instead, he would harness them, let them help him to focus on the best way to ultimately avenge his uncle's death.

As the three men approached Vanat, the engineer

trembled slightly with fear. He had, after all, witnessed the way Wal had roughed up one of the other prisoners and was wary of being the next target. As such, he was stunned when Wal instead took a key and unlocked the manacles around his wrists and ankles.

"My apologies, Dr. Vanat," Nhajsib Wal told the man. "It appears we are in error holding you prisoner."

The moment he heard his name, Vanat's otherworldly gaze was tempered by a flicker of recognition. He glanced up, first at Wal, then Les Marris. Bolan remained a few yards back. His role wasn't yet called for.

"Dr. Vanat," Marris intoned officiously as he extended a hand. "I am Gerald Cook, a senior executive officer at British Aerospace. I, too, owe you an apology, on behalf of our entire organization."

To Vanat, who, prior to his resignation, had driven himself to distraction in his failed attempts to establish a dialogue with the hierarchy at British Aerospace, was stunned by Marris's pronouncement.

"You want to apologize?" he said, his voice quavering. "To me?"

"Quite right, sir," Marris said, gesturing toward the doorway leading back to the command center. "If I could just have a word with you away from these hooligans you've fallen in with, I'm in hopes we can straighten things out and have you back where you belong…at British Aerospace."

Vanat was now speechless. How many nights had he spent awake, playing over and over in his mind the things he felt his superiors should have told him in response to his charges of ethnic discrimination? How many times had he envisioned the grand moment when he would be vindicated, when his charges would be not only acknowledged, but also addressed, promptly and in his favor? Could this really be happening?

"How...how did you find me?" Vanat managed to burble.

"We, sir, have been looking for you, night and day, for the better part of four months," Marris said. "Ever since your packet of letters finally found their way into the right hands. Mine."

"The photo we took of you was sent out on the wires," Wal explained to Vanat. "And, as it happened, Mr. Cook was in Kottayam for the day while en route to Trivandrum."

"To negotiate with them at the space center about replacing their lost Sabre missiles with our Rapiers," Marris added quickly, anxious to lend credence to the incredible coincidence of a senior official being so close at hand within minutes of Vanat's apprehension.

Bolan could see the tentative look on Vanat's face, as if he were, for the first time, beginning to question what he was hearing. It was time for him to move in and play his part of the charade.

"All right, enough kissing up to this bastard!" He pushed his way past Wal and Marris and poked his index finger against Vanat's chest. "Look, Mahatma, these dolts might think you're some poor little victim of circumstances, but if you ask me, I think you're as guilty as the rest of your towel-headed friends here, and I aim to prove it!''

"That's enough!'' Wal said, pushing Bolan back a step and standing between him and Vanat. "This matter is no longer under your jurisdiction!''

"This guy came within a hair breadth of popping our President with a stolen SAM,'' Bolan retorted, playing the role of "bad cop" to the hilt. "That makes him our boy, not yours!''

"He was undoubtedly coerced,'' Marris ventured. "Some sort of brainwashing, no doubt. We have no intention of holding it against him.''

"You guys make me want to puke!'' Bolan shouted at Marris and Wal.

"I think you've said quite enough,'' Marris sniffed.

"Yes,'' Wal concurred. "This matter is no longer your concern. If you insist on trying to make it otherwise, I'll have you brought up on charges.''

"Me?'' Bolan guffawed. "What charges?''

"This is Indian soil,'' Wal reminded Bolan. "You have disparaged a fellow countryman with ethnic slurs. It will not be tolerated.''

"Oh, great!'' Bolan threw his hands up in mock resignation. "Fine. You want to mollycoddle this traitor, suit yourself. Just don't come crying to me when he stabs you in the back first chance he gets.''

"You've said enough,'' Wal told Bolan. "I want you off these grounds immediately.''

"On whose orders?''

"Mine,'' Wal responded coolly.

"And I daresay I'll do what I can to back him up,'' Marris promised.

Bolan looked at Wal and Marris, then smirked. "Hey, what do you know, the Brits and Indies are chums again all of a sudden."

"There's the door," Marris told Bolan. "I suggest you use it."

"Oh, I'll use it, all right," Bolan promised. "But when this guy winds up double-dealing on you, don't come crying to me!"

As Bolan started off, Nhajsib Wal and Marris continued to escort Vanat the other way, toward the command center.

"I'm sorry you had to hear all that," Marris said. "Americans, you know."

"Yes," Wal concurred. "They are proof that the greater one's wealth, the greater their arrogance."

"But you needn't pay him any more mind," Marris said. "You're among friends now. And before we go any further, would you care for some tea? A bite to eat, perhaps? Anything you wish."

"I am a little hungry," Vanat confessed.

Vanat's dossier had been comprehensive down to his dietary preferences, and when they passed through into the command center, the engineer was pleasantly surprised to find a table set out with nearly every one of his favorite foods. As he filled a plate, Marris and Wal exchanged a knowing look behind his back. They definitely had him where they wanted him.

"We'd like nothing better than to show that American just how much he misjudged you, Dr. Vanat," Wal prompted.

"Oh, we can get around to that later," Marris interjected. "Let the poor chap eat!"

"Thank you," Vanat said. "You are both very kind."

"It's just that we understand what you must have been through these past months," Marris said. "That is to say, we think we understand. Of course, I'm sure we actually haven't the faintest clue."

"It has been a difficult time," Vanat admitted as he sweetened his tea.

"How in heaven's name did the mujahideen manage to lure you over to their side?" Marris wanted to know. "I mean, besides the fact that we were so boorish in the way we handled your grievances."

Made comfortable and reassured, what little remained of Vanat's paranoia gave way to an almost euphoric sense of relief. Here at last were men who truly understood him, who were not looking to merely seduce him for their own selfish purposes. Who better to unburden himself of the ordeal he'd been through all these months?

"How did they win me over?" Vanat laughed faintly. "How else? They used a woman."

*Bombay
Maharashtra State*

"YOU ARE AN EVIL woman," Daeon Murawd told Briley.

"So you've told me...at least a dozen times since we left Kottayam," the woman said, sighing. Despite Murawd's pleading, she had been smoking cigarettes almost nonstop the past three hours, flicking ashes on the control panel and littering the floor with crushed filters. Now, as she crumpled an empty pack and tossed it playfully at Murawd, she blew smoke in his face and teased, "What happened to the charming gentleman so eager to flatter me out of my panties?"

"Evil," Murawd repeated.

"Less talking, please," Dehri Neshah called out from the rear seat. "You have a plane to fly."

"I am an experienced pilot!" Murawd snapped irritably. "I can fly and talk at the same time!"

Neshah leaned forward and pressed the cold barrel of his Smith & Wesson revolver against the pilot's cheek. "If you will remember correctly," he told Murawd calmly, "you had the foresight to store parachutes for your valued clients. If need be, we can shoot you and float to safety while you and your precious plane crash to Earth like a spent meteor. Is that the fate you want?"

Murawd stared ahead sullenly but didn't answer.

"I asked you a question," Neshah said. He pulled back the hammer on the pistol. Murawd flinched at the sound.

"I understand the situation," he finally replied, his voice strained.

"And...?"

"And I will not cause any more trouble," Murawd promised.

"A sensible man." Neshah removed the gun from Murawd's face and returned to his seat. Beside him, Penghat Shili had several maps unfolded across his lap. For most of the past three hours, during which they'd traveled northward over one small coastal town after another, the two men had divided their attention between the maps and Murawd's customized radio. They constantly changed stations, seeking newscasts for the latest information on the day's events in Kottayam. It was clear to Murawd that the men—and most likely the woman, as well—were somehow linked to a prison break, the killing of two priests and the takeover of an academy. Insofar as the newscasts kept referring to the incidents as the work of Kashmiri separatists, Murawd also felt certain the two men seated behind him were mujahideen. As such, he wasn't about to take their threats lightly.

And yet, Murawd was also puzzled by much of the men's hushed conversation the past hour. He had only been able to pick up bits and pieces, but as they drew closer to Bombay, again and again Murawd heard the two men speak, not of further insurrection or acts of sabotage, but rather of plans for a movie and the need to make sure the props were ready. True, Bombay, referred to by many as Bollywood, was India's film-making center and home to a number of cutthroat producers who were terrorists in their own right, but Murawd found it hard to believe either man had any intention of turning his sword into film shares. Were they speaking in code? It seemed unlikely. What did it matter to them if he overheard their connivings? He would more than likely be taking their secrets with him to his grave, wherever they wound up deciding that was to be.

Or was he mistaken?

Murawd suddenly began to wonder if perhaps he wasn't marked for death after all. Maybe the muja-hideen were secretly considering him as a possible wingman. They seemed the type likely to have need of a reliable pilot at a moment's notice, and the fact that he was Indian would be a plus for them while they were operating in his country. Perhaps, despite all their taunting and abuse, they secretly respected him for standing up to them. It was a common enough trait among those in power.

Buoyed by his renewed prospects, Murawd tried to think of the best way to go about convincing his captors that he was worth more to them alive than dead. When he saw Briley crush out her last cigarette, he glimpsed an opportunity and took his pack from his shirt pocket.

"Here." He offered her the pack with what he hoped would pass for a teasing grin. "Maybe if you smell up my plane with my own brand I'll be less upset."

Briley snatched the cigarettes from his hand. "Is that supposed to be some sort of joke?"

"You're welcome," Murawd said, the smile still plastered across his face.

"Shut up." Briley lit one of the cigarettes and tossed the match at Murawd. "Asshole."

Murawd turned to the men in the rear seat and offered them a sly wink. "I think she loves me," he confided.

Shili and Neshah both glanced up. Murawd had hoped to get a laugh out of at least one of them, but both men seemed only perturbed by his interruption.

"I told you to keep quiet and fly the plane," Neshah reminded him.

Murawd decided to play out his hand. Instead of

shutting up, he told Neshah. "If you are trying to make a movie, I think I can help you with financing."

It worked. The two men both glanced back up at him.

"My brother is an investment counselor in Bombay," Murawd went on. "He can get his hands on venture capital as easily as you or I could pick fruit from a tree. In fact, he lives only a few miles from Santa Cruz airport. I could arrange for him to meet us."

Neshah and Shili looked at each other as if weighing the offer. Murawd's mind raced. What a brilliant ploy he'd come up with! With all the recent terrorist acts in India, he knew that security had been beefed up at the Santa Cruz facility. Perhaps soldiers would be on the lookout for the men sitting behind him. Even if that wasn't the case, the airport was one of the busiest in the nation. There would be opportunities to make a break for it and lose himself in the frenetic bustle.

Murawd's fantasizing was interrupted when Shili suddenly flicked open a switchblade and lashed out with it, his hand a blur. Murawd felt a sting across his cheek, and when he put his fingers to his face, they came away red with blood.

"Eavesdrop on us again and next time I'll slice off your ear," Shili warned, wiping his blade clean on the fabric of his seat. "As for landing at Santa Cruz to meet your brother, that is not going to happen. You already have your instructions."

And so Murawd's short-lived hopes faded along with the last glimmer of daylight out over the Arabian

Sea. The same darkness that began to cloak the western coastline also draped itself across Murawd's heart and soul. Once again he was filled with a sense of impending doom. Blood from his sliced cheek trickled down onto his shirt, but he made no effort to staunch the flow. What was the point?

Soon the lights of Bombay came into view, illuminating the coastline like a vast, bawdy trove of gems. In the past, it was a sight that filled Murawd with excitement and anticipation. He flew there frequently, usually on weekends when his brother would be off work. For Murawd, Bombay was spirited afternoons of cricket at the Azad Maidan, followed by a feast of specialties at Khyber Restaurant in Coloba. He and his brother would meet up with friends there and then continue their Coloban revelry across town, barhopping and disco dancing at the clubs along Arthur Bunder Road. If they didn't hook up with any women to their liking, it was only a short taxi ride to Foras Road, where there were prostitutes at every street corner. Anywhere else in India, one needed a holiday to celebrate, but as far as Murawd had always been concerned, in Bombay every day was a festival, every night a bacchanal.

Not so this time, however. Now, as the lights of the city grew brighter and more inviting, Murawd could only stare at them with longing and sorrow. As Shili had just reminded him, they wouldn't be landing in the city, much less setting foot there. Those weren't his instructions.

Once he reached the harbor, Murawd veered to his right. Below, the number of lights dwindled quickly.

In time, they would leave civilization behind and find themselves in the wilderness.

As Murawd carried out his orders, Penghat Shili dialed a number on his SAT phone. Murawd listened carefully to the Kashmiri's end of the conversation. Apparently, the mujahideen had established some sort of camp or base near Guiyn Plateau, a long-abandoned Hindu shrine miles from the nearest town or roadway. Murawd regretted having bragged to the woman about his ability to set the plane down in meadows and pastures. Wherever it was they wished to have him land, he knew there would be no airfield, no security, no witnesses. No hope that he would live out the night.

"They will be ready for us," Shili told Neshah as he put the phone aside.

"Excellent."

Neshah called out to Murawd, "You can start to take us down. We will tell you where to land."

"As you wish," Murawd responded demurely, beginning the plane's descent.

As he had several times during the flight, the Keralan toyed with the idea of crashing his plane, perhaps after putting the Ghurka through a few dizzying aerial maneuvers that would prevent the others from bailing out. That way, before dying he would at least have the satisfaction of seeing fear on the faces of his tormentors. Also, he reasoned, taking the mujahideen with him to their deaths would be a noble act, one certain to offset a lifetime of petty transgressions and enhance his stature in the next life.

It was a nice thought, but ultimately Murawd

wasn't quite ready to give up his present life, much less willfully destroy his prized Ghurka. There had to be another way.

Once he had passed over the small towns of Panvel and Karjat, Murawd could see nothing before him but wide black plains and the shadowy outlines of hillocks and small buttes. Experienced or not, it would be impossible to land in such utter darkness, and, judging from his fuel gauge, they would have to land soon. He was about to tell the men as much when, as if by magic, lights began to flicker to life, one by one, atop a nearby plateau. It quickly became clear that they were lined up in two neat rows, creating a makeshift landing strip.

"There you are," Neshah told him, pointing out the small plateau. "It looks like an aircraft carrier in the middle of the desert, yes?"

"How flat is the plateau?" Murawd asked.

"Flat enough for a man of your talents to make a smooth landing," Neshah responded.

Briley snickered. "Just pretend we're going to our little rendezvous."

Murawd held his rage in check. As he drew close to the plateau, he noticed shadowy figures with assault rifles standing beside the flickering oil lamps. Most likely they would douse the lamps as soon as Murawd landed, returning the plateau to darkness. He would be swallowed by the night, most likely never to see the light of another day.

Murawd was lowering the plane's landing gear into position when it occurred to him, for the first time, that he was the only one inside the plane wearing a seat belt. Up in the air they hadn't encountered any turbulence and it hadn't been an important consideration, but now, during landing, restraints were vital, especially for a small plane landing on possibly rough terrain. It was customary for Murawd to advise his passengers to buckle up, but this night, he decided, would be an exception.

Everything seemed in order as the plane leveled off and approached the plateau, so much so that Neshah and Shili turned their attention back to one of the maps. Then, at the last possible seconds, Murawd made his move and veered the plane to one side. Suddenly, instead of coming in between the rows of landing lamps, Murawd had the plane aimed dead center at the men lined up beside the left row of lamps.

Like tenpins being struck by a bowling ball, the first two gunmen bounded away from the nose of the Ghurka. A third and fourth were crushed as they fell under the plane's landing gear. Murawd had already made a point to land rough, and when the plane bounded over the bodies, Briley, Neshah and Shili were thrown around the cabin. Briley struck her head on the windshield and was knocked unconscious, while Shili slammed hard into the stereo cabinet, sending a sharp pain down the length of his arm. Neshah, thrown to the floor, twisted his knee but was otherwise unhurt.

By now the other men on the ground had dived clear of the oncoming plane, but with Neshah and Shili aboard they were wary of firing at the pilot. Murawd let out a raucous whoop as he began to weave the plane back and forth across the runway, hoping to keep his passengers off balance.

Those on the ground began to suspect Murawd's ploy and countered the only way they knew how, by firing at the plane's tires. Shot after shot bit into the dust being thrown up by the plane, and there were muffled explosions each time a bullet found its mark. As rubber gave way and the plane's wheel rims bit into the soft earth of the plateau, the Ghurka began to decelerate.

Inside the plane, Shili had been thrown against the side window, cracking both it and his skull; he was now out cold on the floor. Neshah, also pitched about the cabin like laundry in a dryer, had managed to keep hold of his Smith & Wesson. Once he got the sense the plane would indeed stop short of the plateau's edge, he took aim as best he could and fired at the pilot.

Shots ripped through the seat and burrowed into Murawd until he slumped over the controls, bleeding from half a dozen wounds to the back and neck. The plane continued to roll of its own accord for another twenty yards before slowing to a stop in thick gravel.

Neshah had made a point to leave one bullet in the chamber of his Smith & Wesson. He staggered forward and pointed the gun at the base of Murawd's skull.

"Very clever," he said, pulling the trigger. "But not clever enough."

CHAPTER THIRTEEN

Krula Pass Airfield, Western Ghats

Mack Bolan wasn't sure which was the ruder awakening, the alleged coffee he'd been given to sip on the way to the airfield or the first glare of the morning sun peering over the mountaintops. Deciding it was a toss-up, he turned his back to the sun and spilled the rest of the coffee on the ground, half-expecting it to sizzle in the dirt.

"Pekoe," Les Marris told him. The CIA agent, who'd driven Bolan up to the airfield in a Company minivan, held out his foam cup, sloshing around its contents. "It's really a black tea, not coffee. The secret is plenty of cream and sugar, and even then you've got to keep it stirred up."

"I think I'll just wait until they open a Starbucks," Bolan said.

Along with the rest of the core team looking into the mujahideen's takeover of the youth academy, Bolan and Marris had spent the night in the dormitory, rising shortly before dawn to pick up where they'd left off the previous evening. Little of consequence had come to light while the men slept. The biggest news was confirmation that among the Kashmiri fatalities were two brothers, Vargadrum and Raghubir Shili. Vargadrum, it turned out, had been the man who'd killed Ziarat Wal up near the pagoda, only to be gunned down himself by Nhajsib, Ziarat's nephew. The other brother, Raghubir, had died while impersonating a priest during the prison break in downtown Kottayam. The authorities were intrigued by the latter's death because he'd been stabbed in the chest and then nearly disemboweled—a trademark of the man who'd been sprung from jail, Dehri Neshah, aka the Kashmir Shredder. The irony of Raghubir's death was compounded when the warden at the detention center had identified the second would-be priest taking part in the escape as Penghat, Raghubir's older brother. Dr. Vanat, rousted from his sleep for questioning in the matter, had confirmed that Raghubir and Neshah had had a falling-out several weeks earlier. Vanat also said that all three brothers were extremely close, giving rise to a theory that Neshah had yet to tell Penghat, his alleged right-hand man, about the real circumstances of Raghubir's death. A consensus had yet to be reached, however, on whether to make the information public in hopes of creating a rift between the two mujahideen, wherever they might be.

It was in hopes of determining the whereabouts of Penghat Shili and Dehri Neshah that Bolan and Marris had driven up to the remote airfield overlooking Kottayam and Vembanad Lake. Lying on its side downhill from the grove of hardwoods where the two men stood was a late-model Honda sedan. The vehicle had been spotted shortly after dawn by an amateur photographer who'd come to the airfield hoping to hire a pilot to fly him over the Academy of Arts for some freelance shots he could then sell to the Indian tabloids. Advised that airspace over the school had been declared off-limits, the photographer had climbed one of the hardwood trees hoping to use his telephoto lens for the next-best thing. Instead, he'd spotted the Honda, which, as it turned out, had been stolen the morning before from an upscale Kottayam neighborhood less than three blocks from the hotel where Vanat had planned on having his much anticipated rendezvous with the American call girl known only as Briley. Jack Grimaldi and John Kissinger were presently at the hotel trying to get more information on Briley, who had checked out a half hour before the theft of the Honda.

The Honda, meanwhile, was being searched by the same Intelligence Bureau authorities who the day before had investigated the murder of the two priests downhill from the academy. Marris and Bolan, content to leave the IB to its business, were waiting to speak to one Kalyanar Tendulma, one of the airfield's groundskeepers, who claimed to know how the Honda had wound up halfway down the embankment. When he'd been called at home about the matter, Tendulma had promised to drive up to give a statement. When Marris and Bolan had shown up ahead of him, Marris had cut a deal, giving IB dibs on the car in exchange for first crack at the groundskeeper.

As they waited for Tendulma, Bolan stared downhill at the distant academy. The fires were out and the tanks had been withdrawn, but the academy was still cordoned off to anyone but government officials, sanctioned members of the media and intelligence agents with the proper authorization. The most activity was in the adjacent paddies, where workers angrily labored to salvage a rice crop trampled by tanks and Indian ground forces positioning themselves for the previous night's photo session. So vehement had been their anger this morning that the prime minister had been forced to cancel his belated visit to the grounds. To save face, it was said that the prime minister would be joining the U.S. President in Bombay for an impromptu state funeral procession honoring Ziarat Wal.

Marris was beginning to recount the good-cop–bad-cop routine they'd played on Vanat when he and Bolan were joined by a gangly man in his midforties, wearing a khaki uniform and matching cap, his calves wrapped in puttees. He looked like a caricature of a member of the Indian army dating back to the days of Teddy Roosevelt.

"Kalyanar Tendulma at your service," the man said in flawless English as he extended a hand to Bolan. After the three men exchanged greetings, the groundskeeper explained, "I learned your language from television. Excellent shows like *Dynasty* and *Mannix*." He reached to his scalp and pulled a strand of hair down over his forehead, then cocked an eyebrow and pointed to Marris, drawling, "Book 'em, Dan-o."

"That would be *Hawaii Five-O* not *Mannix*," Marris said.

"Yes, yes!" Tendulma said. "*Hawaii Five-O*, starring Jack Lord!'' As the Indian closed his eyes and bobbed his head, humming the show's theme song, Marris glanced at Bolan and pretended to smoke a joint. Bolan nodded. No doubt about it, their prize witness was stoned out of his mind. They were beginning to think they had traipsed up to the airfield on a wild-goose chase.

Once Tendulma had finished his performance, Marris patiently indicated the disabled Honda and asked, ''You saw how this car wound up down there?''

Tendulma shook his head. ''No, no, no, that's not what I told them. I said I knew whose car it was. Big difference.''

''You can say that again,'' Marris grumbled. ''But fine, I'll bite. Whose car is it?''

''A woman,'' Tendulma said. ''American, like you.''

Marris and Bolan exchanged another look. Maybe they were on to something after all. Bolan turned to the Indian. ''You saw her here?''

''More or less.''

'''More or less' doesn't cut it,'' Marris said testily. ''You're going to have to be a little clearer.''

''Just tell us from the beginning,'' Bolan suggested, though he was wary the man might do just that and launch into his life story, starting with infancy.

''It was last night, a little before sundown,'' the groundskeeper said. ''We have a pilot here, Daeon Murawd, who thinks he is quite the ladies' man, like Hugh Hefner. He drives up and he tells me he knows it's late, but he happened to meet this foxy American woman in a Honda just down the road from here.

She's a real hubba-hubba, he says, and she wants him to take her on a quick tour.

"Now, Daeon, with him 'a quick tour' means he flies a woman someplace where they can be alone and he can park his plane in her hangar, if you know what I mean."

"Yeah," Marris said, "I think I get the picture. Go on."

"He tells me this when I'm heading out to take in some of the cones," Tendulma said, indicating the bright orange markers that lined the nearby runway. "So I have my back turned to him for a while, and then I hear his plane pulling away from the hangar. I guess the woman must have drove up when I wasn't looking, but when I check around, I don't see her car.

"I can't see inside Daeon's plane, either, because it's going the other way. So I don't know if he's got the woman with him or not. And I don't care much, because I want to finish work and go to town and find a woman of my own, yes?

"I go back to my cones, thinking Daeon will be taking off any second. But no. I look back again and I see that his plane has pulled off the runway, by these trees. I don't know why he does this, and when I look, I can see under the plane and I think I see legs…you know, the legs of somebody on the other side of the plane coming from out of the woods to get on board."

"A woman's legs?" Bolan asked.

"If she was wearing pants, maybe," the groundskeeper said. "But a woman wearing pants in Kottayam? I don't think so, even if she is an American."

"Then he was picking up a man," Marris prompted. "Or maybe more than one man?"

Tendulma shrugged. "Maybe yes, maybe no. I'm not playing Jack Lord then, you know? I'm not playing detective. I just want to finish work and have my weekend."

"But you saw the plane take off."

The Indian nodded. "Yes, that I saw," he said.

"But you didn't get a good look at anyone inside the plane," Marris said. "Not even when it was taking off."

"No," Tendulma said. "I finish my business and go home to eat and shower, then I go to the clubs. No luck. This morning I get a call asking if I know anything about a Honda Accord. I tell them I think I know who it belongs to. They say they want to know more, so I say I will drive out. Here I am."

"And on the way you happened to smoke a little breakfast," Marris suggested.

Tendulma looked offended. "That is personal business."

"When you smoke, do you ever see things?" Marris persisted. "You know, like hallucinations?"

"That is personal business," the groundskeeper repeated. "But, if you must know, I do not smoke on the job. I know what I saw, and this Honda is not a hallucination."

"All right, all right," Marris said.

Bolan stepped in and took over the interview. "Do you know when this Daeon fellow got back last night?" he asked. "Obviously, we'd like to talk to him."

"He didn't," Tendulma said.

"He didn't?"

Tendulma shook his head. "I looked in his hangar before I came over here. He never came back last night."

"Is that normal?"

"Most nights, no," the groundskeeper said. "Fridays, though, maybe."

"Why's that?" Marris asked.

"Daeon has a brother in Bombay. Some weekends he likes to fly up there. Who knows, maybe he talked the woman into going with him. It's happened before."

"This brother of his. Do you happen to know his address?" Bolan asked.

The groundskeeper shook his head. "No, but Daeon has an office in his hangar. Maybe the address is there."

"Good idea," Marris said. "Let's have a look."

They were halfway to the hangar when a nondescript Ford Taurus pulled into the airfield. Bolan recognized Jack Grimaldi behind the wheel and left Marris to contend with the groundskeeper. He reached the parking lot as Grimaldi and John Kissinger were getting out of the Taurus, having driven straight from the hotel where Briley had been staying.

"Any luck?" Bolan asked them.

"Sort of," Grimaldi explained. "She paid off her tab in cash—no surprise there—and hasn't been seen since. But we checked a couple nearby stores and hit paydirt at this used bookshop."

"She bought a few travel books on Bombay," Kissinger added. "A couple books on the film industry there, too."

"Film industry?"

"Yeah, I don't get that part, either. How about here? That lead pan out?"

Bolan nodded and relayed the information they'd gotten from Tendulma. "I don't think this Murawd guy's in cahoots with them, though," he concluded. "My guess is he got strung along. If we can get his brother's address and phone number in Bombay, hopefully we can clear a few things up."

"Good," Grimaldi said.

"Speaking of Bombay," Kissinger added, "I got word from the Farm that the President's on his way there."

Bolan frowned. "He wasn't due there until tomorrow."

"I know," Kissinger said, "but there's going to be a service up there for Nhajsib Wal's uncle this afternoon, and the President wants to be there for it."

"That's crazy," Bolan said. "It's bad enough he can't be talked out of canceling his trip. But going to Bombay for a funeral service? He might as well wave a red flag in front of Pakistan and the mujahideen."

"Don't think he hasn't been told that," Kissinger said.

"Needless to say," Grimaldi said, "we've got orders to pull stakes and head for Bombay ourselves."

CHAPTER FOURTEEN

Stony Man Farm, Virginia

"Whoa!"

Stony Man computer expert Akira Tokaido saved the images he'd been viewing and yanked off his headset midway through Sleater-Kinney's "The Swimmer." "Carmen! Get a load of this!"

Carmen Delahunt, an attractive redhead sitting twenty feet away, took off her reading glasses and glanced up from her terminal. "What's up?"

"Come, take a look."

"Be right there."

Delahunt logged a few final notes, then pushed away from her desk. Well dressed and smartly groomed, Delahunt looked far younger than her years. She'd spent more than half her life using her high-tech know-how in the war against crime and global terrorism, first with the FBI, then as a part of Aaron Kurtzman's cybernetic braintrust. Next to Barbara Price, Delahunt was the second-highest-ranking woman at Stony Man Farm and she carried herself accordingly. She wasn't only decisive but also quick-witted and sharp-tongued, traits that tended to be magnified late in the day, when she often skipped dinner in favor of caffeine and sugar-charged snacks. Her vice of choice at the moment was a chocolate-covered PayDay bar, which she dunked in Aaron Kurtzman's patented 30-weight coffee as she joined Tokaido at his computer station.

"Let me guess," she said. "You blew up a SAT-CAM shot of that nude beach you use for a screen saver. Let's see what you got."

Tokaido reloaded the image he'd been observing, taking advantage of the lag time to pack his cheeks with two fresh sticks of bubble gum. "I'm telling you, this is straight out of the *X-Files*."

Peering over Tokaido's shoulder, all Delahunt could see on the monitor screen was a dark blur. "I'm guessing an aerial night view of a desert somewhere out in the boonies."

"Not bad," Tokaido said. "It's some Orion SAT-INTEL footage from last night. We're about eighty miles northeast of Bombay, just across the Ghats. Nothing but an old Hindu shrine site that— Hang on, here we go...."

On the screen, Delahunt saw a series of small, flickering lights begin to appear. The first two looked like fireflies, but once a third light shone, it was clear that they were forming a pattern. Two parallel lines gave off enough light that she could begin to make out bits of landscape and, near each light, a barely discernible figure.

"Landing lights?" Delahunt guessed.

"Yeah, but for who?" Tokaido said. "Like I said, this is the middle of nowhere. Forty miles to the nearest highway and twice that far to Nasik. And it's not just that. There's flat desert all around them, but they set up their landing strip on a plateau.''

''Sounds like drug smugglers,'' Delahunt ventured. ''Or were you maybe thinking more along the lines of Hindu extraterrestrials? Ganesh, the Elephant from Venus?''

''Go ahead, laugh…or, actually, check this out first, then see if you think this is some kind of joke.''

Tokaido advanced through a few seconds of footage, then slowed down the playback. ''Okay, it's coming right up….''

Behind them, the door to the Computer Room opened and in strode Hal Brognola, carrying a few pages of notes scribbled in his notoriously illegible handwriting. Delahunt waved him over.

''What do we have?'' Brognola asked. ''Something on the Briley woman?''

''I've got plenty on her back at my desk,'' Delahunt said. ''This is Akira's baby. He thinks he's found India's Area 51.''

''I'm not talking UFOs, Carmen, all right?'' Tokaido said. ''Here, chief, have a look…''

Brognola and Delahunt eyed Tokaido's terminal just in time to see the shadowy outline of a small plane approaching the plateau. As it touched down, it plowed through one line of the flickering lamps, as well as the figures standing beside them.

''You see that?'' Tokaido exclaimed. ''Freaking plane's mowing down guys like they're weeds.''

''Could be an accident,'' Delahunt said.

''I don't think so.'' Tokaido quickly backed up the

footage and played it back. "I mean, look. It's not like the plane's out of control. The pilot just lines these guys up in his sights and lays into them. Poor bastards probably never knew what hit them."

Brognola glanced down at his notes, then stared at the grisly display on the screen. "Where is this?" he asked. "Anywhere near Bombay?"

Tokaido looked at Brognola with disbelief. "How'd you know that?"

"That's why I get paid the big bucks," Brognola joked. "Now, tell me what this is about."

As the footage continued to play out, Tokaido quickly explained where and how he'd come upon it, adding, "I ran a check to see if anybody'd reported it. Nothing."

"This was last night, huh?" Brognola said, eyes fixed on the screen. He paid close attention to the plane, following it as it slowed to a stop near the plateau's edge after taking out nearly the entire left row of landing lights and the figures standing beside them.

"Run it one more time, would you?" he asked Tokaido. "And if there's any way you can zoom in on the plane, that'd be great."

"I can, but you're going to lose some clarity," Tokaido said.

"Let's try."

"Coming up…"

Tokaido blew a bubble as he readied the footage yet again, this time magnifying the image of the plateau, as well as the plane. As he'd predicted, while the basic shapes were enlarged, the details were grain-

ier and less focused. The sharp lines of the plane soft-
ened until it looked like some giant bird swooping
down onto the plateau; and the figures near the landing lights now looked less like men than large bugs.
Clustering together, those who hadn't been plowed
over started rushing toward the plane. Before they
could reach it, however, the image on the screen
abruptly changed to an aerial view of Bombay's Marine Drive, every bit as bustling as the plateau had
been desolate, its streetlights aglimmer so that, from
the camera's perspective, the thoroughfare looked
very much like its proverbial nickname, Queen's
Necklace.

"What happened?" Brognola asked.

"Orion sends out things in snippets," Tokaido explained. "Unless somebody orders a lock on some
specific view, it jumps ahead and starts taking footage
from another angle."

"Sort of like a surveillance camera panning back
and forth," Delahunt said.

"Personally, it drives me batty," Tokaido said,
"but they figure it's the only way to cover a lot of
ground without launching another twenty SAT-
CAMs."

"Do we come back to the plateau?" Brognola
asked.

Tokaido nodded. "A quick sweep fifteen minutes
later. I checked already, and guess what. The whole
area's cleared away. No lights, no plane, no figures.
You want a look?"

"No, I'll take your word," Brognola said. "If you
could, though, can you pin down some coordinates?"

"No problem." Tokaido fingered his keyboard, bringing back the previous image and overlaying a GPS readout. Along with longitude and latitude—said to be accurate to within fifty yards—the database also spit up a description of the area in question.

"Guiyn Plateau," Carmen said, reading off the screen.

"Nice work, Akira," Brognola said. "Now, let's see if you can factor in a couple more things."

"Lay it on me," Tokaido said.

"I was just talking with Cowboy down in Kottayam," Brognola said, referring to his notes. "He and Jack checked out the hotel where this Briley woman was staying, and it turns out she'd just bought some books on Bombay. Not only that, but Striker just finished talking with some guy at an airfield near the arts academy who thinks she took off from there around sundown last night. In a twin prop."

"Same kind of plane we were just looking at," Delahunt guessed.

"I think so, yes," Brognola said.

While the others were talking, Tokaido had been racing his fingers across his keyboard, factoring in data like a schoolboy tackling a story problem in mathematics class. Once he was caught up, he called out, "You got a specific takeoff time for Kottayam?"

Brognola checked his notes. "Around 6:30 p.m., their time."

"Close enough," Tokaido said. "Make of the plane?"

"Ghurka," Brognola said. "Balsa Twin. I don't have a model number."

"I'll be able to pull that up on my own," Tokaido said.

"You need anything else?" Brognola asked.

Tokaido shook his head. He popped one bubble, then started on another. Once he'd finished programming all the data, he cued up a customized analyzing application. Delahunt and Brognola watched as he pressed a last few keys, then leaned back in his seat. "Abracadabra!"

"Just out of curiosity," Brognola said. "If we didn't have computers, how many hours do you figure it'd take to assemble and go through all that data you just processed?"

"One guy?"

Brognola nodded. "One guy in a library, like in the olden days."

"You should remember, Hal," Delahunt teased. "You were around then."

Brognola smiled. "I'll pretend I didn't hear that."

"One guy," Tokaido mused. "Who knows? Ten hours, maybe twelve."

As they were speaking, Tokaido's computer beeped. All eyes turned to the monitor, In quick succession, a series of images flashed across the monitor screen. First up was an aerial map of India's west coast, over which a mileage graph appeared and automatically calculated the distance between Krula Pass Airfield and Guiyn Plateau, taking into account ten different flight paths. Next came a rotating, 3-D schematic design of a Balsa Twin Ghurka, complete with all pertinent data on engine make and horsepower, passenger and load capacities, maximum cruising speed, fuel capacity and flight range. Lastly, a weather map was downloaded and superimposed over the aerial map. Multicolored shaded areas took into account everything from cloud formations, jet streams and directional winds—along with their velocity—to likely areas for updrafts and any other meteorological variables that could have a bearing on flight time.

All in all, it took the computer fourteen seconds to process the various data and answer the question foremost on the minds of the people clustered around the workstation: if the Ghurka had taken off from Kottayam at 6:30 p.m. with a pilot, a full tank of gas and several passengers, could it have conceivably reached the Indian state of Maharashtra in time to be the same plane the Orion spy satellite had filmed landing atop Guiyn Plateau?

On the terminal, a green line slowly snaked upward along the Indian coastline from Kottayam, veering inland once it reached Bombay. Had any of the aforementioned factors come into play in a way that would likely have slowed the plane down, the indicator line would have turned yellow or even stopped moving and turned red. Instead, the line remained a constant green and smoothly completed its trek, coming to a stop directly atop the plateau. The calculated arrival time flashed across the screen in capital letters. The hypothetical plane had touched down 5.42 minutes ahead of the time posted on the Orion's SAT-intel footage of the real plane's ill-fated landing atop the plateau.

"Does that answer your question?" Tokaido asked Brognola.

"I think so," Brognola said. "Good work."

"It also explains those guys getting mowed down," Tokaido ventured. "This guy whose plane they hijacked must've decided to play hero when he was coming in for a landing."

"Not that he lived long enough to tell the tale," Delahunt guessed. "He probably never got out of the plane alive."

"That would be my guess," Brognola said.

"So," Tokaido concluded, "what we've got now are leftover mujahideen skulking around the mountains playing Che Guevara, is that it?"

"Well, I think we have to keep in mind the mujahideen didn't have all their eggs in one basket down in Kottayam," Brognola said, again glancing at his notes. "We took a good bite out of them, but if our intelligence is correct, there are still enough of them scattered around between Kashmir and Calcutta to make life hell for us."

"But it's the ones in Maharashtra we need to be worried about most, right?" Delahunt said. "I mean, their top two guys were in that plane."

"Exactly," Brognola said. "Striker's already on the way up with Jack and Cowboy. They were going to start looking for leads in Bombay, but I think I'll give them a call and have them check out this plateau first. Even if the mujahideen moved in and out, there's bound to be some kind of trail we can pick up."

"What about this woman who was in the plane?" Tokaido said.

"Briley?" Brognola said.

Tokaido nodded. "What kind of name is that?"

"She put both her names together," Delahunt interjected. "Her real name's Brenda Reilly."

Brognola turned to Delahunt. "You *did* find something."

She nodded. "I was pulling everything together when Akira called me over."

"Let's have a look," Brognola said.

"I came up with a lot," she forewarned him again as they started back to her station. Tokaido said he'd catch up with them and went off to get coffee at Kurtzman's station.

"How about just the headlines to begin with," Brognola said.

"Fair enough." Delahunt sat at her computer and pulled up the file she'd been working on. "We took the Identi-Kit composite from this Govankrishna Vanat guy and ran it through Aaron's archives," she explained. "Good thing the poor guy was so sappy on her. His description was damn near camera perfect."

Brognola eyed Delahunt's monitor, which she'd split into two separate screens. On the left was Vanat's Identi-Kit image of Briley. Far more than most facsimiles, the simulated head shot was nearly identical to a file photo of Brenda Reilly, taken following a prostitution bust two years ago in Las Vegas.

"I don't want to hear any wisecracks about red hair," Delahunt advised.

Brognola smiled. "Fair enough."

She switched to the file where she'd merged all her findings into a single document. "Brenda Michelle Reilly," she said, racing through her notes, touching on only those that seemed most significant. "Born 1976, Lancaster, Pennsylvania. Clean record through high school. Even graduated class salutatorian.

"She got a drama scholarship at UCLA but dropped out after two years to do the modeling-actress thing. An agency signed her but nothing came of it." The screen filled with the agency's black-and-white comp sheet of Brenda, showing her in various poses, always smiling, eyes still shining with a sparkle of small-town innocence.

"Has that girl-next-door look," Tokaido said as he rejoined them.

Delahunt nodded. "Probably why modeling didn't pay off. This was during the height of that heroin-chic look in all the fashion mags. She looked too wholesome.

"But that changed quick enough. She must've fallen on hard times, because next I've got her down for two arrests over an eight-month period, one for substance abuse, the other for check forgery. She wriggled off the hook both times, but must've figured she'd worn out her welcome, because after the second arrest she moved out of state to Vegas."

"I'm sensing a downward spiral here," Tokaido observed.

"Textbook," Delahunt said. "She trimmed her name to Briley when she got a showgirl gig at the Tropicana. She only lasted a few weeks."

"Why's that?" Brognola wondered.

"Let's see..." Delahunt sequenced some data and brought up an entry form the Clark County Sheriff's Department, including a booking mug shot of Briley staring sullenly out at the camera. "She fell in with a dealer who was scamming at the blackjack tables. He brought her in on the act and they got caught. Again, no prosecution, but she lost her work permit and wound up lap dancing at a place called Olympic Gardens, just north of the Strip.

"From there it was prostitution, first on the street, then operating out of a condo on the west side with four other girls. Twelve arrests, but she usually made bail and was out before her mattress cooled."

"Is that where that first photo of her came from?" Brognola asked.

Delahunt nodded. "She went to trial three times and got off with fines and a slap on the wrist.

"At some point, she must've hooked up with a major player, because next thing we know, she's in D.C. living rent free at some choice digs in Georgetown. Gossip rags link her to some business bigwigs, a couple ranking senators and a member of the Joint Chiefs of Staff."

"Taking care of his joint, no doubt," Tokaido wisecracked.

"Yeah, I'm guessing escort work," Delahunt said. "She's there two years, then there's a six-month gap before she turns up last spring in London.

"Now life is definitely good for her. Rents a million-dollar penthouse off Trafalgar Square, drives a Bentley, does the club scene four, five nights a week, usually with up-and-coming politicos or finance geeks."

"Not to mention our friend Dr. Vanat," Brognola said.

"I don't have anything putting them together," Delahunt commented, skimming through the documentation. "But seeing how the two of them dropped off the map around the same time, you have to figure he was one of her clients and wound up getting sweet-talked into running away to join Dehri Neshah."

"Which means she probably knew he could help out with these missile shenanigans the mujahideen were putting together," Brognola conjectured.

"Ten points for the big guy," Delahunt joked.

Tokaido had been doing his best to keep up with the flow of information, but there was something that puzzled him. "What I don't get is how she wound up in bed with the mujahideen, so to speak," he said.

"Good question," Brognola said.

"And I wish I had a good answer," Delahunt responded. "But I ran half-a-dozen word searches on her files and came up blank."

"Maybe it had something to do with that six-month gap between Washington and London," Brognola said.

"You're probably right. If you want, I'll dig a little deeper."

"If you could, sure," Brognola said. "But first, tell me, did you turn up anything on her that had to do with the movies? Especially in India?"

"Bollywood?" Delahunt thought it over a moment. "I don't think so... Or wait a minute, maybe I do."

"I'm asking," Brognola explained, "because Briley apparently bought some books on the India cinema at the same shop where she picked up the guidebooks to Bombay."

Delahunt reworked the screen, pulling up a no-frills search engine she and the rest of the entire cybernetic team had been developing over the past five months. The program was designed primarily to help locate criminals and terrorists suspected of operating under assumed identities and therefore untrackable by means of a paper trail. It scanned head shots of an individual—in this case the file photo from Brenda Reilly's Vegas arrest—then configured a three-dimensional model, incorporating as many as two dozen distinguishing facial characteristics. Once converted to a .bmp file, the model was run through a gauntlet of graphics databases for matchups. As with conventional word searches, one often ended up with a lot of matches that were either off the mark or totally irrelevant, but as Delahunt quickly demonstrated, the program just as often succeeded in the photo-scan equivalent of pulling a rabbit out of a hat.

"My first run-through turned up over six hundred hits," she explained, "but after some quick weeding I was able to throw out all but thirty that were clearly her. You know, things like passport photos, driver's licenses, yearbook pics, her Vegas shot. And then there's these."

Delahunt brought up a block of photos taken at a variety of nightclubs. "These are Fleet Street tabloid shots of various celebrity spottings in London last spring, right before Briley most likely hooked up with

Vanat. She turned up mostly as just a face in the crowd, you know, two people away from whoever the paparazzi were really going for.

"There're three shots here, taken the same night at different nightclubs, where she's on the dance floor with the same entourage. See the guy in the middle of each shot? He's some big-shot Indian film producer by the name of Jahan."

"Abdul Jahan?" Tokaido interjected. "Are you kidding me?"

"You know him?" Brognola asked.

"I know of him," Tokaido said.

He turned to Delahunt. "He did that cheesy thriller about the queen's brother-in-law making his own A-bomb, right?"

"*Nuke of Earl,* Yeah, that's him," Delahunt said.

"What a great flick!" Tokaido said. "I mean, it was one of those movies that was so bad it was good. You know, like those Italian spaghetti westerns. Hell, I think he even won something at Cannes with it. Most popular or something like that."

"I don't know a thing about it," Brognola confessed.

"Yeah, well, what's the last movie you saw, Hal?" Tokaido asked. "*Patton?*"

"What can I say?" Brognola responded with a shrug.

"Anyway," Delahunt went on, referring to the on-screen file, "Jahan was in London a few weeks trying to line up financing for a sequel to *Nuke.* From the looks of it, Briley got hooked up with the crowd he took out clubbing every night."

"Any follow-through?" Brognola asked.

Delahunt shook her head. "Like I said, this is just before she and Vanat pulled their disappearing act. There's no link between her and Jahan after this, so I figured it was just socializing on her part."

"That probably would have been my guess at first, too," Brognola conceded. He checked his notes, then looked back at the image on the screen. Briley no longer had a look of innocence about her. She seemed hardened, the type who liked to party mostly because it was an easy way to make inroads with the wealthy and powerful. Brognola suspected her profile—professional sex object—was, as with many other similar women he'd encountered over the years, misleading. Women like that would give the impression they were being used, but when push came to shove, it often turned out that they were the ones pulling the strings.

"I might be wrong," Brognola predicted, "but something tells me we might have a Lady Macbeth on our hands."

CHAPTER FIFTEEN

Bombay, India

From the beginning, Briley had been charmed by Dehri Neshah's unpredictability, but there were times when it got to be too much for her.

This was one of those times.

Here it was, not even ten o'clock in the morning the day after his escape from prison, and what did he want to do? Check out the remaining Sabre missile launcher? Plot strategy with Penghat Shili and his other top confidants? Make passionate love with her and then sleep in until noon? No, what Dehri wanted to do was dress up like a tourist and roam the grime of Chowpatty Beach and then trek down to some place called Nariman Point. And why? Oh, he claimed this was important, that he wanted to see how security was shaping up for the state funeral taking place later that afternoon near Malabar Hill. But was that really necessary? Did they really have to get up early and straggle down here to realize that, especially after the missile scare in Kottayam, no expense would be spared to keep the mujahideen from getting close to the President or prime minister? No. Briley knew the real reason Dehri had insisted that they come here and risk detection was that he wanted to look at a statue. A statue! Had he gone mad?

This was only her first visit, but Briley already hated Bombay with a passion. The guidebooks she'd bought in Kottayam had talked up the city's boisterous vitality and diversity, but all that Briley saw was nearly twenty million wayward souls crammed into a space far smaller than Manhattan, most of them poor and unsightly, living off the streets, loud, scabrous, needy. Even now, with the sun barely up, they were already out by the thousands, wading into the bay with their clothes on, then straggling out to watch a shabby clot of street performers do tricks while their children scrambled about the sand with their hands out, begging for rupees. It all disgusted her to no end. Forget about the strategic targets Dehri was always talking about. Bombay, she thought, was where a few well-placed warheads could *really* do some good.

She kept these thoughts to herself, of course. As Neshah led her by the hand past people vending food on the beach from rickety carts, Briley's face was locked with a faint smile and a look of contentment. It was no easy feat, especially as her senses cringed at the oppressive smells around her; not just the good—spiced curd, fried vermicelli, chutney, roasted chickpeas—but also the rank odor of unwashed bodies. It was enough to make her nauseous. Hadn't these people heard of soap? Deodorant? Toothpaste? How much more of this was Dehri going to subject her to?

Oblivious to Briley's discomfort, Neshah slowed, eyeing the food selections as if he were a gourmet viewing a culinary feast. Please don't stop, Briley pleaded silently, but to no avail.

"You have to try some of this!" Neshah enthused, steering her toward a grizzled-looking vendor scooping dark-colored globs from an unsanitary-looking deep fryer and stuffing them into a white, doughy roll. Neshah bought two, holding one out to Briley. *"Pao bhaji,"* he told her. "Potatoes and chiles in batter."

Briley shook her head demurely, still smiling. "I would, but my stomach's still a little unsettled from the flight."

"Too bad." Neshah chewed down one of the treats, humming to himself with contentment. "Perhaps later. This or maybe some *bhel puri.*"

"Perhaps."

Briley watched him happily devour the second *pao bhaji.* Despite her paranoia, she had to admit Dehri was unlikely to be recognized. Last night he'd cut off his beard, trimmed his eyebrows and had his head shaved. Now, wearing sunglasses, a straw hat, floral-print shirt and Bermuda shorts, he looked even less formidable than he had in prison with his bleached beard and unkempt hair. And with her beside him in her modest capri slacks and a cotton blouse, Briley was sure they could pass for any number of middle-class American couples out steeping themselves in the wonders of India.

As he ate, Neshah raised the binoculars strung about his neck and peered past the crowd toward Malabar Hill, where the funeral of Ziarat Wal would take place. Briley looked in the same direction. She'd read in the guidebooks about how the Parsi dead were disposed of at the Towers of Silence, but the spires weren't visible from the beach. All she could see that hinted of the funerary ritual were several large, black-winged vultures circling lazily in the vicinity, no doubt waiting for their dinner to be served.

"You think it's barbaric, don't you?"

Briley looked at Neshah, startled that he'd realized what she was thinking.

"I know it's some kind of custom," she answered tactfully.

Neshah nodded. "The Parsis are Zoroastrians. They hold earth, water and fire as sacred. For them, it's wrong to violate the elements by cremation or burial."

"I understand that," Briley said. "But still...to feed their dead to the birds..."

"It's very ecological," Neshah told her. "And when you think about it, what's so smart about stuffing people in boxes and burying them in holes?"

"Maybe so," Briley conceded. Not that she was convinced. She sympathized with the wealthy who lived in the expensive apartments nearby and had to deal with vultures dropping half-eaten limbs and bits of flesh into their patios, not to mention the local reservoirs. It all struck her as every bit as barbaric as the antics of the acrobatic troupe performing nearby. Incredibly, they were using an old circus catapult to launch children no more than ten years old far out into the bay so that they could swim their way toward various floating plastic statues of Ganesh and local saints that had been tossed into the water last night to mark the end of Ganesh Chaturthi, which, as near as Briley could figure, was India's week-long answer to Halloween or New Year's Eve.

Seeing that Briley was watching the performance, two younger children scampered over. Their hands were out and they pleaded to her as they gestured out into the bay.

"For a donation," Neshah explained, "their brother will touch a floating likeness of Ganesh and make your dreams come true."

"I'll pass," Briley said, trying to keep a smile on her face as she shook her head at the children. Neshah, however, crouched before them and handed them a few rupees. As he spoke with them, Briley watched another youngster let out a whoop as the catapult sent him hurtling out into the sea, arms and legs flailing. The bay was shallow, and even though the boy flew more than fifty yards through the air, at the last second he straightened his body and hit the water at a flat enough angle to avoid striking the bottom. Briley was amazed; it was like watching the cliff divers in Acapulco, only here the dives were horizontal rather than vertical, and performed by children. The youth surfaced quickly and swam to the nearest statue, a Ganesh the size of a refrigerator sitting cross-legged in a pose of meditation. Holding on to the bobbing effigy while he caught his breath, the boy waved back to shore, smiling.

Behind the boy, Briley noticed that the sky had turned leaden. Far out to sea, she could see heavy rain streaking from large swollen clouds that seemed to have materialized out of nowhere. In moments, as if to announce the storm's coming, a strong, salty breeze rolled across the bay. Briley shuddered.

"Monsoon," Neshah said, rejoining Briley. "Long overdue."

"It'll rain out the parade, won't it?" Briley said.

Neshah laughed. "It will come, and for an hour it will seem like Bombay is ready to sink under such a downpour. Then the storm will move on and the sun will come out. All the while people will go about their business. If there is enough of a wind, the streets might even be dry again in time for the parade."

"I guess I have a lot to learn about this part of the world," Briley said.

"Come," Neshah told her, taking her by the hand, "I want to show you the statue before it rains."

"You're not forgetting our meeting, are you?" Briley wondered.

Neshah checked his watch. "We have time," he said.

"When you paid those children, what did you wish for?" Briley asked him as he led her to the street and flagged down a passing taxi.

"For success with our mission, of course," he said, opening the back door of a dilapidated cab and gesturing for Briley to get in. "And," he added, "that you will one day come to love this part of the world as much as I do."

Briley had no ready answer for Neshah, so, as she moved past him into the back seat of the cab, she merely smiled again and stroked his cheek, letting him draw his own conclusions. Neshah sat next to

Briley and put his arm around her, then called out for the driver to take them to Nariman Point.

It was slow going. They were on the main thoroughfare, and traffic, even for a weekend, was every bit as congested as it had been in Kottayam when Neshah and Penghat were fleeing the detention centre. Adding to the slowness was the presence of troops and city workers setting up barricades for the funeral procession that would later carry the body of Ziarat Wal to the Towers of Silence.

Neshah scowled at the sight, directing most of his anger at the troops. Puppets of the Shiv Sena, he called them, his anger flaring. How dare they appropriate the name of the great Shivaji Bhonsole! How dare they desecrate the great man's legacy to justify their agenda of Hindu nationalism and Muslim oppression. They needed to be stopped, at any cost. And stop them he would. Soon, he claimed—sooner than anyone suspected.

Listening to Neshah's rantings—whispered in her ear so the cabbie wouldn't overhear—Briley was lulled into a familiar reverie. At times like this, when Dehri talked of the future with such passion, determination and confidence, she would do her best to forsake her cynicism. If she could manage to get caught up in his fervor, it was like an aphrodisiac. She would find herself thinking of all that would come her way should he succeed: wealth, fame, a life of idle leisure. No longer would she have to ply her sexual wiles in the name of Neshah's cause. She could indulge in passion for passion's sake alone, the way she liked it. Let Neshah pursue his desire to rule

over these teeming, heathen masses. Let him feel he
could crush them, then, by force of will, teach them
to love and respect him. Briley could live with this.
She would gladly fuel his hunger for power, his desire
to be enthroned. She would be content with the spoils
that fell her way as the power behind the throne.
When Briley put her life into this perspective, any
sacrifice seemed tolerable. And so she listened, rapt,
until at last the cab pulled to a stop in front of the
Oberoi Towers.

"So many dreams," Neshah said, sighing. With a
grin, he added, "Perhaps I should have paid those
children a few more rupees, eh?"

Briley clasped his hand and told him, "I believe in
you."

"I know you're just being kind," Neshah said.
"But let me show you that it is all really possible."

Neshah paid the cabbie, then led Briley along a
newly built promenade leading out to Nariman Point.
Located halfway down the peninsula, the promenade
overlooked not only Back Bay, but also, jutting inward toward the heart of the financial district, a large,
rectangular expanse of water left over from the latest
reclamation project by which Bombay, over the centuries, had claimed land from the sea to build upon.
All in all, it wasn't the ideal place to erect a statue
that Maharashtra's ruling party hoped would one day
rival America's Statue of Liberty—most had favored
something on the other side of the peninsula, near the
Gateway of India—but, once completed, the pedes-
taled, forty-foot-high likeness of folk hero Shivaji

Bhonsole would be visible not only to ships approaching Bombay Harbour, but also throughout Back Bay.

The statue, rising from the tip of the promenade, was supposed to be completed in time to celebrate the fiftieth anniversary of Balasahek Thackeray's founding of the Shiv Sena Party, but Briley could see that was never going to happen. The forty-foot-high pedestal seemed finished, but as for Shivaji and his majestic, rearing stallion, both were for the most part mere skeletal outlines through which the morning sun glared, silhouetting the flocks of pigeons that were apparently of the opinion that India's ruling party had made them a fanciful birdhouse. There were no workers in sight, and a few hundred people were slumbering around the base of the pedestal, having moved their sheets and bedrolls so that they could sleep a while longer in the relative coolness of the statue's shadow. They looked to Briley like beached seals.

"Isn't it magnificent?" Neshah extolled, taking a step back. The wind had picked up, forcing him to take off his hat and use his hand for a visor as he eyed the statue from top to bottom.

"It will be when it's finished," Briley suggested.

The Kashmiri nodded. For what, to Briley, seemed an eternity, Neshah stared silently at the guano-splattered edifice. Then, taking off his sunglasses, he dabbed the corners of his eyes. Briley couldn't believe it; Dehri was weeping!

"Are you all right?" she asked him.

"Fine," Neshah said, nodding. "Tears of pride, that is all. You know how I feel about Shivaji. He is proof that my dreams can come true."

Briley nodded back, offering an indulgent smile. "Tell me about him again."

"Are you sure?" Neshah asked.

Briley was actually tired of hearing about Shivaji, but she knew how much Dehri liked to expound on his own particular take on the founder of the Maratha Confederacy, which overthrew the Mogul Empire in the late seventeenth century and ruled western India until being, in turn, subdued by the British. Although most historians tended to focus on Shivaji's technological foresight and his penchant for religious tolerance, Neshah was more fascinated by his hero's military prowess, particularly in his clashes with the Mogul emperor Auranagzeb. Never mind that Shivaji had been a Hindu and Auranagzeb a Muslim like Neshah; to Dehri, that was beside the point, an unfortunate miscasting that could be overlooked.

The previous year, before Neshah had put her up at her town house in London, he'd taken Briley to Pune, Shivaji's birthplace seventy miles southeast of Bombay. There he'd told her how the great Shivaji had reclaimed his hometown from the Muslims by teaching lizards to carry up the ropes by which his troops scaled the steep walls of Simhagad fortress. And Neshah's escape from the detention center in Kottayam had been, in part, inspired by his hero's escape from custody in Agra shortly after the completion of the Taj Mahal. In Shivaji's case, however, instead of smuggling himself out disguised as a priest, he'd hidden himself in a large basket of sweets and waited for the authorities to deliver him to his freedom.

"Once we have finished our mission," Neshah predicted, "I will go down in history as the Shivaji of my time."

"And then, in a thousand years, there will be those who aspire to be the next Dehri Neshah," Briley assured him.

They had spent only a few minutes before the statue, and yet, as she looked around, Briley suddenly noticed that they were surrounded. Where moments before there had been only hundreds of people on the promenade, now there were thousands, with thousands more on the way, flowing forth from the city, the women's saris snapping loudly in the breeze. Briley was stunned, concerned. She doubted anyone had overheard Neshah's ramblings—how could they have, chattering as everyone was in their noisy slew of incomprehensible dialects—but why risk the chance?

"Don't forget," she gently reminded Neshah, "we're meeting Abdul in an hour."

"Yes, yes, of course," he said. Taking a cell phone from his pocket, he led her away from the mob. "What would I do without you?"

The Kashmiri called one of his Bombay contacts, who owned a powerboat and was idling out in the bay, pretending to fish as he awaited the call to pick up Neshah and Briley and take them around Malabar Point to the north part of the city, where Abdul Jahan had converted one of the old textile mills into a motion picture facility. Neshah told the other man where to meet them, then stopped at a nearby kiosk to buy a half-dozen different morning papers. As they started

down a wide wooden staircase leading back down to
the beach, the newspapers rustled loudly in Neshah's
hands as he tracked down stories and photographs
about yesterday's events in Kottayam. Briley knew
he was eager to see what the press had made of his
escape and the discovery of a missile launcher at the
Academy of Arts, and to her it looked as if he were
skimming the print for two key words only: Dehri
Neshah.

Neshah cursed several times when he came across
accounts painting the mujahideen in a negative light,
but he was amused by the boastful claims of authorities eager to take credit for having supposedly dealt
a death blow to the Kashmiri separatists.

"Fools," he scoffed. "They would think they'd
killed a octopus if they nipped off one of its tenta-
cles."

Rounding Nariman Point, they came to the mini-
harbor remaining from the Back Bay reclamation project. The shoreline had been taken over mostly by
Koli fishermen, descendants of the aboriginals who'd
first settled Bombay. Though more prevalent fifteen
miles to the north, in Versova, the Kolis had en-
trenched themselves here, as well. Clapboard shanties
bordered the beach, creating a squalid, makeshift village that contrasted sharply with the gleaming sky-
scrapers across the water. Fishermen—as well as the
notorious Koli women—were already out in force.
Some were preparing to head out for the day despite
the approaching monsoon, while others were unloading boats filled with fish pulled from the sea during
the night. The stench made the other smells Briley

had thus far endured seem like perfume. She worried that she and Neshah would wind up reeking of fish when they met Abdul.

"How long before the boat is here?" she asked.

Neshah didn't respond. Briley saw that he was transfixed on an article in one of the papers. He shook his head to himself as he read, and under his breath he cursed—not like before, but more in alarm.

"What is it?" Briley asked.

Neshah, clearly troubled, handed the paper to Briley, pointing out a paragraph in a story about the prison escape. In describing how Neshah had managed to walk out of the prison disguised as a priest, the article described, in detail, how the man who'd provided him with his clerical robe and hat had been left behind in the cell, stabbed in the manner of the so-called Kashmir Shredder. They'd made a point of printing Raghubir's name and pointing out that he had two other brothers in the mujahideen: Vargadrum, who died in the siege at the Academy of Arts, and Penghat, who had participated in the escape and was presumed still at large with Neshah.

"I should have told him," Neshah muttered, staring into space.

"Penghat?" Briley said.

"How could I have thought it wouldn't come out?" the Kashmiri wondered. "What was I thinking!"

"I'm sure you did what you had to," Briley assured him.

"I know that!" Neshah retorted. "But will

Penghat? You saw how devastated he was when he learned about Vargadrum.''

Briley nodded, recalling the fit of wailing Penghat had unleashed last night when, at the hotel they'd checked into for the night, he'd learned of his younger brother's death on the television news. He'd not only wept but also spit and fumed, swearing vengeance on whoever was responsible for shooting Vargadrum more than thirty times.

"I need to see Penghat," Neshah decided. "Before he finds out from someone else."

Briley nodded. "I understand. Go. I'll take the meeting."

"Are you sure?" Neshah said.

"I can handle Abdul," Briley said.

"That's what I'm afraid of." Neshah's grin was strained.

"Dehri," Briley replied tenderly, "that was a long time ago. Abdul and I are friends, nothing more."

"I want to believe that."

"Then do," Briley said. "We've been through too much not to have trust in each other."

Dehri stared at Briley. "Yes, of course."

Briley leaned forward and kissed him lightly. "Now go. Do what you have to. Everything will be fine."

Neshah smiled again, this time with more ease. "You are an amazing woman, Briley."

Briley winked back at him. "What would you do without me?"

CHAPTER SIXTEEN

Guiyn Plateau

"You gotta hand it to Akira," Jack Grimaldi said, checking his watch. "We're damn near right on the money."

Grimaldi was at the controls of Daeon Murawd's Ghurka Thresher. Though smaller, less powerful and nowhere near as well maintained as the Twin Balsa Murawd had flown from Kottayam the previous night, the Thresher—helped along during the last leg of its flight by strong tailwinds from the approaching monsoon—had reached Guiyn Plateau only five minutes later than the ETA Tokaido had put together back at Stony Man Farm.

"And not a moment too soon." Sitting up front beside Grimaldi, Kissinger peered westward at the large swollen clouds massing on the far side of the Ghats. "Looks like a doozy coming in."

"Sure does," Grimaldi said. "What do you think?" he asked Bolan. "Still want to put her down?"

Bolan glanced up from the topo map he and Les Marris were analyzing in the back seat. "I think

we've got time," he said after sizing up the storm.
"And if there's any evidence down there we better
get a look at it before the rains wash it away."

"Good point," Grimaldi conceded. "In that case,
let me make a quick pass and get a better look at our
runway."

In the morning light it was clear why Murawd had
landed atop the plateau the previous night. The surrounding desert was pocked with gullies and ridges
of deep sand that shifted readily under the wind's
forceful hand. And as for the need for landing lights,
as Grimaldi brought the Thresher over the plateau, he
saw a series of deep shafts dotting the surface.

"What are those?" he wondered. "Sky lights for
the caves?"

"They're kind of all-purpose shafts," Marris explained.

"You say those shafts are bad mothers?" Grimaldi
called out in the deepest voice he could muster.

"Right on," Marris replied, playing along. "Back
when this used to be a shrine, the monks used them
for light, air, plus a way to get rainwater down into
holding pools inside the caves."

"Thank you, Professor," Grimaldi said.

"Hey," Marris replied, "if you're stationed somewhere long enough, you eventually get to know a few
things about the place."

"Whatever the case," Kissinger told Grimaldi,
"those pits'll eat the hell out of your landing gear if
you give them a chance."

"Not bloody well likely," Grimaldi said, imitating

the fake British accent Marris had used last night on Vanat.

Marris chuckled. "Not bad. Better than your Isaac Hayes at any rate."

"Shut your mouth," Grimaldi said with a grin.

Kissinger scanned the area around the plateau through his binoculars, then called over his shoulder to Marris, "I thought you called ahead and made sure the welcome mat was out for us."

"I did," Marris said. "Must be we beat the reception committee."

"Fine by me," Kissinger said.

"Man, do I hear that," Grimaldi agreed. "How are we supposed to do covert ops when we always get stuck playing buddy-buddy with the legits? No offense, Les."

"Har-har," Marris deadpanned. "Is this the part where I'm supposed to ooh and ahh because you guys are more covert than CIA...whoever you are."

"Hey, we're special task force for the Secret Service," Kissinger reminded him.

"Yeah, and I'm Wild Bill Donovan," Marris said.

Bolan grinned at the bantering, but he could share Grimaldi's sentiment about always having to deal with outsiders. There was a part of him that longed for the earlier days when there were fewer players on the field and it was easier to operate alone. Now it seemed that every country in the world had followed America's lead and exhausted their alphabet with acronyms for various crime-fighting agencies whose main function was tripping over each other's toes while the bad guys got away.

India was no exception. Once it had been determined that they would be flying up to inspect the plateau, Marris had to pull his CIA clout to get India's Intelligence Bureau to turn around and call in some favors from the Shiv Sena Party's intelligence arm in order to make sure any military in the area wouldn't mistake the Thresher for enemy aircraft and start heaving ordnance once it entered Maharashtran airspace. Thankfully, at least that part of the equation had panned out, allowing the Thresher to come in for a landing without interference, save for a few small bumps and dips on the hardpan. Once he touched the plane down, Grimaldi had no problem veering around the shafts and bringing the plane to a stop well short of the plateau's edge.

"Passengers may now deplane," the pilot joked in an officious tone, "and thank you for flying Air Thresher."

"All right," Marris said as he unstrapped himself. "Call me superstitious, but I get nervous when I'm in a plane named after a doomed submarine."

"I think this baby's named after the bird," Grimaldi said. "That or those folks who work the paddies."

"Whatever," Marris said, rising from his seat. "Let's go see what kind of souvenirs we can pick up."

From the moment the men stepped out of the plane, it became clear that the mujahideen had been careful to cover its tracks. Though packed and hardened by the sun, the surface of the plateau still had enough play to leave footprints and plane tracks, but none were to be found except for those made by the Thresher. Everywhere else, the earth bore only widespread swirls and scratches, and even those were fading as wind whipped across the plateau.

"Bastards must've swept the place with tree branches," Grimaldi guessed.

"That only works so well, though," Bolan said, crouching over a dark stain on the ground. "Got some blood here, probably from those guys who got mowed down."

"That or the poor schmoe who did the mow—Hey!" Grimaldi grabbed at his head, but the wind had already plucked off his trademark baseball cap and was carrying it back toward the plane. As he jogged after it, Kissinger called out to Bolan and Marris.

"Hey, get a load of this." Kissinger was squatting before one of the shafts. As the wind gusted across the opening, it gave off an eerie, moanful wail.

"Vishnu's ghost?" Marris guessed.

"Not that," Kissinger said. He pointed to a series of rungs chiseled out of the rock, leading into the shaft. "They don't look new, either. What do you think, Professor?"

"Ladders," Marris said, straight-faced. "The monks would use them to sneak up to see if any pilgrims were on the way."

"Get out," Kissinger said.

Marris pretended to scout the horizon, then called down into the shaft in a Hindi accent, "Hurry, boys, get dressed and put away the chess set! We got customers!"

Kissinger smirked at the CIA agent. "You're a real stand-up guy, there, Marris. Maybe you should get your own sitcom."

"While you two work on your material," Bolan told the other men, "I think I'll check out this hole."

Bolan was about to crawl down the shaft and see where it led when they were interrupted by a stream of epithets from Grimaldi. Glancing back at the plane, they saw the pilot—retrieved ball cap pulled down tight over his head—angrily kicking one of the Thresher's tires. As they headed over to the plane, the men saw that the tire was flat.

"Damn," Marris said.

"'Damn' is right," Grimaldi agreed.

"Puncture?" Bolan asked.

Grimaldi nodded, pointing to a metal shard, as thick as a pencil, jutting from between the tire's treads. "Probably part of one of those landing lamps that guy bowled over."

"Is it fixable?" Bolan asked. He had to raise his voice to be heard over the roar of the wind buffeting the side of the plane. "This storm's coming in quicker than I expected."

"If there's a repair kit and some kind of compressor stashed away in the hold," Grimaldi said, "I can get us out of here in fifteen, twenty minutes."

"How about if I give you a hand and see if we can get it done in ten," Kissinger suggested, eyes on the storm front. "I'd just as soon wait until later to take a shower."

"Let's go for it," Grimaldi said.

"While you two are doing that, I think I've found

something to keep us busy,'' Marris told Bolan. He was facing away from the plane, glancing downhill toward the desert floor. About fifty yards from the base of the plateau, the windswept sand was undulating almost like an ocean shoreline. As the grains were pushed eastward, away from where the men were standing, they left exposed a tangled heap of what, to the CIA agent, had at first looked like firewood. Now, however, as more and more sand fell away, he and the others could see that the pile wasn't made of branches, but rather the arms and legs of at least six men tossed together into a shallow grave.

Bombay

GROWING UP in Pennsylvania, Briley had experienced her share of fast-moving summer storms. There had been plenty of times that she would stand atop the hill a quarter-mile from the family farm and watch the clouds drift toward her. Once she felt the first drop of rain, she would turn and race downhill, trying to outrun the storm. She would rarely succeed; the storm would overtake her and she would wind up drenched by the time she got home. Not that she minded. As a child, Briley loved the rain and nothing pleased her more than to stand out in the yard after her run, laughing as she panted for breath, letting herself get soaked. Her mother would rush out onto the porch and tell her she was crazy and yell for her to come inside. Her mother was so clueless. She had no idea that the last place she ever wanted to be was inside the house, especially if her father was around, awaiting a chance to be alone with his precious little Bren-Bren. No, she preferred the rain. Somehow the rain always made her feel clean again.

But Briley was no longer a child. The thought of ever being clean again seemed laughable to her, and as she watched the monsoon rake its way toward shore, she felt nothing but annoyance. She wasn't sure which she dreaded more, being pelted by the rain or spending another minute suffocating on the stench of dead fish. The smell was everywhere, but it seemed worse whenever one of the Koli women trudged by, round shouldered, sullen faced, saris knotted tight around their waists, arms weighed down with gigantic fish, some as large as pillows. They glared at her, shouting oaths, occasionally spitting in her direction. Now Briley understood why the guidebooks had called them contentious.

She looked past them out to sea. Where the hell was the boatman who was supposed to take her away from all this? Had Dehri given him the wrong directions? Had the man become intimidated by the storm and taken the boat ashore elsewhere? If he didn't come soon, Briley was going to get wet, and she doubted any amount of rain could wash away the foul smell invading every pore of her body. She wanted to get aboard the boat and call Abdul to delay their meeting so that she could have a chance to take a shower and change. She hated to admit it, but she wanted to look her best for him. She tried to tell herself it was all political, that it was always easier to contend with men if they could be compromised with desire, but deep down she knew there was more to it than that. *She* was the one filled with desire. Stop it, she told herself. She was with Dehri now; if he succeeded, he would be better able to provide for her. So what if he was impotent? He was always willing to look the other way and let her tend to her needs, especially when they served his, as well. Of course, he drew the line when it came to Abdul. Abdul for her was off-limits except for business. Maybe that's why she had these stirrings inside her. Abdul was forbidden fruit.

A clap of thunder startled Briley. At the same time, the monsoon reached shore. This was nothing like the rain in Pennsylvania. There were no warning sprinkles; it hit her with the sudden force of a cold, stinging shower.

"Goddammit!" she cursed.

Briley was about to head for cover beneath the promenade when one of the Koli women veered toward her, shouting curses of her own. She gave Briley a sharp push and sent her staggering backward.

"I wasn't talking to you!" Briley shouted back at the woman. "Get away from me!"

The other woman lurched forward, pushing Briley again. She was joined by a second, older woman, who was carrying a small wooden bucket filled with fish bait. After conferring with her younger friend, the older woman turned to Briley, her eyes filled with hate. Without warning, she jerked her bucket forward, soaking Briley with brine and bits of chopped fish. Overhead, another peal of thunder resonated above the sound of the rain. Another three Koli women joined in the fray, surrounding Briley on all sides.

Most slapped at her with opened palms, but one woman swiped at Briley with one of her fishes, while another struck Briley's shoulders and forearms with the flat edge of the knife she used to gut fish. Amazingly, save for a handful of curious children, no one else paid any attention to the altercation. They ignored the pounding torrent, as well, going about their business as if such things were an everyday occurrence.

"Stop it!" Briley pushed the women away. They kept coming after her, however, some of them laughing scornfully. Finally, Briley was able to grab the bucket away from the woman who'd doused her. She swung it sharply, hitting the woman on the arm. The woman with the knife responded by taking a more vicious swipe at Briley. With a loud thunk the blade bit into the bucket and stuck. Tugging hard on the bucket, Briley managed to yank the knife from the other woman's hand.

As she tossed the knife and bucket aside, the Koli women closed in on Briley once again. Now, as well as slapping, they began clawing at her. Some grabbed at her purse, slung across her shoulder.

"Get away!" Briley screamed. "Get away."

She punched one of the women with her fist and flailed with her elbows until she'd managed to ward the others off. Her purse had come unclasped and she quickly reached inside, pulling out her derringer. The older woman had just pried free the knife from her bucket and she waved it menacingly at Briley. When the woman started to take a step toward her, Briley fired. Dropping the knife, the woman sagged to her knees. As the others rushed to her side, Briley saw her chance to escape and ran.

There were too many people around the staircase leading back up to the promenade, so she went the other way, bowling over an old man mending his fishing net and then bounding up a wide dirt path between two rows of shanties. Behind her, she heard the angry cries of the Koli women as they began to chase after her. The loud slapping of wet saris against the women's legs sounded like the flapping winds of a bird. Like vultures, Briley thought. She ran faster.

Soon she had left the fishing village behind and was running up Free Press Journal Road toward the heart of the financial district. In sharp contrast to the ramshackle shanties on the beach, the buildings here were tall, modern structures made of steel, brick and concrete, testimony to Bombay's place as the economic heart of India. Though it was Saturday and the stock exchange was closed, the streets were nonetheless busy. Rain quickly inched its way up to the curb, slowing traffic to a standstill and allowing Briley to dash between cars as she tried to put more distance between herself and her pursuers. Once she crossed the street, she paused to catch her breath and glanced back over her shoulder. She could see the women, half a block away, slowed by their saris, haranguing passersby and pointing Briley's way as if seeking help in the chase. As on the beach, however, everyone either shook their heads or ignored the women altogether. Still, Briley wasn't about to let up. She broke into a run again, taking the sidewalk.

She thought of seeking out one of the museums in

hopes it would provide a refuge, but, realizing she might not be admitted smelling the way she did, she went the other way and soon found herself caught up in the sea of Indians trying to cram their way into Churchgate Station. Rather than try to get past them, she waded into their midst, doing her best to mingle in and worm her way forward. By the time she passed through the turnstile into the train station, she felt confident that she had managed to elude the Kolis.

Of the two train lines servicing Bombay, Churchgate served the western side of the island, away from the safehouse where she'd hoped to shower and change. There was a stop within two blocks of Adbul Jahan's studio, however, so Briley paid her fare and followed the attendant's directions to the loading platform. At this point, gussying herself up for Abdul seemed petty and trivial. She was just glad to have escaped her brush with the fisherwomen. Besides, she figured she could play on Abdul's sympathy when she recounted her close call.

The crowd outside the terminal was nothing compared to what Briley encountered when she reached the loading platform. People were packed in so tightly they covered every square inch of the platform, and there was chaos when the train pulled in. People stormed for the nearest doorways of each rail car, waiting for them to open after arriving passengers had departed on the other side. Still concerned the Koli women might show up, Briley wedged herself into the mob and let herself be carried along. Somehow she managed to find her way into one of the cars. The Bombay train system typically ran 150 percent ahead of capacity, and today was no exception. All the seats had been taken and Briley was forced to stand near one of the vertical handholds, hemmed in on every side by other passengers, all of them Indian, all of them soaked by the monsoon. When the train began to pull out of the station, Briley felt herself being nudged and jostled. She knew it had nothing to do with the Koli women or any attempt to molest her; people just had nowhere else to move. Still, the confinement was stifling, and when they'd reached their first stop at Marine Lines, two passengers boarded for every one that got off. Briley felt herself squeezed in even tighter. She was close to tears. Shutting her eyes, she tried to calm herself. This, too, would pass, she told herself. This, too, would pass....

CHAPTER SEVENTEEN

Guiyn Plateau

"It's got to be the guys who got hit by the plane," Les Marris said.

"Seems that way,' Bolan agreed.

The two men had just made their way down a steep path leading from the plateau. The monsoon had cleared the mountains and was sweeping toward them, forcing them to shield their faces against the sting of windswept sand. They'd already decided that even if Grimaldi and Kissinger managed to repair the tire, there was no way they were going to be able to take off until the storm had blown over. Once they checked out the graves, they figured they'd duck into the caves and wait for the others to join them.

Halfway to the unearthed bodies, Marris lost his footing and fell to his knees. He was pushing himself back up to his feet when he felt something just below the surface of the loose sand.

"Holy shit."

Bolan backtracked and saw that Marris had literally stumbled onto yet another mass grave. Though shallow, it had been dug a good two feet deeper than the one they'd seen from the plateau, and it was only when Marris and Bolan started scooping away handfuls of sand that they could get a good look at the bodies. There were eight of them and, unlike the others, they had been laid to rest neatly, in rows, wrapped from head to toe in what looked to be parachute material.

"Fucking bizarre," Marris said.

"Sure is." Bolan peeled the shroud off the head of one of the dead men and saw that his face had been crushed by brute force. Rigor mortis had set in and sand fleas swarmed over the exposed flesh, which was discolored but had not yet begun to decompose.

"These guys haven't been down long," Bolan surmised.

"Agreed," Marris said, inspecting another of the corpses. "Lots of blunt trauma going on, too, which makes me think *these* are the ones who got run over."

"Makes sense," Bolan said. "It didn't seem like the mujahideen would just dump their people in the ground, no matter how much of a hurry they were in."

"Okay, but if that's the case," Marris countered, "then who are those other guys?"

"Good question."

Bolan and Marris moved away from the first grave and headed toward the second. As it had appeared from atop the plateau, the dead men had been tossed haphazardly atop one another. Unlike the mujahideen corpses, not only had they been deprived of burial shrouds, but they had also been stripped to their shorts, not unlike the slain priests back in Kottayam.

Bolan reached for his Desert Eagle. "Something tells me this is the reception party that was supposed to meet us."

"Shit," Marris muttered. "If that's the case—"

Before he could finish, a gunshot ripped through the desert air, striking him in the side. Marris let out a groan as he pitched to the ground, bleeding. Bolan whirled, tracing the direction the shot had come from. More than ten men were charging out of the caves beneath the plateau, half of them wearing the familiar tracksuits of the mujahideen, others the olive-colored fatigues of the Shiv Sena militia. Even with the poor visibility caused by flying sand, Bolan could see that most of the uniforms didn't fit the men wearing them. It was obvious they'd ambushed the men whose bodies Bolan and Marris had just discovered, no doubt executing them after taking their clothes.

"Sons of bitches!" Marris fumed, hauling a 9 mm Browning pistol from his shoulder holster. The gun was covered with blood, but Marris had no trouble firing it. He sprayed a burst at the advancing mujahideen, dropping two of them. Bolan had equal success, but that still left them outnumbered. The Kashmiri terrorists were better armed, too, most of them firing MP-5s. They returned fire as they fanned out, clearly intent on surrounding Bolan and Marris.

With no other available cover, Bolan and Marris had no choice but to take up positions behind the bodies of the slain militia.

"How bad did you get hit?" Bolan asked the CIA agent.

"It smarts," Marris said with a grimace, "but I'll be fine."

Besides being outnumbered, Bolan and Marris were put at a further disadvantage by the wind, which was in their faces, forcing them to constantly blink away flying bits of sand. Several enemy rounds, meanwhile, struck the bodies they were crouched behind, making them twitch as if they were stirring back to life.

Knowing they had to ration their shots, both men held their fire, waiting for the mujahideen to make a better target of themselves. The Kashmiris weren't playing along, however. The odds stacked in their favor, they were content to lie lower in the sand and make their way slowly forward on their bellies. Behind them, the storm clouds looked ever more menacing in contrast to the sunny sky to the east.

"Rain'll be here any second," Bolan said. "Hopefully we can make some use out of it."

When Marris didn't respond, Bolan glanced to his side. The CIA agent lay still, gun in hand, his face buried in the mesh of human limbs he'd taken cover behind.

"Marris?"

Bolan reached over and checked the man's pulse. He didn't have one. Glancing down, the Executioner saw blood pool out from underneath Marris's body, turning the sand red. He was gone.

There was no time for mourning. Another volley of gunfire rattled the corpses, forcing Bolan to drop lower to the ground. He took the Browning from Marris's hand and rolled sideways, then came up firing.

A mujahideen less than twenty yards away took three hits across the midsection and toppled to the ground. Behind him, another Kashmiri stopped his retreat and flattened himself behind a ridge of sand. This close, Bolan could see the man's legs trailing back from the ridge and lined up a shot, firing through the sand. The other man flinched and started to rise to his feet, only to keel over, his scalp turned crimson by a kill shot to the head.

Sheets of rain began to slam into the earth with a muffled sound like popcorn bursting inside a microwave. Bolan, anxious to get his hands on one of the submachine guns, prepared to bolt from cover, using the rain as a screen. He hesitated, however, when he heard another sound, far louder than the storm, issuing from inside the cave. A car engine.

Moments later, a British SAS Land Rover charged from the cavity. It was an older model, its "Pink Panther" salmon coloring faded but still an effective camouflage. The vehicle had two 7.62 mm machine guns, mounted fore and aft, and there was a man in back serving as tail gunner. Bolan had no idea whether the mujahideen had seized it from the militia or had otherwise appropriated it. All that mattered to him was the fact that the Rover would have no trouble navigating through the sand toward him, neutralizing any gains he'd just made by felling two more of the enemy. When he saw the gunner pivoting the machine gun his way, Bolan abandoned any thought of going after the MP-5 and dropped to the ground, awaiting the deadly hail.

The machine gun barked out rounds as fast as they

could be fed into its firing chambers, but to Bolan's surprise, none of the shots seemed to be striking anywhere near him. When he heard the mujahideen's MP-5s join in the chatter with the same ineffective results, Bolan risked a glimpse above the corpses.

"I'll be damned," he muttered, grinning despite the gravity of the situation.

It was Grimaldi at the wheel of the Rover, Kissinger manning the tail gun. They were attacking the mujahideen from the rear. At one point Grimaldi idled the vehicle and made use of the front-mounted gun, drilling 7.62 mm hellfire into a Kashmiri about to lob a grenade. The terrorist recoiled, dead on his feet, and the grenade exploded in his hand, fragging another gunman several yards away.

Emboldened, Bolan broke from cover, emptying his Desert Eagle and then switching to Marris's pistol as he charged through the pummeling rain toward the gunman he'd nailed moments before. Once the Browning was depleted, Bolan tossed it aside in favor of the MP-5. When gunfire whistled past him, he spun, fanning a spray of 9 mm Parabellum rounds at the last standing would-be ambusher. The mujahideen fired an errant burst, then slumped to the sand.

It was only then that Bolan realized he'd taken a hit at some point. His forearm was bleeding, and when he let the rain wash away the blood, he saw that he'd been grazed near the elbow. Considering his prospects less than a minute ago, he wasn't about to complain.

Bolan turned as the Land Rover approached. Grimaldi flashed a wave while Kissinger remained vigilant in back, on the chance that there might be survivors still lurking out in the sand.

"How the hell did you pull that off?" Bolan shouted over the rain and the sound of the engine as Grimaldi pulled up alongside him.

"This?" Grimaldi said, indicating the Rover. "We were about to take some potshots from up by the plane when Cowboy said maybe we ought to try taking one of the shafts first. We climbed down and—voilà—Pink Panther, keys in the ignition, ready to rock and roll. Why the hell *they* didn't use it is beyond me."

"No element of surprise," Bolan said. "When you started that thing up it was like thunder."

"Maybe so." Grimaldi glanced around. "Where's Marris?"

"He didn't make it," Bolan said.

"Shit." Grimaldi slammed his hand against the steering wheel. "Where's the body?"

"Back with the others," Bolan said. He was indicating the shallower of the two graves when Kissinger interrupted.

"We got a problem, guys. Big time."

Bolan and Grimaldi glanced toward the mountains and saw what Kissinger was talking about. Surging across the desert toward them, every bit as fearsome as a phalanx of mujahideen, was an eight-foot-high wall of water, crushing and submerging everything in its path.

"Flash flood," Bolan said.

"NO WAY I CAN outrun it!" Grimaldi said as the floodwaters raced forward.

"The caves!" Kissinger shouted through the rain, giving Bolan a hand up onto the rear of the vehicle.

"Let's go!" Bolan urged.

Grimaldi slammed the Land Rover into gear and jerked hard on the steering wheel. Wet sand fantailed behind the vehicle as he sped away, cutting as sharp a turn as he could without tipping over. The plateau was a good fifty yards away, far closer than the flood. The water, however, was racing faster than the Rover could ever hope to. It was going to be close.

As they sped toward the nearest cave, Bolan saw the water close in on the nearest of the mujahideen fighters. The body rose up for a brief moment, then was pulled under by the force of the wave, disappearing from sight. Next the flood surged toward an aged acacia, one of the few trees on the desert plain, so old its trunk was nearly as wide as the Land Rover. The tree resisted a second or two, then snapped loudly, becoming little more than an oversize piece of driftwood dragged along by the water's sheer force.

"Faster!" Kissinger shouted.

"Pedal's to the metal!" Grimaldi announced, steering around a ridge of sand. They were now twenty yards from the black maw of the cave. The flood was, at most, thirty yards from the Rover and gaining fast.

Kissinger clutched the machine gun's mount for support. "We're not going to make it," he said.

He was only partly correct. Grimaldi powered the Rover forward, managing to get halfway into the cave before the water hit them, slamming the rear end hard against the mouth of the cave. Kissinger and Grimaldi were both ejected from the vehicle and thrown against the cave wall. Grimaldi managed to get an arm up to blunt the impact, but Kissinger was off balance and struck his head and shoulders against the hard rock. Unconscious, he fell to the ground and was nearly crushed by the Rover as it toppled onto its side. Though shaken, Grimaldi had the presence of mind to grab the Stony Man armorer and yank him clear.

The flood was moving at such a pace that it raced by the cave rather than surging into it. Still, enough water coursed into the cavity that Grimaldi was hard-pressed to drag Kissinger from its path. Finally, as the water came up to his waist, he gave up and slung one arm around his friend, leaving the other free to tread water. The water lifted both men up to a ledge, and when the level ceased rising, Grimaldi helped Kissinger onto the shelf and then crawled up beside him. His arm was scraped and he was bruised all up and down his right side, but he was alive and thankful for it.

He was dragging Kissinger farther from the edge when the man sputtered and came to.

"Sit tight," Grimaldi told him. "We got through it."

Kissinger winced. His skull was throbbing.

"Mack?" he asked.

Grimaldi stared out at the lapping waters and the crushed heap that had been the Land Rover. There was no sign of Bolan.

"I don't know," Grimaldi confessed, the cold truth coming to him. "I think we lost him."

DON'T FIGHT IT.

That was Bolan's first conscious thought as he

found himself being swept along by the floodwaters. Unlike Grimaldi and Kissinger, he'd been thrown away from the cave when the water had caught up with the Land Rover. At first he'd been pulled down beneath the surface and pushed along the outer facing of the plateau, and for a brief moment he'd even been pinned to an outcropping for so long that he felt his lungs were about to burst. The rock had finally given way, however, and he'd found himself pushed upward until he was able to get his head above the waterline. Now, as he struggled to stay afloat, the plateau fell away from him. The battlefield where he and Marris had discovered the graves was underwater, and there was no telling where the bodies were or where they'd wind up. There was nothing but uninterrupted plains stretching westward, and the flood, constantly nourished by the monsoon, showed no signs of abating. Bolan had no idea how long his strength would hold out, but he saw no choice but to let himself be carried along and hope that he wouldn't be pulled back under.

The water was cold and brown and littered with debris, mostly uprooted shrubs and small trees. Occasionally, a body would pop briefly to the surface, only to disappear moments later. Bolan could feel himself weighed down by his boots and clothing, but he wasn't in a position to do anything about it; he had to kick and tread water constantly just to keep going with the flow.

It was difficult to have any sense of time or distance, but after what seemed like miles and hours—though he knew it was neither—Bolan felt the current diminishing beneath him. The storm was moving past, too, and patches of blue actually began to appear overhead. Bolan wasn't about to celebrate, however. His legs were beginning to cramp, and his arms, especially the one that'd been nicked by gunfire, were weakening. He doubted that he could ride out the flood much longer.

Forty yards to his right, the old acacia—or what was left of it—floated by like a crude ship, its gangly branches the masts, scraps of leaves the shredded sails. Summoning his strength, Bolan began to swim at an angle toward the tree. He was hindered by the fact that he was being swept along at a faster pace. It would do him no good if he aligned himself with the tree, only to find himself too far ahead for it to be of any use to him. And so he narrowed the angle of his approach until he was swimming almost perpendicular to the flood's course. His strength was sapping, but he refused to give up. Pushing himself, he lengthened his strokes until, finally, he was within reach of the tree.

"Yes," he gasped as his fingers closed around one of the branches. The euphoria was short-lived, however, as the limb snapped under his weight and he was pulled away from the tree again. Twice more he tried to gain a hold, with the same results. Finally, however, he reached a branch thick enough to support him. Hand over hand, he pulled himself closer to the tree's trunk, half of which was above the waterline. It was only when he reached the trunk and clambered up onto it that Bolan allowed himself to collapse. He gasped for breath, his lungs aflame, his arms and legs both numb and throbbing at the same time. He told himself he would rest a moment, then try to stand up and support himself against one of the upward-thrusting branches. His body had other ideas, however, and within seconds he'd passed out.

Bombay

TWO BLOCKS into the Muslim quarter, the cab Dehri Neshah rode in sputtered to a stop. Given the car's condition, he was surprised he had made it that far. As he was paying the driver, a throng of street urchins waded through the knee-high water, volunteering to help push the taxi uphill to where the street was only flooded a few inches. The driver waved them away angrily, accusing them of having stuffed rags in the gutter to keep the street from draining properly. Neshah suspected such was the case but he wasn't about to intervene. He paid the driver and opened his door. The water was so high it nearly flowed into the cab. Neshah had to crouch, then leap to the sidewalk to keep from getting wet.

In the aftermath of the downpour, merchants were just beginning to haul their wares back out for display, having already used brooms to sweep the grimy water from the sidewalks in front of their storefronts. The sun was out, and far to the east the remnants of a rainbow hung over the Ghats. Neshah hoped it was a good omen.

As with every other city the mujahideen had encamped at during their months-long mission across the subcontinent, Neshah had arranged for Spartan living quarters, this time in a two-story hovel just down the block from the Minara mosque. He'd chosen a safehouse in town rather than on the outskirts because he felt his men were less likely to draw notice here, where the neighborhood's population was almost exclusively Muslim. Given that between three and four hundred new arrivals set foot in Bombay any given day, he'd doubted that anyone would question the sudden appearance of the few men he'd brought with him from their larger base at Guiyn Plateau.

Neshah stopped to buy a bag of fruit from one of the vendors, then made his way to the safehouse. Though their second-story quarters faced the street, to reach the private entryway he had to pass down an alleyway. He looked around. One of his men, disguised as a homeless beggar, was supposed to be standing guard near the rickety staircase at all times, but there was no one about save for a pair of cats fighting over one of the countless millions of rats that thrived off the substandard sanitation in everywhere but a few elite pockets of the city.

Neshah glanced up to the second story. The blinds were closed at the safehouse, and there was no one out on the balcony that faced the street. As he warily started up the staircase, he unzipped his fanny pack, allowing him quick access to his gun, a World War II Japanese-made Taisho-14 8 mm pistol one of his men had won in a poker game back in New Delhi. Neshah had helped himself to the weapon after arriving at Guiyn Plateau, preferring it to the Smith & Wesson he'd taken during his jail break. He waited until he was up the steps and inside the building before pulling the gun out. The apartment his men were staying at was halfway down the deserted hallway. All of the other apartments were vacant. Neshah's men had coerced the landlord into displacing the other tenants, claiming that a beggar afflicted with leprosy had broken into the building and died in the hallway, contaminating the entire floor. It was quiet and Neshah approached the doorway cautiously, cursing the floorboards when they creaked under his feet.

He had a key to the apartment, of course, but he wasn't sure he wanted to use it. He was deliberating his next move when the door to the apartment swung open. Instinctively, Neshah took a step backward, into the shadows. He saw that it was one of his men, Lata, a doe-eyed, frail-chinned Kashmiri in his early fifties. The man was unshaved and dressed in rags, carrying a small wooden flute and a ratty turban filled with small change.

"Dehri?" he said, peering into the shadows.

Neshah stepped forward, glaring at Lata as he slipped the Taisho back into his fanny pack.

"Your post is downstairs, Lata!" he snapped. "In the alley."

Lata nodded. "I'm on my way. I had to use the bathroom."

Neshah lashed out with the back of his hand, slapping Lata across the face. "You're supposed to be a beggar! Use the street!"

"I would have, only—"

"No excuse!" Neshah interrupted, striking the man again. "What if I was IB? I could be standing here with twenty men behind me and no one would know it, because you left your post!''

''He left his post because I asked him to,'' came a voice from behind Lata. Lata stepped to one side as Penghat Shili stepped into the hallway. Penghat was armed, and he was aiming his gun at Neshah. There was hatred in his red-rimmed eyes. With a jerk of his head, he gestured for Lata to leave. The man was only too happy to oblige.

''What is the meaning of this?'' Neshah demanded, though he already suspected the answer.

''Let me ask you a question first, Dehri,'' Shili responded coolly. ''Can you give me one good reason why I shouldn't kill you right here, right now, for the dog you are?''

''I understand your anger,'' Neshah calmly told him, ''but this will solve nothing.''

''I will have avenged Raghubir. That is something.'' He tried to sound as dispassionate as Neshah, but there was a quaver in his voice. Neshah knew there was still hope for him, if only he could bide more time.

''I came as soon as I saw the papers,'' he stated.

''Why? So you could kill *me,* too?''

''I didn't kill Raghubir,'' Neshah claimed.

''Lies!''

''It's the newspapers that lie!''

''For what reason?'' Shili demanded. ''Why would they want to lie?''

''Because they were told to. Because they, too, were lied to.''

Shili laughed. ''What kind of answer is that?''

"You are distraught, Penghat," Neshah said. "You are filled with grief and rage, so it is not easy for you to see that—"

"Don't talk down to me!" Shili raised his weapon, pointing it at Neshah's face. His arm was trembling. "Don't you dare talk down to me!"

"I did not mean to—"

"I'm not one of your little sheep!"

"That is true," Neshah said. "You are my oldest and closest friend."

"More lies!" Shili retorted. "Vikrab and Andesh, safely back in Zalam. *They* are your close friends. You let them stay home, out of harm's way, while you led the rest of us to slaughter!"

Neshah felt it was time to assert himself, before Shili became one with his anger and steadied both his aim and resolve. "You just told me you were not a sheep," he replied firmly. "That you are not a child. Then prove it to me! Put down your gun so that we can discuss this man to man." Gesturing at the doorway behind Shili, he added, "Inside, so that this does not become a spectacle."

"You mean so that I don't expose you to the world for the fraud you are!"

Neshah stared hard into the man's eyes. "If you have no interest in the truth, then go ahead, pull the trigger! Kill me and be done with it! Take charge of mujahideen or call it all off and send them all on their way, if that is your wish. Make it so that your brothers died in vain."

Shili hesitated a moment, then slowly lowered the gun. He kept it in his hand, however, using it to wave

Neshah into the apartment. Neshah complied. As he passed through the doorway, he saw that the apartment had been ransacked. Newspapers were strewed across the floor, most of them ripped into tatters. The cots had been tipped over, as had the only other pieces of furniture, a plain card table and five folding chairs. It looked like the work of vandals, but Neshah guessed this was Shili's doing, no doubt his first reaction upon reading the details of Raghubir's death. Neshah wasn't about to trigger another outburst by attempting to right a chair to sit in.

"Where are the others?" he asked.

"I didn't want anyone around," Shili said. "As you say, I wanted us to be able to talk man to man. You'll excuse the mess."

Neshah nodded. "Of course. You felt provoked, which is exactly what they want."

"So we are back to that, then," Shili said caustically. "Explain it to me, this 'provoking.' Help me to understand."

"They have provoked you in hopes it would come to this. You taking sides against me." Neshah let his voice sound pleading. "Can't you see, Penghat? They're using you, to drive a wedge between us."

Shili said nothing, but Neshah could see that his cohort was buying into it.

"They are afraid," Neshah went on. "They are afraid of our power, afraid of the threat we pose."

Shili let out a deep sigh. Some of his rage left him, as well. "I wish that I could believe you, Dehri."

"I tell you, it's the truth. On my life! Before God!" He risked turning his back and went to the window, drawing open the blinds so that Shili could see the Minara spire down the block. "Here, in sight of the mosque! I'm telling you, I did not kill your brother! I loved him."

"You resented him," Shili retorted. He stepped back from the harsh glare pouring into the room, trying to hide the fresh tears welling in his eyes. "You despised him because he was willful, because he spoke his mind."

"We were past that. You know that," Neshah said. "I heard him tell you as much."

Shili glanced away, casting his eyes to the floor. As if trying to rally his anger, he snatched up one of the newspapers and held it out so that Neshah could see the headlines, which told of new developments in the breaking story out of Kottayam. Kashmir Shredder Kills His Own In Brazen Escape!

"If you didn't kill Raghubir, then who did?" Shili demanded. "And why did they do it with a dagger?"

Neshah felt trapped. He thought fast.

"Who is to say they used a dagger?" he said. "Are there photos showing that he was stabbed?"

"No, but—"

"That is what they want you to think," Neshah interrupted. "They probably shot him, then thought of this way to put the blame on me."

"Why go to so much trouble?"

"I've already told you," Neshah said. "So that you would turn against me. It's their only chance of weakening us, of stopping us just when we are about to succeed."

Shili turned the newspaper around and stared at it

as if seeing it in a new light. He cast it aside and waved at the other papers. "What about the other news?"

Neshah was genuinely puzzled. "I don't know what you mean."

"The news about Vargadrum." Shili swallowed hard. A tear streaked down his cheek. He wiped it aside. "They say he was shot more than thirty times, at close range. Thirty times!"

This was the first Neshah had heard of it. "I didn't read that," he said. "I had no idea."

"Shot thirty times!" Shili repeated. "By the nephew of that defiler they are holding a parade for today."

"I am sorry, Penghat." Neshah felt his own rage building. He willed tears to his eyes. "This is a terrible thing that has happened," he said.

"Raghubir and Vargadrum, both dead." Shili's voice was thick. "My brothers. They are dead because of me."

"No."

"Yes! They joined the mujahideen because of me. I talked them into it. 'To hell with acrobatics' I told them. 'To be part of a circus when there is work to be done for Kashmir? It is a disgrace!' This I told them! They were happy at what they were doing, but I changed all that. I brought them into the mujahideen. I badgered and bullied until they agreed to join. Now their blood is on my hands. I might just as well have killed them myself."

"That is madness, Penghat. You mustn't think that way. They died for a righteous cause."

"So we keep telling ourselves," Shili scoffed. "Meanwhile, more and more of us just die."

"Sacrifices are difficult to accept, I know," Neshah said, "but they are necessary."

He ignored Neshah. "All morning I tried to reach the others at the plateau," he went on, indicating the antiquated Mk III suitcase transceiver lying on the floor near the overturned table. "Nothing. What if they've been killed now, too?"

"You're forgetting, Penghat," Neshah reminded him. "The monsoon. They were probably forced to take cover. They may not be near the radio."

"Or they may be dead."

Now that Shili had given himself over to despair, Neshah felt that he was reachable, that he could be brought back into the fold and made use of.

"Penghat," he said tactfully, "if you must dwell on death, make it worthwhile."

"How would I do that?" Shili responded bitterly.

"By helping to strike back," Neshah said. "We have to strike back at those responsible for Raghubir's death and especially Vargadrum's."

Shili's eyes narrowed suspiciously. "Why do you say especially?"

"The parade today," Neshah explained. "The ceremony at the Towers of Silence. Vargadrum's killer will be there, mourning his uncle. And not just him. The Yankee President will be there, too. And India's prime minister."

"Ha! What are we supposed to do about it? The parade route will be teeming with Shiv Sena, with American CIA. Anyone who looks Muslim will be singled out." Shili pointed out the window. "They are probably watching the streets here, right now, ready to follow anyone suspicious who heads in that direction."

"We can't just give up," Neshah insisted. "We have come too far for that."

"I don't see how we can do anything."

"There is a way," Neshah told him. "If it is important enough, there is always a way."

"Not always," his cohort responded bleakly.

"Penghat, I was there this morning," Neshah said. "I have had a look at the route they will be taking for the parade. It can be done."

Shili glanced up at Neshah, a glimmer of hope in his eyes. Almost without thinking, he holstered his weapon, caught up in the familiar camaraderie. "How?"

Neshah smiled. He'd done it. He had Penghat back on his side. He braved a step forward and put an arm around the other man's shoulder, physically drawing him into his confidence.

"I have a plan."

CHAPTER EIGHTEEN

Guiyn Plateau

There was still a job to be done, a mission to be carried out, so John Kissinger and Jack Grimaldi went through the motions. But their hearts weren't in it. As they explored the cave while waiting for the flood-waters to subside, they told each other that Bolan was all right, but their words sounded hollow. They'd fought side by side with the Executioner for what seemed like an eternity, cheating death at every corner, yet resigned that one day, for each of them, the odds would go against them and this would be the result. Already it had happened with other members of the Farm, and one day it would happen to them. But somehow they always thought that Bolan was different, or at least that he would be the last of them to go. Obviously, they were wrong. Mack Bolan *was* Stony Man Farm. The notion of carrying on without him seemed absurd, a travesty. And yet, there was still an enemy out there to be fought, an enemy that would lose no sleep at the thought that one of their fiercest adversaries had been taken out of the game. With or without Bolan, the Kashmiri insurgents would have to be brought to justice or put out of operation. And since they'd come to Guiyn Plateau to search out clues as to where the mujahideen would strike next, search they did.

There was little left of what had been the old Hindu temple. All of the most important sculptures and artifacts had been extricated from the caves and shipped to museums where they could be shown in an environment safe from vandalism and desecration. Where there had once been miniaturized temples and shrines carved out of the cave walls, now there were only scalloped chisel marks. And the monks' quarters, once breathtaking in their Spartan simplicity, were now strewn with litter and smelled of bats.

"Looks like they were using this as a base camp," Grimaldi said, walking among the cheap, soaked cots and bedrolls in the largest of the dimly lit underground rooms. Though elevated from the floor of the cave and spared the wrath of the floodwaters, the quarters had nonetheless wound up under a few inches of rainwater that cascaded down one of the shafts reaching up to the plateau.

"But why?" Kissinger wondered. "The closest town is Nasik, and that's a good fifty miles away. I know they're theoretically close to Bombay, but to get there they'd have to play Hannibal and cross the Ghats. It doesn't make any sense."

"I'm sure they had their reasons."

Grimaldi ventured toward another of the air shafts, this one used as a chimney, set as it was over a crude stone hearth. Next to the fireplace was a crate filled with foodstuffs—fruit, rice, spices, sacks of flour and dried meats. A plastic tarp had been thrown over the crate, but rainwater had collected in pools and soaked through, ruining everything. A second crate rested on a stone bench nearby; inside was an array of weapons and ammunition along with large containers filled with lamp oil. As he inspected the crate, Grimaldi's attention was drawn, not to the wares, but to the box itself.

"Should've known," he muttered. Glancing over his shoulders, he called out, "Yo, Cowboy, I think I found something."

His voice echoed off the walls, as did Kissinger's when he answered, "So did I."

Kissinger had disappeared, but he returned moments later, passing through a large, carved archway leading to one of the adjacent caves. "There are truck tracks over there," he told Grimaldi. "Bigger than the Rover's."

"Big enough for something capable of hauling a major load?"

"Like the other Ghurka?" Kissinger said.

"Not exactly," Grimaldi said.

"I figure it was at least an eight-wheeler," Kissinger said as he joined the pilot. "Why do you ask?"

"These boxes," Grimaldi said. "They didn't get them from behind the nearest supermarket."

Kissinger glanced at the crate on the bench. Grimaldi pointed to markings stamped on the side. There was lettering, both in Hindi and English. They had no clue what the former meant, and the English lettering spelled out words that both men assumed had to be Hindi, as well. Certain key words jumped out at them, however, as they were easily translatable. One was "Trivandrum," home of the Vikram Sarabhai Space Centre. The other was "Sabre."

"SAMs," Kissinger said.

Grimaldi nodded. "I think we found the other missing launcher."

"Or at least where they were keeping it," Kissinger corrected. "The horse has already left the corral."

"That explains why they didn't mind setting up shop here in the boonies," Grimaldi said. "With those surface-to-airs they can reach out and touch anybody within, what, a five-hundred-mile radius?"

"Something like that."

"Can they rein them in any?" Grimaldi asked. "You know, shorter range?"

"As in hurling one at Bombay?"

Kissinger nodded. He knew what Grimaldi was getting at. "Down in Kottayam they only had the President to take a crack at. Here they can take down the prime minister, too."

Kissinger mulled over their options, then told Grimaldi, "Why don't you go check on the plane? If it's still in one piece, try to patch through to the Farm and give them the news."

"That's one call I'm not looking forward to making," Grimaldi said, thinking once more of Bolan.

Kissinger made it clear he wasn't in for a picnic himself. "Yeah, well, while you're doing that," he told Grimaldi, "I'm going to be out looking for his body."

Thoughts of Bolan putting a damper on their discovery, the men split up. Grimaldi started climbing the wet, chiseled rungs leading up through the chimney. Kissinger checked the munitions crate for some field glasses and found a British Simrad day/night bino-scope. The batteries were still good, so he slung the strap over his shoulder and waded through ankle-deep water out of the cave.

Outside, the desert looked like the surface of another planet. Denuded by the flash flood, the ground—where it wasn't still underwater—bore trenchlike culverts and small, smooth hills of sand. All the bodies, both from the graves and the earlier skirmish with the mujahideen, had been swept from sight. How far they'd been carried away was anyone's guess. When he scanned the eastern horizon with his bino-scope, Kissinger couldn't spot any of them and he suspected most had been reburied under the displaced sand. A shadow sweeping across the ground drew his attention skyward. The vultures were already out, circling overhead. Kissinger realized there was a good chance he would have to wait and let the birds do his searching for him. Once they drifted down and began poking through the sand, he could track after them and scare them off, then tend to whatever remains he came across.

"What a life," he murmured.

Kissinger was about to call up to Grimaldi when something caught his eye off in the distance. He squinted against the sun's glare, trying to get a better look. It was a figure, far off, maybe two or three hundred yards away, moving slowly across the sand toward him.

"Son of a bitch!" Kissinger raised the bino-scope

again and peered out, shifting the focus ring until he had a clearer view. "Son of a bitch!" he repeated. It wasn't a curse, however, so much as a cry of elation.

Heading toward him across the desert, back from the dead, was Mack Bolan.

Bombay

VULTURES WERE also in the air eighty miles west of Guiyn Plateau, haunting the skies over the wooded section of Malabar Hill. Staring at them, Nhajsib Wal was beset by the same uneasiness he'd felt every time he'd come to the Towers of Silence. He was no longer the devout Zoroastrian he'd been as a boy, but he understood and respected the philosophy behind this, their chosen way of dealing with mortal remains. But understanding something and being comfortable with it were two different things. Since childhood, when he was first brought here to attend rites for his parents—victims of a car accident—Wal had been plagued by recurring nightmares in which vultures the size of pterodactyls would swoop down at him out of nowhere, champing beaks lined with razor-sharp teeth eager to sink into his flesh. The image lingered with him during subsequent funerals, when, as was custom, friends and family watched the deposition of the dead from a pavilion in the adjacent park. There, landscaped gardens blocked the towers from view, so that all that he could ever see of the proceedings was the coming and going of the birds. From a distance, they still seemed frighteningly large.

This day, however, Wal was, for the first time, on his way to see the birds up close.

The deposition of his uncle's body would not take place until later in the afternoon, following the funeral parade—which he had opposed, only to be overruled by other family members—but given the need for heightened security, IB had been ordered to inspect the towerlike structure that bore the exposed corpse and arrange for guards to be stationed to prevent their use as possible sniper posts when the prime minister and America's President came to attend the final rites. There were those who found Wal's request to be part of the inspection team sacrilegious, but he didn't care. He had to see for himself the fate that awaited his uncle and would one day await him.

Besides, it gave him an excuse to get away from his relatives. He was disgusted mostly by his aunt and two uncles—Ziarat's sister and brothers—who throughout his uncle's life had mocked him for his decision to devote his life to the teaching of *kalaripayattu* but now were overeager to sing his praises to the media, all dressed in their finest clothes and freshly primped after trips to the barber and hairdresser. That morning, when he'd stopped by the hotel where they were staying, there had been a heated argument about who would get to sit where in the open convertible that would follow the hearse carrying Ziarat's body down the parade route. For Nhajsib, that had been enough.

Now, standing before the gates to the tower where his uncle would be brought, Nhajsib Wal put aside his loathing. Less than ten feet away, atop the arch-

way through which he would soon pass, perched a
row of vultures, as still as statues save for their eyes,
which seemed trained on him. His heart began to race,
and beads of cold sweat ran down his forehead. He
forced himself to stare back at them, to eye them in
detail, in hopes he could overcome his fear. The first
thing he noticed was their size. Up close, they were
still large, but no more so than pheasants, and certainly nothing close to pterodactyls. They were ugly,
too, from their bald, wrinkled heads and hooked beaks
to their seemingly withered necks. More than fearsome, they seemed deformed and pitiable. It was only
when they were joined by another and Wal saw the
flapping of the familiar dusky wings that he had any
sense of the grisly majesty that had haunted him all
these years. Even then, he was able to shed—at least
for the moment—his fear of the birds.

By custom, the only ones allowed to enter the
tower were select pallbearers who came to their position by way of heredity. There had been vehement
protests within the local Parsi hierarchy when they'd
learned of the proposed inspections, but IB had insisted and, as a compromise, Wal and several other
Parsis within the bureau had been given permission
to enter. Still, as one of the white-clad pallbearers
opened the metal gates, he stared at Wal with disap-
proval. The man followed Wal inside, closing the
door behind him.

After three steps into the circular tower, which
measured some thirty yards across, there was a
pitched incline leading down to a central pit. It was
there, in the pit, that the bones of the deceased were

tossed after they'd been picked clean by the vultures. The pit was lined with charcoal and sand so that, in the event of rain, the decomposing remains wouldn't leach into the earth, contaminating it in violation of the same tenets that had given rise to the ritual in the first place.

The platform was still damp from the monsoon, which had washed away most traces of the deposition that had taken place earlier in the morning. That didn't prevent a few vultures from fluttering down and pecking at the stone slope in places where small bits of flesh had to have become caught in the ribbed bands of stone where the bodies were placed to keep them from rolling into the pit. To see the scavengers in action, to hear the persistent click of their beaks against the stone, unnerved Wal. He turned away from the sight, drawing a deep breath to collect himself, then quickly carried out his inspection.

The enclosure's high stone walls rose straight upward, then tapered slightly outward. The vultures had an easy footing, but there was no way snipers would be able to take up positions along the walls. At best, they could perhaps lob grenades or fire a mortar launcher from where he was standing, but if guards were stationed outside the gates and adequate aerial surveillance was provided, Wal doubted the mujahideen would even consider approaching the grounds, much less the towers.

Forewarned that speaking was prohibited within the walls, Wal signaled to the pallbearer that he was ready to leave. The other man, now expressionless, turned and opened the door. As he left the enclosure, vultures staring down at him, Nhajsib felt the hairs on his neck stand on end. He wasn't sure if he'd rid himself of his nightmares, but one thing he was certain of was that he would never again set foot in the Towers of Silence.

The pallbearer remained behind as Wal headed for the park. IB had set up a command post near the pavilion. One of his fellow agents waved him over and said there were two new developments to report.

"First, there was a shooting at the fishing village near Nariman Point," the other officer said. "A Koli woman was shot at close range by another woman. An American, by most accounts."

Wal's mind flashed at once to the briefing he'd received that morning before leaving to meet with his relatives, word from the CIA that Dehri Neshah had fled Kottayam the previous night in a plane, accompanied not only by Penghat Shili, but also a woman. An American woman.

"How is the Koli woman?" he asked.

"She died in surgery," the other man replied.

"Was there a description of her shooter? Other than her being American?"

"Contradictory descriptions, yes. All that anyone agrees on is that she wore a scarf, slacks and a light-colored blouse."

"Which she's probably not even wearing now, thanks to the rain," Nhajsib said. Still, he felt certain there had to be a link between the woman and Neshah. And if she was in Bombay, then the odds were so was he, which meant that the mujahideen terrorists, undaunted by their defeat in Kottayam, were indeed in the city.

As a precaution, he told the other man to double the guards at each of the Towers of Silence and to call in more men to help the Shiv Sena militia reinforce the perimeter around the park.

Then he asked, "What was the other matter?"

"It's unrelated, but no less important," the other man said. "I just received a call from RAW. Over the past twelve hours they have intercepted several SIG-INTEL communiqués from Pakistan ISI concerning a proposed attack on Jaisalmer."

"Jaisalmer?" Nhajsib frowned, puzzled. "There must be a mistake."

"That was my first thought," the other man said. "But they put the messages through eleven different encryptions, and each time it was clear. They're targeting Jaisalmer."

"But why?" Wal said. "Jaisalmer has no strategic significance. There's nothing there but the old fort and tourist shops."

"You're forgetting, just like I did," the other man said. "This year they are celebrating Ganesh Chaturthi there."

Nhajsib muttered an oath. Yes, he *had* forgotten. There had been a new resort built on the outskirts of Jaisalmer, with a large man-made lake using water siphoned from the Rajasthan Canal. There was a lot of controversy over the development, as well as its plans to inaugurate a local celebration of Chaturthi, using the lake as a place where revelers could haul their replicas of Ganesh and other deities. The fear had been that the event would turn into a carnival catering primarily to tourists, but once the schedule had been locked in place, it became clear that citizens throughout Rajasthan had become fascinated by the concept and planned a pilgrimage across the Thar Desert to attend.

"How many people showed up?" Wal asked, figuring the number would run into the tens of thousands.

"More than half a million," the other man responded. "There are so many they have extended the festival through the weekend."

"Half a million! Where are they staying?"

"The fort, the town, the desert... Wherever they can set down tents. Already it is the third-largest gathering for Chaturthi next to here and Pune."

Now it made sense to Wal. Five hundred thousand Hindus camped out in the open desert. What better target for a Muslim attack? Jaisalmer was less than a hundred miles from the Pakistan border. Pakistan had a whole arsenal of land-based SRBMs that could clear that short distance and turn the desert into a killing ground. And if Pakistan chose to follow up with ground and air forces...

"Are they just out to butcher Hindus," he wondered aloud, "or could they have their eyes on the canal?"

"I can't believe they'd try either one," the other man responded. "Neither can the prime minister. He is convinced there has to be some kind of mistake, but until he knows for sure he has put the armed forces on high alert."

"This is absurd!" Wal exclaimed. "All this focus we have put on stopping the mujahideen, and now we have Pakistan preparing an act of war? It's madness. There's been no warning, no sword rattling in Islamabad. They are supposed to be meeting with us to discuss peace, not war!"

"Put yourself in Pakistan's shoes," the other man countered. "What better time to strike at us than when we are preoccupied, not only with the mujahideen, but also Chaturthi and the presidential visit."

"And the funeral," Wal added grimly. He glanced back at the Towers of Silence and the hovering vultures, who, like Pakistan apparently, were in hopes that any hour soon there would be dead to swoop down and feast on. It was only now beginning to set in. No longer was India's main concern the isolated terrorism of Kashmiri separatists. No, now the country, unbelievably, seemed on the brink of all-out war.

CHAPTER NINETEEN

Stony Man Farm, Virginia

Once he passed through the security checkpoint, Huntington Wethers drove his Lincoln TownCar down the access road that passed through Stony Man Farm. The moonlit grounds looked deserted, but Wethers knew if he looked hard enough he would see blacksuits stationed strategically throughout the farm, maintaining their around-the-clock vigil over the compound.

Just as the land had been painstakingly planted, landscaped and cultivated in the manner of a legitimate farm, so did the main house look like any number of sleepy country estates dotting the Shenandoah Valley. Beneath its rural facade, however, the house was a veritable armed fortress, complete with not only reinforced steel doors and walls and bulletproof glass, but also antiaircraft guns mounted beneath a retractable roof.

Wethers yawned as he was admitted through the front entrance of the farmhouse. He was still battling the fog of deep sleep he'd been roused from nearly an hour ago by an urgent call from Hal Brognola. Of course, there was no such thing as a call from Brognola that wasn't urgent, especially at this hour.

Once in the building, Wethers was escorted down to the tunnel linking the house with the Annex. A blacksuit had brought up one of the tram carts. Wethers exchanged perfunctory greetings as he climbed aboard, then both men traversed the tunnel silently.

Tall and distinguished, his short-cropped hair turning grayer with each passing month, Wethers looked as if he'd never left his former job as a university professor at Berkeley. Stick a piece of chalk in his hand and put him behind a lectern facing an auditorium full of students, and most of his co-workers felt he could readily pick up where he'd left off, attacking the chalkboard with deft strokes as he expounded on cybernetic theory and drummed home his neverending campaign to make sure the world put the science back into computer science.

On the phone, Brognola had mentioned wanting to tap Wethers's encryption expertise, a sideline pursuit that appealed to his professorial side, rife as it was with patterns, mathematics and formulations. Whenever Kurtzman, Tokaido and Carmen Delahunt were stumped trying to decipher foreign intel or looking for a way to help another agency beef up its own dissemination, they invariably turned to Wethers.

Tokaido was off napping after a fourteen-hour shift, but Kurtzman and Delahunt were still at their computers when Wethers entered the room and made a beeline for the coffeemaker. Brognola was present, too, rolling an unlit cigar between his fingers as he stared at the largest of the computer monitors lining the wall farthest from the workstations. On the screen was a SAT-CAM photograph of the South Asia sub-continent overlaid with graphics delineating borders and major cities. It took Wethers a moment to see that he was looking at the India state of Rajasthan, as well as portions of Gujarat, Madhya Pradesh, Harvana and the Pakistani states of Punjab and Sindh.

"Another snag in the peace talks?" Wethers guessed.

"Hunt!" Brognola turned and shook Wethers's hand. "I appreciate your coming on such short notice."

"Anything to help," Wethers said. He exchanged greetings across the room with Kurtzman and Delahunt, then told Brognola, "Now what's this about an encryption problem?"

"We're under the gun, in more ways than one," Brognola said, "so I'll cut straight to the chase.

"Over the past hour," the big Fed went on, "we've tapped into communiqués passed between India's RAW and their Intelligence Bureau. For their part, they're claiming they've done the same thing with ISI in Pakistan, unearthing some plot to fire a missile at some religious gathering in the Thar Desert near Jaisalmer."

"The Ganesh festival," Wethers said. "I was monitoring that earlier in the week. It's turned into something like a Hindu Woodstock, correct?"

"In terms of people showing up, yes," Brognola said. "Half a million. But it's looking like they have more in store for them than peace, love and music. If a missile crashes their party, it'll be wholesale slaughter."

"What about interceptors?"

"India's working on it, ground and air," Brognola said, "only they've got a split focus, given the situation in Bombay."

"They're canceling the parade, I assume."

"With the President, you never assume," Brognola said with a shake of his head. "He got the prime minister to back him."

"Then I take it none of this has been made public."

"Absolutely not," Brognola told Wethers. "They don't want to raise a panic, either in Bombay or Jaisalmer. That many people crammed together, you trigger any kind of stampede and they'll start trampling each other trying to get away."

"Not a pretty sight."

"Besides, there's a chance it's all a false alarm."

"How so?"

"Pakistan just came out saying they have no such plans, that a prank call somehow found its way into the loop."

"That's some prank," Delahunt called out from her station, having overheard.

"We'd expect Pakistan to deny anything, though, wouldn't we?" Wethers suggested.

"We're looking into that angle," Brognola said. "In fact, that's what we need your help with. But first let me finish, because it gets more complicated."

"I'm following you so far," Wethers said.

"Good, then stay with me," Brognola said as he moved over to the map on the large monitor. He used his cigar as a pointer as he talked. "While you were on the way over here, Aaron tapped into an ISI feed out of Islamabad, and in Pakistan the shoe's on the other foot."

"I'm not sure what you mean."

"They're countercharging that they've seized a RAW interoffice memo analyzing strategy for a missile strike at two key nuclear weapons sites in Punjab." Brognola pointed to a cluster of dots on the map, all centrally located in the Indus River Valley. "Multan's a heavy-water facility. Dera Ghazi Khan is less than ninety miles away. They've got a uranium mine there, Baghalchur, that's nearly played out but still produces enough to be processed into twenty metric tons of yellow cake a year. That plus they're scouting for more uranium deposits in neighboring areas."

"If India takes out the mines around Dera Ghazi Khan, they still have Lakki up north."

"True," Brognola said, "but there are reports Lakki is underproducing, too. As far as long-term planning for yellow-cake reserves goes, for Pakistan, the new sites around Dera Ghazi Khan are the future. If India takes them out, it'd be a major blow to their nuclear programs."

"Not to mention dusting monsoon clouds with uranium," Kurtzman added, wheeling over to join the two men.

Wethers stared at the map a moment, putting things into perspective. "If all this is true, we're saying the President flew over there to talk peace and is going to wind up getting caught in a cross fire."

"It's looking that way," Brognola said. "And I don't need to remind you both India and Pakistan have nuclear capacity. It's not likely to stop with one exchange."

"Mutually assured destruction," Wethers intoned, trotting out the scenario that had led to the first wave of global arms proliferation back in the cold war.

"Not a pretty picture," Brognola said.

"Not at all," Wethers agreed.

"Provided the threats are legitimate," Kurtzman reiterated.

"Why should we think they aren't?" Wethers wondered.

"For starters," Kurtzman said, "there's the timing. Out of nowhere, we have both India and Pakistan pointing fingers at each other based on intel that both claim is fabricated."

"India's denying these strike plans in the Indus Valley?"

Brognola nodded. "RAW and IB both claim it's all new to them, and the prime minister has assured the President no such plans are on the table."

"Again," Wethers countered, "you'd expect a denial from them."

"Normally, I'd be the first to agree with you," Brognola replied. "But let me throw the last bit of fat into the fire."

The big Fed signaled to Kurtzman, who'd brought along his remote keyboard. He clicked out a few commands and, as he had the day before when accessing the President's vulnerability to a missile attack in Maldives, he overlaid the computer view of Rajasthan with a shaded circle with a five-hundred-mile radius. He adjusted the circle's placement until the afore-mentioned target sites in Pakistan fell within its up-permost crescent. Other cities located within the circle included Bombay, New Delhi, Jaisalmer and two of India's valuable nuclear sites.

"Consider this," Brognola told Wethers. "Suppose someone got their hands on a short-range launcher and decided to heave missiles at both Pakistan and India, like that kid in that fairy tale who dropped nuts from a tree onto the heads of two giants and got them to kill each other."

"Because each thought the other had hit him first," Wethers said.

"Exactly."

Wethers looked at Brognola and Kurtzman. "We're talking about the mujahideen, aren't we?"

Kurtzman nodded. "We just got word from Striker at Guiyn Plateau," he said. "He and the guys had a close call that I'll get into later, but the bottom line is they figure the Kashmiris had that second missing Sabre system stored at the plateau as late as last night, when Neshah was flown in from Kottayam after his jail break."

"And they've set up there on the Aravalli Moun-tain Range?"

"We don't know that for a fact," Brognola inter-jected. "We've checked all aerial surveillance and haven't pinpointed anything looking like a launch site. We only speculated Aravalli because it's the closest place they could have gotten to that would put them within striking distance of both Jaisalmer and the Indus Valley. Depending on what they've got hauling the launcher, they might have been able to cover more ground, in which case we have to consider this target area could be a little off.

"Wherever the hell Neshah plans to fire from, our theory is this—he's had his people plant these rumors about missile strikes to bait India and Pakistan into prepping for any option ranging from preemptive to retaliatory strikes. With everybody's finger close to the button, all he has to do is fire some Sabres near Jaisalmer and the Indus and he'll have both countries ready to go to the mat."

Kurtzman finished the scenario. "Pakistan and India self-destruct and Kashmir not only has its independence. It could also make a play to expand its borders while the dust is settling."

"This is worst-possible scenario," Wethers said. "To have things come to this is quite a stretch."

"You're probably right, but we can't afford to fiddle around and let Rome burn."

Wethers nodded. "Understood. Where do I fit in?"

"The communiqués that started this whole escalation," Brognola said. "What we have to do is trace them back as best we can and hopefully prove that they were sent out from the same source."

"Some hacker working for Neshah."

"I'd work on that presumption, yes," Brognola said.

"I've assembled most of the data already," Kurtzman said, "and I'm making some headway with it, but I think you can cut through some of the codes quicker than I can, which'll leave me more time to tend to any other fires that pop up."

"If we can come up with some kind of proof that Neshah planted those rumors trying to play Jack the Giant Killer," Brognola said, "then we can go to India and Pakistan and tell them to back off any plans for full engagement should the mujahideen get off a shot before we track them down."

"I'll certainly do the best I can," Wethers replied.

"Good." Brognola patted Wethers on the back. "I'm counting on you."

"Come on, I'll show you what we have so far," Kurtzman told Wethers, leading him back to his station. Brognola, meanwhile, stared at the large screen a moment longer. He could only hope there wouldn't come a time when Kurtzman had to start calling up graphics tallying body counts in what could well be the worst global bloodbath since World War II.

Carmen Delahunt was unwrapping the last chocolate PayDay bar in her wholesaler's twenty-pack when Brognola joined her.

"You're going to have peanuts sprouting out of your ears if you keep putting those away," Brognola joked quietly.

"I'm worried more about working them off at the gym before they go to my thighs," Delahunt responded between bites. Once she'd finished the candy bar, she took off her glasses and pinched the bridge of her nose, stifling a yawn.

"Once Akira comes back on, you're down for forty winks, okay?" Brognola told her. "I'll make it an order if I have to."

"Yeah, yeah. I just wanted to finish what I was doing while everything was still fresh in my mind, or what's left of it. I know this Briley woman's small potatoes compared to what's come up, but I managed to come up with a few new things on her."

"Good," Brognola said. "And, who knows, it could wind up being more important than you think. Especially if it turns out she's this woman they're looking for in that shooting in Bombay this morning."

"I sure hope so."

Delahunt had printed out most of the documentation she'd compiled on Brenda Reilly, but there were still a couple items up on the screen being run through search engines to fill in the still considerable blanks in her dossier.

"Remember how we were speculating that she must have made some kind of connection before she moved from Vegas to Washington?"

Brognola nodded. "She went from call girl to top-dollar escort."

"You'll have to explain to me what the difference is sometime, but if it has anything to do with making more money, that's what happened. And her benefactor?" Delahunt cued up a still photo obviously taken from a casino surveillance camera. It showed a dealer passing out cards to four players at a blackjack table. Two of the players had their backs turned to the camera, but the other two, a man and woman sitting two chairs away, were clearly visible.

"Briley and Dehri Neshah."

"In the flesh. It looks like she's the better player

of the two. He went bust drawing to twelve when the dealer was showing three. She stayed on fourteen. This was culled from footage at Caesar's Palace two and a half years ago, about a month before Briley split for Washington.''

"How the hell did you get your hands on that?"

Delahunt smiled. "You asked me to dig deep. I dug deep."

"You're amazing."

"Remember that when I hit you up for a Christmas bonus. This is all circumstantial, of course, but as you'll see here, they left together once Neshah went through all his chips.'' She called up another photo, taken a few minutes later than the earlier shot. Briley had slipped her arm through Neshah's and was laughing at something he'd said to her.

"I wonder how Neshah managed to get to Vegas without throwing up any red flags,'' Brognola wondered.

"I don't have anything on that, but there's any number of ways,'' Delahunt explained. "My guess is he used forged credentials and came in with a players' junket. They're usually all high rollers, so the casinos aren't likely to look too closely at anything but their bankrolls. They rake it in off these guys because once they start losing, they aren't going to hop back on the plane and fly halfway around the world back home.''

"Monte Carlo's a lot closer than Vegas,'' Brognola observed.

"Like I said, Neshah's not much of a gambler,'' Delahunt reminded him. "If you ask me, he takes Vegas over Monte Carlo because he's specifically recruiting somebody for Washington and figures he's better off going American. Or, to put it another way, Brenda Reilly fits the profile as far as the kind of woman her first john in Washington goes for.''

Delahunt switched from her Vegas file to a gallery of photos she'd put together of Briley out on the Washington social circuit. She'd come up with fourteen different shots covering the two-year period. In the first five photos, she was accompanied by the same man, a *GQ*-looking type in his midforties who in all but one of the shots was wearing a different tailored Armani suit.

''He looks familiar,'' Brognola said.

''Name's Martin Gerard,'' Carmen told him. ''He was with NSA for a few years, then came into some money and started up a think tank specializing in Eurasian socioeconomic studies. I sniffed through State Department records, and his passport's stamped heavily on the side of South Asia.''

''Pakistan and India,'' Brognola guessed.

''And Kashmir,'' Delahunt added. ''If you're Neshah, here's a guy whose brain you'd like to pick.''

''So he had Briley pick it for him,'' Brognola said.

''It fits. They were together on and off seven months. Time for a lot of pillow talk.''

''You said Gerard was with NSA before he went private,'' Brognola said.

''Yep. Seven years.''

''What area?''

''I think it was communications.'' Delahunt switched screens, highlighting the pre-think-tank portion of Gerard's résumé. "Yeah. Looks like mostly SIG-INTEL work."

"Encryption," Brognola murmured to himself.

"What's that?"

"Can you sidebar the Gerard material and do a file transfer over to Hunt?" Brognola asked. "I think he might be able to get something out of it."

"Not a problem but let me finish first."

"There's more?"

"Hey, I'm like those monsoons," Delahunt wise-cracked. "When it rains it pours."

"Rain away," Brognola told her.

"It's the six-month gap between Washington and when Briley wound up in London. Turns out she made a little side trip to India. A place called Pune. Seems she'd done such a good job in Washington that Neshah had decided to indulge her." Delahunt uploaded a video player on the computer and loaded a file into it. "Look at this."

Brognola eyed the monitor. Briley, dressed to look like a cross between Wonder Woman and a domina-trix, stood before a clapboard being held by a stage-hand. Written on the chalkboard was a film title: *Spy Lass*, as well as the name of the film's director and producer. The latter name jumped out at Brognola.

"Abdul Jahan," he said. "The guy she winds up clubbing around with in London."

"The same. Apparently, Briley wanted to try her hand at acting and… Well, judge for yourself."

Onscreen, the clapboard sounded and was pulled away, at which point Briley proceeded to deliver the worst example of bad acting Brognola had seen. Trying to speak her lines in phonetic Hindi, Briley sounded as if she were reading the back of a cereal box with a mouthful of Rice Krispies. Brognola got the idea that she was supposed to be in the process of seducing someone, but her movements were stiff and herky-jerky; she looked more as if she were flashing hand signals from the deck of a Coast Guard cruiser.

"Ouch," Brognola said.

"The worst part is she got the gig," Delahunt said.

"I think I'm beginning to understand why they call it Bollywood."

"Amen. Anyway," the woman went on to explain, "the film was only supposed to be a quickie—you know, one of those straight-to-video numbers—but it wound up taking six months."

"Because her acting was so bad?"

"That, plus the fact she was sleeping with the producer."

"Jahan?"

Delahunt nodded. "It turned up in the India cinema magazines. Jahan's a notorious womanizer, and he's got a reputation for taking his female stars a little more under his wing than most."

"Funny," Brognola said, "I was under the impression Neshah was doing the same thing. I mean, why else would she have been in on his getaway from Kottayam?"

"I can't help you on that one, chief," Delahunt said. "Maybe Neshah was just an employer and didn't care about her personal life."

"Then why'd he bother playing Svengali and put her in the movies?"

Delahunt shrugged. "I don't think I'm going to be able to find out the answer to that one in cyberspace, either."

"Of course, you're right," Brognola said. "What happened with the movie?"

"It's supposedly in postproduction, but I'll bet you anything it winds up getting shelved indefinitely. This Jahan guy's already moved on to other projects. I've got him down with eighteen different movies in the pipeline. Eighteen. My favorite is *Moon over Mars*. About a computer geek who invents a time tunnel and winds up on a lunar colony under attack by Martians."

"I bet he kicks ass and gets the girl," Brognola said.

"Without a doubt."

"At this point, I'd love it if this whole showdown between India and Pakistan turned out to be just another of Jahan's harebrained fantasies."

"Wouldn't that be nice? Look, I figure I've got another few minutes to pull everything together, then I'll run off a hard copy for you to look over while I catch those forty winks."

Brognola didn't respond. Delahunt glanced up and saw him looking across the room at the main computer screen.

"Hal?"

Brognola turned to her. "Do me a favor, would you? Before you go on break, could you go over all the production info on the films Jahan's doing?"

"It'll cost you a box of PayDays," Delahunt bartered.

"Done," Brognola said.

"What am I looking for?" she asked.

"I want to know if Jahan's filming on vacation anywhere in Rajasthan."

CHAPTER TWENTY

Bombay, India

"Abdul, this is incredible!" Briley exclaimed.

Abdul Jahan smiled modestly. "My men just followed the designs and specifications you sent us."

"Along with the money," Briley reminded the producer with a smile.

"Please, I am a filmmaker," Jahan said. "I never discuss money. That is why God created the accountant."

They shared a familiar laugh as they circled the large, futuristic-looking space tank taking up the better half of the work space. A crew of prop masters was busy finishing a few final touches: painting the tank's foam cannon a gunmetal blue, applying decals to give the impression that the weapon was part of India's moon colony arsenal in the year 2555, and adjusting the central hinges that allowed the would-be vehicle to be split in half for easy transport and reassembly on location. Though in reality little more than a shell of plastic and fiberglass, once mounted over a Hummvee framework and filmed in the right light, it would pass for the difference between life and death for the colonists under assault by the deadly forces of Martian warmonger Zogg-7.

Or so Jahan had been led to believe.

Paid the outrageous equivalent of eleven million dollars to be the hands-off producer of *Moon over Mars,* Jahan's involvement in the film had been negligible. He'd laughed over the script, provided the props and costumes and used his clout to secure use of various film sites. Other than that, he'd turned a blind eye to the venture, figuring it was yet another mad whim of the man he knew as Kumar Boze, the supposed computer-chip recluse who'd thrown away his money on *Spy Lass.* Meanwhile, he'd funneled his fee into projects closer to his heart. It never crossed his mind that Kumar Boze was an alias for Dehri Neshah and that the lunar space tank he'd built to such demanding specifications would be fitted over, not a Hummer, but rather a Sabre missile launcher presently cloistered in the hold of an eight-wheel semitruck bound for the film's location in the Thar Desert twenty miles north of Jodhpur.

"You'll still be able to get this to us by this afternoon?" Briley asked Jahan. "Our first day of shooting is tomorrow, and we don't want to wind up behind schedule coming out of the starting gates."

"I've made all my deadlines so far, haven't I?" Jahan said.

"For this film, yes," Briley repeated. "I'm still waiting to hear about a release date for *Spy Lass.*"

Jahan sighed and held his hands out in a gesture of resignation. "What can I say? Sometimes great art must evolve at its own pace."

Briley laughed. "You are such a liar. That movie will never see the light of day, and we both know it."

"One never knows." Jahan eyed Briley intently. After arriving at the studio, she'd mentioned how drenched she was, and Jahan had suggested she shower in one of the changing rooms and help herself to something from wardrobe before their meeting. She'd chosen a low-cut red sequin cocktail dress with a slit skirt and black high heels—the only things that fit her, or so she'd claimed. With a fresh application of makeup and her damp hair pulled up in a knot skewered by long wooden pins, she looked like a high-priced hooker ready to hit the executive lounge at the nearest Hilton. And she knew it. To her own amazement, despite everything that was going on around her, every since hearing Jahan's voice on the phone, Briley's one thought had been getting alone with him and rekindling the passion between them. Dehri wouldn't have to know.

"Perhaps we could negotiate a release date," she suggested coyly, returning the Indian's stare with one every bit as brazen.

"What would Kumar have to say about that?" Abdul inquired.

"I told you, he's been detained elsewhere. He won't be coming."

"How unfortunate."

"One man's misfortune is another's paradise," Briley said. She reached out and dragged a fingernail across the producer's arm. Jahan, who'd gotten his start in the Indian film industry as a leading man, was still a handsome figure, with a well-sculpted physique he maintained through daily workouts with a personal trainer in a minigym adjacent to his office on the top floor of the converted textile mill.

Jahan took Briley's hand and kissed it, then told her, "Let us finish our business first."

"Bastard," Briley teased. She reached into her purse and withdrew the next payment due Jahan for his services. "It's a little wet," she said, handing him the check. "And I'm afraid it smells a little of fish."

"What's a little fish among friends?" Jahan took the check and put it into an envelope he found lying on the nearby workbench. "Besides, once the bank cashes it, it will smell like rupees."

Briley smiled and glanced back at the prop shell. "How do you plan to get that to the film site anyway?"

"Cargo plane," Jahan told her. "I promise, it will be in Jodhpur within the hour."

"Speaking of an hour," Briley said with a wink, "that's about how much free time I have on my hands."

Guiyn Plateau

JACK GRIMALDI SNIPPED off the tip to the plug he'd used on the punctured tire and stepped back to admire his handiwork. The Ghurka Thresher had withstood the brunt of the monsoon with minimal damage, and after transferring gas from the reserve fuel tank, Grimaldi figured they were good for a few hundred miles before needing a fill-up.

"Ready with that compressor?" he asked Kissinger.

"One way to find out."

They'd found the unit among the mujahideen's provisions in the caves, and though it had been partially submerged by the floodwaters, Kissinger had done a good job of drying the spark plug. When he tugged the crank star, the compressor rattled noisily to life, startling a pair of vultures perched above the cockpit. They took to the air, heading out over the desert.

"Good riddance," Grimaldi said. "Another minute of those ugly bastards sizing me up and I was going to let them have it."

"I had the same idea," Kissinger said, "only I was thinking more along the lines of roasting one on a spit. I'm starving."

"There's some grub back in the cave that might still be edible," Grimaldi suggested.

Kissinger shook his head. "I don't eat anything I can't recognize."

"Bull," Grimaldi taunted. "I've seen you scarf down your share of mystery meat back at the Farm."

Kissinger grinned. "Stew doesn't count."

The compressor nozzle was a poor fit on the plane tire's stem, but enough air found its way in to slowly inflate the flat. Grimaldi spit on his finger and rubbed the plug, looking for bubbles. There weren't any.

"Hot damn!" he exclaimed. "Now let's hope this sucker doesn't conk out before it finishes the job."

Kissinger said, "I'm going to check the laptop and see if Aaron's gotten back to us."

"Go for it," Grimaldi told him.

Moments after Kissinger climbed inside the cockpit, Bolan appeared, looking drained from his long climb up the side of the plateau.

"No luck?" Grimaldi called out.

Bolan shook his head. "The birds led me to a couple mujahideen, but there's no trace of Marris."

"It seemed like a long shot."

"Yeah." Bolan dropped tiredly to the ground and inspected his arm. He'd cleaned the bullet wound and dressed it with gauze from a first-aid kit inside the Thresher. It still hurt like hell, but there was no blood showing through the gauze, so he figured he'd get off with just another battle scar to add to all the others he'd collected over the years.

Grimaldi finally shut down the compressor, then snapped the inflated tire with his fingertip. It sounded like a ripe watermelon. "Music to my ears," he said.

Kissinger emerged from the cockpit, carrying the laptop.

"A couple of things," he reported. "Hunt tracked down the origin point for that bogus first-strike intel Aaron was talking about."

"That fast?"

"Well, Carmen lent a hand," Kissinger said. "She turned up some ex-NSA guy in Washington that our girl Briley had her hooks into when she was working D.C. Some guy named Gerard. Turns out he was ground floor on the Orion project and stationed here a few years figuring out code intercepts on both sides of the fence."

"What'd Briley do, blackmail him into going turncoat?"

"He's not the one," Kissinger said. "Hunt honed in on SIG-INTEL coming out of the cities Gerard was stationed at. Bingo, he finds out one of Gerard's old cronies is still working out of New Delhi. We're not sure how yet, but he managed to hack his way into both ISI and RAW's intercept systems.

"IB's on their way to take him in for questioning, but my guess is the mujahideen fed him the bogus info when they were in Delhi rigging that car bomb."

"And he waited for their signal to plant it on the grapevine," Bolan surmised.

"Adds up that way to me," Kissinger said. "I say things got put on hold when Neshah wound up in the slammer. They decided to go with their Kottayam option first, and when that didn't pan out, it was on to Plan B. Once they sprang Neshah and flew him here last night, it was all systems go."

"Got to hand it to our cyber guys," Grimaldi said. "Once again they earn their keep."

"As for where the Sabre might be right now," Kissinger went on, "it's a long story, but they're going with the theory that the mujahideen are using a film site in Rajasthan as a front for launching the missiles."

"A film site?" Grimaldi said. "Where'd they come up with that one?"

"Like I said, it's a long story," Kissinger said. "Something about Briley and a film producer."

"That woman gets around."

"She sure does," Kissinger said. "We've got a report she might've killed some woman in a fishing village a few miles from the parade site in Bombay."

"Is Neshah with her?"

"Don't know."

"Let's get back to this film-site business," Bolan said. "Do we have people moving in on that?"

"They're trying to, but there's a problem," Kissinger said.

Grimaldi snorted. "Gee, that's a first."

Kissinger went on. "This producer—I think his name is Jahan—has seven different movies filming in Rajasthan, and they're using a dozen different locations, scattered all over the place. India's sending out recon planes and NSA is repositioning Orion's SAT-CAMs so we can hopefully get a bird's-eye once they bring the launcher out into view."

"Do we have enough fuel to get to any of these sites?" Bolan asked.

Kissinger checked the computer. "Closest ones to here are just outside Jodhpur and some backwater place called Pachpadra. Pachpadra's about sixty miles closer."

Bolan thought it over and went with a hunch. "Let's try Jodhpur."

CHAPTER TWENTY-ONE

Bombay

From the Mahim train station, Dehri Neshah boarded a motorized trishaw for the short trip to Adbul Jahan's film-production facility. This was one of Bombay's worst pockets of abject poverty, surpassed only by the squalid conditions a few blocks away. Should Neshah manage to extend his sway as far south as Bombay, one of his first orders of business would be to rid the city of slums like this. He would have mass housing built across the water in New Bombay—small homes, yes, but with plumbing and electricity—and if the people were reluctant to move, he would force them, for their own good. And then he would level the whole area here, burning everything in sight to the ground if he had to, so that they could start from scratch, this time using some sort of enforced planning. People would be made to understand that they could not just swarm in like rats and make nests out of trash anywhere they pleased. Yes, they might resist at first, and perhaps he would have to initially rule with an iron hand, but Neshah was certain that once he'd rehabilitated the people—made them less willing to accept conditions like this—Bombay would be the better for it.

Less than ten blocks away, Neshah came upon just the sort of new community he was thinking about. The refurbished textile mill that housed Jahan Filmworks was surrounded on all sides by landscaped gardens and a ring of clean, modest apartments, each complex in turn having its own plot of land where children could play and tenants could grow crops. It hadn't always been like that. Ten years ago the mill had been surrounded by the same squalor as everywhere else in the area. But during the 1993 riots, when thousands died and the city burned in skirmishes between Hindus and Muslims, the slums Abdul Jahan had been forced to look down on were reduced to smoldering rubble. He'd bought the land, creating this island of new development. There were those who said Jahan had taken advantage of the riots and had the land torched by the same organized-crime bosses who'd financed most of his early films. Jahan denied it, of course, but Neshah suspected otherwise and had admired the Hindu's resourcefulness. Figuring the producer was a kindred spirit and potential ally, Neshah had arranged a meeting with Jahan several years ago, introducing himself as Kumar Boze and asking to invest in one of the man's next films. A friendship of sorts had been formed, and in exchange for continued funding Neshah had been granted a number of favors, most notably Briley's would-be film debut in *Spy Lass*. And, of course, now Jahan had been duped into providing a needed pretense that would allow the mujahideen to set up a

Sabre missile launcher in Rajasthan and, if all went well, trigger an outbreak of war between Pakistan and India.

When he reached the main entrance to the filmworks, Neshah—now wearing the plain white shirt and tan slacks that was his uniform of sorts while posing as Kumar Boze—presented a forged business card and said he wished to speak to Jahan. The Boze name was well-known around the facility and had already been cleared in conjunction with the meeting he'd missed earlier, so Neshah, as he'd hoped, was admitted without being searched and having to explain the Taisho pistol concealed in his fanny pack.

The main lobby was large, the floor laid with marble, skylights allowing bright light to shine down on the walls, where posters from all of Jahan's films were prominently displayed, framed in gold, with small signs boasting the impressive box-office numbers for each release. Neshah went to the receptionist's desk and introduced himself, again as Boze, saying he wanted to belatedly join the meeting his female associate was having with Abdul.

"I'm not sure where they are right now," the receptionist told Neshah, picking up the phone. "Let me check for you."

"Thank you."

Neshah walked away from the desk and pretended to admire one of the posters. Beneath his pleasant facade, however, Neshah was concerned, agitated. The boatman who was supposed to have brought Briley here from Nariman Point had reported that he'd been unable to find her when he showed up after the

monsoon. He'd assumed she'd ducked out of the rain
and waited on shore for her, only to learn there had
been a shooting not long before his arrival, during
which a female Koli fishmonger had been shot to
death by a white woman who'd subsequently fled the
scene. Neshah had learned all this while at the safehouse with Penghat Shili, plotting an attack on the
funeral parade for Ziarat Wal. He'd promptly called
the studio and had been told that Briley had indeed
shown up for the meeting and was currently with Jahan. When he'd asked to speak to Briley, they had
paged her, but for some reason, neither her nor Jahan
had responded. The operator had suggested that perhaps Briley and Jahan were out touring the back lot.
Neshah, however, had other suspicions. He'd quickly
finalized plans with Shili, then had given the man a
grateful embrace and sent him on his way so that he
could change and come directly to the studio.

"Abdul and I are just friends, nothing more." That
was the way she'd put it, and despite his reservations,
Neshah had believed her. Now, he felt he had been
right to have his doubts. Women—they couldn't be
trusted.

Neshah glanced back at the receptionist. She smiled
at him, phone to her ear. "Still trying," she said.

Neshah nodded, but his patience was wearing thin.
He took a cigarette from his fanny pack and blew
smoke as he paced the lobby. When the twin doors
leading to the ground-floor production facilities
opened, he turned and saw workmen wheeling out a
large cart filled with old props and a mobile wardrobe
rack filled with costumes. A man in a snug-fitting suit

was supervising the activity while at the same time talking with a reporter who frantically scribbled notes. From what Neshah could pick up of their conversation, the items were on their way to a charity auction for victims of the latest cholera epidemic north of the city.

As the workers headed out of the building to bring up a truck, the supervisor led the reporter across the lobby, where he pointed out several of the movie posters featuring some of the props and costumes that would be in the auction. Neshah glanced at the abandoned cart. Something caught his eye. He casually walked over and picked up a set of steel adamantine claws.

Neshah was admiring the craftsmanship that had gone into the making of the claws when the supervisor came up behind him.

"Mr. Boze," he said, extending a hand. "What a pleasure."

Neshah smiled and shook the man's hand, then drew his attention to the claws. "How much for these?" he asked.

"The auctioning was to start at twenty thousand rupees," the supervisor said. "But, of course, if you would like them, they are yours for the taking."

"Nonsense." Neshah went to his pockets and withdrew a money clip. He peeled off bills worth thirty thousand rupees and handed them to the other man. "For a good cause."

Neshah exchanged pleasantries with the supervisor until the workers returned. Then he excused himself, placing the claws in his fanny pack as he approached the desk again.

"I'm sorry," the receptionist apologized, "but I can't seem to reach them. Perhaps they left for lunch through the back way."

"I see." Neshah smiled at the woman. "Perhaps while I'm waiting I could have a look at some of the sets. I won't be a bother."

"Of course." The receptionist handed Neshah a visitor's tag and pointed out the doors behind her. "You know where they are. I'll keep trying to reach Mr. Jahan."

"Thank you," Neshah said.

He passed through the doors. It was like passing into another world. In contrast to the quietude of the lobby, the production hallways were abuzz with activity. The soundstages were all the way down the corridor, but Neshah had no real interest in looking at movie sets. He had other business on his mind. He milled around an alcove lined with vending machines, waiting for a moment when no one was looking. Then, with purposeful strides, he crossed the hall and entered a little-used stairwell. Up the steps he climbed, making his way to Abdul Jahan's office on the top floor.

SATED, THEIR PASSION spent, Briley and Jahan lay entwined on the couch across from his desk. Briley stroked the hair on Jahan's chest and smiled.

"I'm curious," she murmured. "How many women have you had on this couch?"

"None that rival you," Jahan replied, stroking her hair.

Briley laughed. "Always the silver-tongued devil!"

"You will notice I haven't asked how many men you've been with since we were last together."

Briley nuzzled her lips against the Indian's ear, whispering into it, "None that rival you."

Jahan's chuckle was interrupted by a sound overhead, a low rumble like thunder. With a curse, Jahan glanced at his Rolex watch. "My helicopter," he said. "Prompt as ever, damn them."

"Where are you going?"

"I need to check on the site for a film we're doing near Thane Creek," Jahan said, untangling himself gently from Briley's embrace and reaching for his slacks. "And after that I have to attend a charity auction. I want to see how much your outfit from *Spy Lass* will fetch."

"A costume from a movie no one has seen? Not much, I'd think."

"Ah, but can you imagine how many housewives will thrill at the thought of greeting their lovers dressed like that?" Jahan said. "Though, of course, no one could possibly fill it out as well as you."

"It's getting awfully thick in here." Briley snickered, grabbing her dress and undergarments off the floor. As she began to dress, she asked Jahan, "When do you think we'll see each other again?"

"That depends," Jahan said as he threw on his shirt. "As long as you're on Kumar's leash, I think it will be difficult."

"He doesn't own me," Briley insisted.

"So you say."

"We are involved on a lot of projects together at the moment," Briley said. "When that is over, I will be more able to come and go as I please. You'll see."

Overhead, the ceiling jostled slightly under the weight of the helicopter. Jahan slipped his feet into his sandals and finished buttoning his shirt, then moved close, running his hand along Briley's bare shoulder. "I'll count the days hungrily, but in the meantime, my empire awaits me."

They kissed briefly, then Jahan gathered his things and pressed a button next to a dumbwaiter dating back to the building's textile days. Jahan had had the interior enlarged and fitted with a tooled leather bench so that he could sit in comfort as he was whisked up to the heliport or down to the production facilities. He ducked into the opening and winked back at Briley as the doors closed.

"We all have our empires waiting for us," Briley whispered to herself as she finished dressing. She was stepping into her pumps when she heard a knock at the door. Thinking it must be one of Jahan's assistants, she threw the door open to tell them they'd just missed him. Instead, she found Neshah standing in the doorway.

"Dehri!" she gasped.

"Hello, my love," he said, smiling pleasantly. "I see you managed to make it here on your own."

"Yes, yes, I did," she stammered, her mind racing. How long had he been standing outside the door? How could she keep him from coming in? The couch was disheveled. He would know. Gathering her wits, she stepped forward and embraced him. "I'm so glad you made it," she said after kissing him. "How did it go with Penghat?"

"Well enough."

"Let me just get my purse and we can go."

"I'm in no hurry." Neshah gently pulled her arm away from him and strode past her into the office. There was nothing Briley could do to stop him. "Where is Abdul?"

Briley glanced up at the ceiling. She could still hear the helicopter idling on the roof. "He was called away," she said. "You know Abdul. There's always some crisis to attend to. I was just on my way out."

Neshah nodded. "Abdul is a busy man," he said.

Briley saw that he was staring at her dress. She quickly explained, "I had to change when I got here. The boat never came and I was caught in the monsoon on the way to the train station."

"A nice choice," Neshah said, still eyeing the dress. "Very...fetching."

"It was all they had available," Briley said.

"One of the straps is tangled," Neshah observed.

"Oh." Briley glanced at her dress. "You're right. It is." She straightened the strap. Her hand was trembling.

"How did you like the fishing village?" Neshah asked. "Quaint, yes?"

"I guess that's one way of putting it."

"And the people there," Neshah went on. "Very friendly."

Briley stared at Neshah. "You heard."

"Heard what, my love?"

"The shooting. I was attacked by a group of women. One of them had a knife."

"That's not the way they're telling it."

"It's the truth," Briley said.

Neshah ignored her. "The way they're telling it around the village, the woman was shot for no reason. Or perhaps it was because she was one of the unwashed masses. I know how much they repel you."

"It wasn't like that!" Briley said. "I'm telling you, I was attacked! They threw water on me, tried to steal my purse. And the woman with the knife—"

"Fine," Neshah interrupted. "If that's what you want me to believe, I will."

"Why would I lie to you?"

Neshah laughed. "You're right, of course. You being such a woman of your word, I have no right to be suspicious. Forgive me, please."

"Why are you acting like this?"

"I don't understand."

"You know what I mean. The way you're accusing me."

"I haven't accused you of anything." Neshah went over to the couch, humming to himself as he straightened the cushions. "You'd think a man like Abdul would keep his office presentable, or at least have someone do it for him."

"He was napping when I arrived," Briley lied. "He said he was up all night making sure the tank was ready for delivery on schedule."

"And…?"

"He's having it flown out to Jodhpur," Briley told

him, seeing some hope now that she'd steered the subject from Abdul to the mission in Rajasthan. "It may already be there."

"Very nice."

Briley wanted to get away from the office, the sooner the better. "I'm starving," she said. "My stomach's settled. Why don't you take me out to lunch and let me try some of those foods you were showing me at the beach?"

Neshah didn't answer at first. He glanced around the office, filled with film memorabilia and a few objets d'arts. He picked up a large ceramic vase resting on its own stand under a fixed ceiling light. It was a present from Neshah to Jahan, a token of appreciation prior to the first day of shooting for *Spy Lass*. Neshah had bought it at an art gallery down the block from Chor Bazaar. He couldn't remember the price, but he remembered it was roughly the same as he'd paid for the Bentley Briley had at her disposal to use while she was in London. Neshah looked at it briefly, then turned to Briley. When he saw that he had her attention, he held the vase out, then let go of it, letting it crash into shards on the floor. Briley flinched, startled.

"Why did you do that?" Briley asked.

"I never claimed to own you," Neshah told her.

Briley's blood froze. My God, he knew. He'd heard them.

"And I wasn't aware that I kept you on a leash," Neshah went on. "I was more than happy to look the other way when you were with other men. I understand you have your needs. All I asked was that it be with strangers, men whose eyes I would not have to look into afterward. A simple request, easy enough to honor.''

"I can explain," Briley said.

"But Abdul?" Neshah went on, ignoring her. "Abdul is another matter. We are friends. I do not care to look into the eyes of my friends and know they have been with my woman. That is crossing the line."

"It wasn't anything like that!" Briley pleaded. "You have to believe me."

"Believe you?" Neshah grinned savagely. "What is that saying you Americans have? 'Fool me once, shame on you. Fool me twice, shame on me.'"

"Dehri! Listen to me!" Briley said. "He forced himself on me! He lured me up here and then he—"

"I heard laughter between you!" Neshah shouted back at her. "Laughter! Laughter and talk about when you could do it again! Forced himself on you? I don't think so."

"Please, Dehri. Give me a chance..."

"Dirt!" Neshah spit at Briley's feet. "That's what you are to me! Dirt! And to think I cared for you!"

He turned his back to her and strode to the window overlooking the back lot. Briley stared at him, shaking. She had seen Dehri angry before, but nothing like this. She knew there were many things he couldn't tolerate, and above all the others, he couldn't tolerate betrayal.

Briley glanced down at her purse. The derringer, she thought. If she used the derringer on him, she could flee to the roof. The helicopter was still there. She could throw herself at Abdul's mercy.

"Briley?"

She glanced up. Though he'd spoken to her, Neshah was still looking out the window. "Do you love me?" he asked.

Briley was taken aback. She didn't know what to say. She fumbled with her purse.

"Do you?" Neshah asked again, his back still to her. His voice was quiet.

Briley's hand slipped inside the purse, fingers closing around the small gun. "Yes," she called out to him. "I've been trying to tell you that."

"Then perhaps we can work things out," he said.

"I'd like that," Briley agreed.

"Come here. Let me hold you."

Briley hesitated, then stepped toward Neshah, keeping her hand inside the purse, derringer at the ready. With her other hand, she reached out and tenderly touched the back of Neshah's neck. The tension seemed to go out of his back. He started to turn toward her.

"I'm so sorry I hurt you," she told him.

Neshah faced her. His expression seemed tranquil. He was doing his best to smile. "It's all right," he told her. "I know it won't happen again."

Briley nodded, relieved. She let go of the derringer and drew her arms around Neshah. Maybe they would get through this after all. "I promise," she told him.

They kissed, then Neshah drew her closer into his embrace. Briley looked over his shoulder and saw her reflection in the glass. She hadn't realized how badly her lipstick was smeared from her time with Abdul. She was reaching up to wipe a smudge from her cheek when she felt a sudden burning, stabbing sensation in her sides. Letting out a cry of pain, she tried to pull away from Neshah, but he continued to hold her close. The pain increased and it became difficult for her to breathe. Finally, she felt herself getting dizzy and light-headed. Her legs gave out beneath her and she sagged against Neshah.

"I will hear no more lies from you," he whispered in her ear. "Never again…"

Neshah eased his grip on Briley. She fell away from him, blood coursing down her legs, her dress clinging to her in tatters. As life fled from her eyes, the last thing she saw were Neshah's hands dangling above her, blood dripping from the razor-sharp talons with which he had dug his fingers into her.

"YES, I KNOW!" Abdul Jahan barked into the cell phone so that he could be heard over the sound of his helicopter. "I have no idea what it's about, but I certainly aim to find out!"

Jahan clicked off the phone and unfastened his seat belt, telling the chopper pilot, "Keep it running! I'll be right back!"

The heliport straddled two ridges of the textile mill's roof, which was made up of glass triangles to better let light into the upper floors, where Jahan's production staff had their offices. The elevator shaft for his private dumbwaiter rose up like a chimney next to the heliport, but before he climbed in, he put through a hurried call to his production manager.

"Look, I don't know what's going on out there," he said once he had the other man on the line, "but we've got military planes and helicopters flying all over the place above our sites in Rajasthan. They're making so much noise we can't film!''

"Why Rajasthan?" the manager wondered.

"I just told you, I don't know!" Jahan snapped. "I've been trying to get off the ground to Thane Creek but my phone won't stop ringing! And it's not just aircraft! We've got troops roaming around the set in Sikan turning everything topsy-turvy!"

"What are they looking for?"

"Are you deaf?" Jahan roared. "I don't have answers. Answers are what I'm looking for! I want you to get on the phone and start making calls. Get the film commissioner first, and if that doesn't work, try the military or whatever else you have to. Every hour that goes by with our cameramen standing by picking their noses is money out of our pockets!"

"You'll be at Thane Creek if I come up with anything?"

"Yes," Jahan said. "I forgot the shooting script back at my office, but once I pick it up, we'll be on our way."

The production manager promised to start looking into matters immediately. Jahan warned him to get results or any more cost overruns caused by shooting delays would be coming out of his pocket. As he hung up the phone and got into the dumbwaiter, Jahan deliberated whether to call the prime minister. He had the man's private number, but given the funeral parade and the visit by the American President, Jahan doubted it would be a good time, even if he managed to get through.

Jahan fumed to himself as he rode down to his office. Why did this have to happen to him? This day, of all days. Five minutes ago he'd been feeling on top of the world—five minutes after being on top of Briley—and he'd hoped to at least be able to savor the moment. But, no, he had to deal with the military harassing his film sites. What was with them? Were they trying to disrupt things so he'd have to pay them off to get out of his way? He wouldn't put it past them. As far as he was concerned, the only thing in India more corrupt than the politicians were the generals. Bribes for this, bribes for that…who needed it?

When the dumbwaiter's doors opened and he stepped into his office, Abdul Jahan was suddenly no longer concerned about graft and disrupted filming schedules. The first sense he had that something was terribly amiss was the sight of his prize vase lying in shards on the floor.

"What the devil?" He scrambled out of the dumbwaiter, then crouched over the broken pieces and tried to put two of them together. He quickly realized it was a hopeless task; the vase was ruined. What had happened? Had Briley taken offense to something he'd said and thrown one of her tantrums? If so, he'd have to teach her a little more respect. Or maybe it was vibration from the heliport. Looking up, he could see the ceiling shaking slightly. He would have to tend to that.

He was still glancing upward when he detected movement out of the corner of his eye. He slowly turned and let out a gasp.

Ten yards away, before the window, Neshah—the

man he knew as Kumar Boze—was hunched over Briley…or at least Jahan thought it was Briley. There was so much blood it was hard to tell. When Neshah glanced up at him, Jahan shrank back in horror. All around his mouth, Neshah's face was smeared with blood, and when he raised his arms, Jahan saw that he was wearing the metallic claws from *Ghost of Shivaji*; they dripped, not only with blood, but also entrails.

Fighting back a wave of nausea, Jahan staggered toward his desk, reaching for the intercom. Before he could get to it, however, Neshah was upon him, his right arm a sweeping blur. Jahan wailed as the weapon ripped into his arm with so much force that his hand was nearly severed from his wrist. With his other hand, Neshah took a swipe at Janan's face, shredding it in five different places and taking out one of his eyes.

"Let us see how attractive the women find you now, Abdul," Neshah growled, shoving Jahan back onto the couch. "Let us see how many of them will want to come lie beside you when you look like this!"

Jahan was barely alive, in no position to defend himself, but Neshah wasn't finished. He raised his talons one last time, then buried them in the filmmaker's groin. There he left them, unstrapping them from his fingers and pulling his hands away.

Neshah looked back and forth at his two victims for a moment, then he moved swiftly to the dumbwaiter. He climbed in and pressed for it to go up. By the time he reached the heliport, he had his pistol out.

He aimed it at the pilot as he climbed into the passenger seat of the chopper.

"Take it up!" he commanded.

The sight of the gun and Neshah's bloody countenance was all the convincing the pilot needed. He jockeyed the controls and lifted the chopper up into the air.

Staring out his window, Neshah saw a handful of military jeeps pulling into the back lot. Soldiers poured out and began to rush toward the building. But, Neshah reflected triumphantly, they would be too late.

"Where are we going?" the pilot asked, his voice tinged with fear.

"To Jodhpur."

CHAPTER TWENTY-TWO

Bombay

Penghat Shili knew the reason they had chosen Marine Drive for the parade route. To have sent the President and prime minister through the middle of the city would have subjected them to potential assassins on both sides of whichever street they traveled down. By contrast, from Nariman Point to Malabar Hill, Marine Drive, for the most part, hugged the shoreline of Back Bay, cutting in two the land area that security forces would have to watch over. Granted, there were people on the beach, but there were far fewer than the tens of thousands who crammed the other side of the street. Also, those on the beach were out in the open and easy to monitor, especially from the air or out in the dozen or more military boats moored in the bay. On the beach there were no multistory buildings, rooftops, or towers to provide cover for lurking snipers.

And yet, it was at Chowpatty Beach that Shili and ten of his fellow mujahideen planned to stage their attack on the caravan as it passed by en route to the Towers of Silence.

Getting there hadn't been easy. There had been checkpoints where anyone wishing to view the parade from the beach had been walked through metal detectors and, if deemed necessary, frisked for weapons. Shili and the others had outwitted the authorities using the same ploy by which Nhajsib Wal had created a diversion during the early stages of the siege in Kottayam: they had paid children to throw firecrackers on the ground twenty yards away from several of the checkpoints, and during the ensuing chaos— which in nearly every case drew soldiers and inspectors away from their posts—the mujahideen, dressed in the ragamuffin attire of street performers, had slipped past the metal detectors and quickly disappeared into the throngs already cleared to go to the beach. The ploy's success had been particularly gratifying to Shili, as it would mean Nhajsib Wal had provided an unwitting assist to his own execution as well as that of his beloved prime minister and the American President.

They'd crossed Marine Drive just west of where it officially changed names and became Walukehwar Road. And as they'd crossed the street, each of the men had strategically dropped what most certainly would pass for an innocent wad of chewing gum. The pliant substance, however, wasn't gum at all but rather high-grade C-5 plastique, each piece embedded with a remote-detonation sensor no larger than a thumbtack. Separately, the charges, when activated, would give off only the weakest explosions, capable, at best, of crippling anyone walking nearby or disabling the drive train of any vehicle passing over it.

Triggered simultaneously, the explosives would not only do considerably more damage, but they would also force the parade to an abrupt halt, making each vehicle a stationary, rather than moving target for the follow-up barrage, which the men would be launching from the beach.

As the fanfare of a marching band announced the beginning of the parade, five of the Kashmiris spread out among the other celebrants, each of them carrying with them Chinese-manufactured F-44 spigot mortars. No larger than coffee cups, the mortars, encased in shield cowls, could be pulled out and readied for firing in a matter of seconds, and each came equipped with focal lenses, viewing apertures and calibrated adjustment arcs to insure accuracy far greater than one would expect from so small a weapon. The shells they fired were filled with both explosives and frag scraps that, within a ten-yard radius, would likely maim anyone they didn't kill outright.

As for Shili and the others, they took up their positions around the catapult Neshah had watched heave children into the bay earlier that morning. When he'd spoken with the children who'd come to him begging for donations, Neshah had paid them ten thousand rupees—a week's wages for their entire family—to let some of his friends come by later to use the catapult. For some tricks, he'd told him.

Now that they were here, Shili had paid the family the same sum to remain nearby during their ''performance,'' the better to give the impression that the mujahideen were part of an extended family, thereby decreasing the chance they would draw scrutiny from

the shore police and security forces out in the bay.
The family was more than happy to play along. After
all, most of the effigies of Ganesh had either already
sunk out in the bay or been claimed by souvenir hunt-
ers, not to mention the fact that everyone was now
more interested in the parade than sideshow theatrics.

Be that as it may, Shili felt it was important that
he and his men maintain their cover as street performers, and so perform he did. It had been years since he
had done most of the routines that had made the Shili
brothers a crowd favorite back home in Kashmir, but
the instincts were still there, and as long as he didn't
get carried away, he knew he could competently pass
himself off as a practicing gymnast and acrobat. He
juggled, did handstands and, with his fellow mujahideen holding a thick rope taut between them, he even
got up and did the easier portions of his old high-wire
act, balancing himself as he walked, lay and even
danced five feet above the sand. He performed in trib-
ute to his slain brothers, Raghubir and Vargadrum;
perhaps, he thought, he could earn their forgiveness
if, in carrying on in their behalf, he could use the
ways of the circus to meet the ends of the mujahideen.

All the while Shili was performing, two of the other
Kashmiris gradually turned the catapult so that it was
aimed at the street rather than the bay, all the while
laughing and gesturing at the children, as if to show
them that they could climb up on to the apparatus to
get a better view of the parade when it came by.
Though they drew a few curious stares from the shore
police, the authorities had been given no reason to

suspect foul play was in the making and they left the mujahideen alone.

It took the parade nearly twenty minutes to wend its way around the bay. The funeral music of the marching band grew louder and closer, as did the cheering of the crowd. All along the beach, people moved away from the water, elbowing one another as they vied for a view of the street. The five mujahideen with the spigot mortars stayed toward the rear of the crowd. At the right moment, they would take several steps back so that no one was near them. Then, once they'd detonated the plastique in the street and the parade was brought to a halt, they figured they would have ten, maybe fifteen seconds to break out the mortars, line up their sights and fire. They knew it was possible some of them would be spotted, even gunned down before they could launch their volleys, but if even two of them managed to get off a decent shot, it could likely be enough. Besides, there was a still larger payload likely to be added to their assault. The one Penghat Shili himself would deliver by way of the catapult.

UNDER ANY OTHER circumstances, Nhajsib Wal most likely would have been as excited as he was proud to be there, riding in the same open-air car as the prime minister and the President of the United States, the eyes of a hundred thousand of his fellow Indians upon him, their cheers honoring the man who lay in the hearse before him, Uncle Ziarat.

But Nhajsib felt removed from it all, almost as if he were outside himself, watching from a distance. It all seemed unreal to him. All this celebration, this sense that India was congratulating itself for having triumphed over Kashmiri insurgency. If these people only knew the real situation, that as they gawked and waved and shouted their rallying cries and sang their praises, the surviving mujahideen were out there, still conspiring, perhaps even on the verge of wreaking far greater chaos than they would have if they'd succeeded in Kottayam. How could the President and prime minister sit back there, acknowledging the crowd while trying to maintain the solemnity of the occasion, knowing that they were deliberately misleading everyone, playing along with the popular delusion that the cause of Kashmiri separatism had been squashed, leaving one less obstacle on the road to peace in South Asia? That they justified the facade in the name of maintaining order wasn't enough for Wal. Better to be up front, he thought, to err on the other side of caution. To him, the risk posed by the surviving mujahideen was far greater than the notion that the truth would lead to a widespread panic. This was India, after all, the land of *bindaas,* the ability to shrug off misfortune and move on with one's life. Muslims and Hindus might go for each other's throats in a heated moment, but run screaming into the streets at the thought of terrorists striking close to home? He didn't think so.

Gazing in the side mirror, Wal could see his relatives in the car behind him. Only Aunt Nur bore any sort of look approaching grief; the others were waving back to the crowd, and though they weren't smiling, from the glow on their faces and the sparkle in their eyes it was clear they were loving every minute of this.

The caravan had just rounded the bend near Chowpatty Beach when, less than fifty yards ahead of the car Wal was riding in, the street suddenly erupted in a series of small explosions. Just as quickly, the world around him began to move as if in slow motion and he was able to take in a dozen things at once: two members of the marching band pitching sideways to the ground, instruments flying from their hands; chunks of asphalt leaping from the street into the crowd; horrified faces, mouths hanging open in terror; his car and the hearse in front of him slowing to a stop; armed soldiers and Secret Service agents drawing their weapons and looking in all directions, trying to figure out what was happening.

The next thing he knew, Wal was on his feet, scrambling over his seat into the back of the convertible. The President and prime minister both looked numb, incredulous.

"Down!" he shouted, reaching out to both men and grabbing them by the shoulder. At his urging they bent over and he laid himself across them. Within seconds, three others, two Secret Service and one IB field agent, were on top of him, creating a human shield over the two leaders.

Moments later there was another blast, this one directly behind them, followed by screams. Wal peered through the web of limbs engulfing him and saw that the car his relatives were riding in had been hit by some kind of explosive. The hood had been blown off, and there was nothing left of the front windshield.

The driver was slumped over the shattered steering wheel, a portion of his skull missing. Beside him, Wal's aunt was halfway out of the car, blood spewing from the stump where her right arm had once been; she wasn't moving. He could see only one of his uncles, Arvad, in the back seat, his skull crimson. He was staring down at the seats where the others had been sitting, calling his other brother by name. It looked to Wal as if Uncle Donai had to have slumped from view and that Arvad was shaking him, trying to get some response. Two soldiers soon approached and bounded onto the trunk, yelling for him to get down.

On the heels of this, yet a third blast ripped through the air to Wal's right. Pinned down as he was, he couldn't tell where it had struck, but the chorus of shrieks and wails and cries of pain told him that this time the crowd itself had been rent by an explosion.

"What's happening?" Wal heard the President cry out beneath him. It wasn't a question so much as a mantra, the only words the man could spit out in his state of shock. "What's happening?" he repeated.

BY THE TIME the mujahideen had triggered the first explosions on Marine Drive, the children had climbed down from the catapult and run into the crowd, more interested in getting close to the parade route than being able to see it. In their place, Penghat Shili had climbed up onto the end of the swing arm. With him he had taken a flat packet the size of a seat cushion, divided by five different elongated pockets. At various times during his performances, the other mujahideen had carefully removed strips of C-5 plastique strapped to their shins and fit them into the pockets, readying a combined charge that would pack more explosive force than all of the other charges and mortar shells combined.

Dehri Neshah's plan had been to have the packet folded into a ball and hurled by catapult in the direction of the convertible carrying the President and prime minister. His feeling had been that God would help guide the bomb to its mark. At the time, Shili had agreed that it was a good plan, but secretly he'd decided that God might appreciate a helping hand. Now, as bedlam reigned over the parade in the wake of the smaller blasts, Shili was ready to deal the decisive blow.

He'd already discussed with his men in detail how it was to go down. Two of them would hold the catapult secure while another two racheted back the swing arm with him perched on the cradle. Then, on his signal, the catapult would be sprung. When performing with his brothers back in Kashmir, Penghat Shili had been known as the Human Artillery thanks to a routine in which he was shot through the air from a modified cannon, landing in a large circus net. This, he figured, was but a variation of a stunt he was a master at. Once propelled through the air, clutching the makeshift bomb to his chest, he felt he could time the release and even direct its fall so that, as he passed over the parade, he could increase the chances that the President and prime minister—and hopefully the nephew of his brother's slayer—would bear the brunt of the explosion, If need be, Shili was prepared to keep a hold on the plastique and, like a Japanese kamikaze, plummet with it toward the leaders' vehicle. It would be a glorious death, and afterward he would rejoin his brothers in the other world and they would have a good laugh over the whole thing.

He was about to signal his men when gunfire sounded along the beach. He looked over his shoulder and saw that the shore police had drawn their weapons and fired at the mujahideen who had yet to unleash their mortar rounds. Two of the Kashmiris dropped to the sand, mortars tumbling to the ground beside them, unfired. Another whirled and aimed his mortar at the police, getting off a shot even as bullets were ripping through him. His shell flew wide of the mark, landing in the shallow water of the bay before exploding.

"Now!" Shili yelled to the men surrounding the catapult. "Now!"

As planned, the catapult was held secure while he was lowered into firing position. However, he'd only been ratcheted halfway down when more gunfire—this time from one of the military boats out in the bay—whistled his way. He grimaced as he felt a slug rip into his leg. Around him, the other four mujahideen fared even worse, all taking direct hits, not only from the boat, but also the shore police, who now had joined in the fusillade.

Desperate to carry out his mission, Shili twisted about in the cradle and tried to reach the catapult's trigger on his own. In doing so, however, he leaned his chest against the framework, nudging the detonator switch to the bomb pack. Realizing what he'd done, he tried to pull himself back, but it was too late.

With a deafening roar, the explosives clutched to his chest detonated.

THEY WERE TAKING down the command post near the Towers of Silence so that they could move the men closer to Chowpatty Beach to sort through the carnage. The toll so far was forty-six dead, including the ten mujahideen killed on the beach. Injuries ran in the thousands, mostly shrapnel wounds. Marine Drive was closed off, and additional troops had been called in to cordon off the parade route while bomb squads scoured for undetonated explosives. The crowd had been dispersed, with Kamala Nehru Park set up as a way station for those who'd been separated from loved ones during the course of the mayhem. As for Dehri Neshah, the word was that he had been nearly captured at Abdul Jahan's film studio after slaying both Jahan and the woman who'd aided in his escape from Kottayam. It was presumed he was on his way to rendezvous with whatever of his force remained with the second Sabre missile launcher. On that front, inspections at several film sites in Rajasthan had turned up nothing; the search was still on.

Nhajsib Wal was within hearing distance of the command post, but he had tuned out the updates. His focus was on the nearest tower, where his uncle's deposition had been carried out only a few moments before. There had been the suggestion that Wal's other family members be laid out at the same time, but he'd refused. They would have their own service at another time; he wasn't ready just yet to say when.

Behind Wal, the pavilion was empty, as were most

of the folding chairs set out in the adjacent park. With all that had happened, attending Ziarat Wal's service had become a low priority for most and deemed a security risk for the President and prime minister, who had been put aboard one of the surveillance helicopters and spirited away to safer ground. Their planned eulogies would no doubt be delivered later, far from the Tombs of Silence.

Not that Wal minded. His uncle, after all, had been a very private man and would probably have disapproved of all the attention. This way was fine. A favorite nephew bidding farewell to his favorite uncle. Nice and simple.

For the ceremony, Wal had brought along two items, both from the *kalaripayattu* hall back at the academy in Kottayam. He stared at them thoughtfully: the portrait of Ziarat Wal in his military regalia after the liberation of Bangladesh and the painting of him sitting beside his young nephew, who, all those years ago, looked out at the world with an eager confidence.

The sound of flapping wings drew Wal's attention from the portraits to the clear blue sky above the tower. The vultures were on their way. To Wal, they looked small.

CHAPTER TWENTY-THREE

Thar Desert, North of Jodhpur

From the moment orders had gone out to begin searching Abdul Jahan's film sites in Rajasthan, the maddening shell game had been at the mercy of the weather. For all their sophistication, the Orion spy satellite and India's various orbiting UAVs were of limited use when it came to peering through monsoons. Similarly, a collaborative field force made up of the Indian military, IB, CIA, Secret Service and Rajasthan National Guard had given deference to the storm in determining which sites they would first take a crack at. They'd begun in the eastern part of the state, ahead of the storm, coming up empty at sites in Churna, Sikar, Jaipur and Bikaner. To the west, another contingent had hunkered down as the torrents passed overhead. The mujahideen, meanwhile had found the monsoon to be their saving grace, as the staging locale for *Moon over Mars* was located midstate, and other than aerial surveillance by recon planes, the authorities had yet to take their ground search to Jodhpur.

Twenty miles north of the former capital, a 5.8-

acre tract of the Thar Desert had been converted to a lunar landscape, mostly by way of prefab whirlpool tubs embedded in the sand and then partially filled with sand and layered with taupe plaster until they could pass for moon craters. A Quonset hut was dressed up to pass for the main base of the moon colony, and the colonists' main form of ground transportation were low-slung, unarmed Desert Patrol Vehicles painted the same metallic silver as the hut. The DPVs had been bought at a military auction, along with the handful of rust-colored U.S. LVTP-7 Amphibious Tractors representing the formidable Martian invasion force.

As was common in moviemaking, scenes had been scheduled to be filmed out of sequence, and the first day's footage would actually appear at the end of the picture—given, of course, the mistaken assumption that the mujahideen had any interest in adhering to the dummied-up production schedule once they'd used the site to mask their release of the Sabre warheads.

There were nearly sixty extras on the set suited up as warring factions. It was easy enough to tell who was who. The "Martians" wore crimson-dyed ghillie sniper suits, jackets and helmets covered with tattered material so that they looked like a cross between mountain yaks and devils sporting dreadlocks. Opposing them were the noble colonists, sweltering inside their surplus World War II SOE jumpsuits. There'd been a problem getting the silver spray paint to stick to the fabric of both the suits and helmets, and through the camera viewfinders it looked as if their outfits were made of aluminum foil. Of the sixty men, less than half were mujahideen. The rest were bona fide extras, plucked from the streets of Jodhpur during an impromptu casting call during which prospective actors were briefly interviewed to weed out anyone of passing intelligence. The mujahideen wanted dullards, men who wouldn't ask too many questions as they were moved around the sand like chess pawns to give the impression a battle scene was being choreographed for cinematic posterity.

The extras may have been simpletons, but they understood the concept of flash flood, and there were grumblings as they glanced nervously westward at the black clouds crossing the desert toward them. How long would the filming take? they wondered. Would they be taken to high ground once the storm hit? Did they get paid extra for working under bad weather conditions?

Umaid Bhawan, the top-ranking mujahideen at the site quickly took control of the situation. He picked out the extra who was doing the most complaining, paid him the agreed-upon fee for his services, then told him to take off his outfit and go home.

"Home?" the man said. "It is twenty miles back to Jodhpur!"

"Enjoy the walk," Bhawan told him.

The man had a sudden change of heart and decided perhaps he would stick around for the shooting after all. The others fell in line, and the mutiny was quickly quelled.

Six minutes later, an Antonov An-12 cargo plane dropped below the cloudline and came to a landing on a flat stretch of desert adjacent to the film site. Stenciled on the rear tail fin was a large *J* in the shape of a flexing bicep, the logo for Jahan Filmworks. The Antonov, a one-time Aeroflot workhorse, had an up-swept tail to accommodate its rear loading ramp, and by the time Bhawan and two other mujahideen posing as prop masters reached the plane, the cargo crew was already unloading the fancified shell for the colonists' war tank. They'd gone ahead and affixed the shell to a Humvee, allowing them to drive it down the ramp. Behind the ''tank'' was a late-model Dodge Ram pickup, its rear bed stacked with smaller clip-on attachments designed to give a futuristic look to a range of .50-caliber and 7.62 mm machine guns.

While Bhawan was signing off on the delivery, the cargo foreman wondered if it would be possible for his crew to stick around and watch some of the filming. Bhawan's first reaction was to tell the man that wasn't possible, because the plane would be in the way of some of the shots. But when he glanced up the ramp and saw that there was room inside for all his men, he decided the Antonov might be a more useful, and less conspicuous, escape vehicle than the Aero Spacelines Guppy that was doubling as the Martian warship.

Bhawan made a deal with the cargo carriers. They could watch the filming for a few minutes, provided they would then board their craft and have it ready to take off at a moment's notice. ''In case we need to evacuate because of the monsoon,'' Bhawan explained.

The cargo foreman glanced back at the storm front

and figured that gave them a good half hour. Bhawan
indicated an area they could watch from without getting in anyone's way, then headed off to assist in the
delivery of the new props.

"Incidentally," he called back over his shoulder,
"under no circumstances are you allowed anywhere
near the white tent. It is the stars' quarters and they
do not care to be disturbed while they are preparing
their roles."

The cargo foreman nodded and promised his men
would keep their distance.

There was room in the back of the pickup for Bhawan. He climbed aboard and signaled for the driver
to circle around the costumed Hummer and lead the
way to the tent. On the way he checked his watch.
Half an hour was cutting it close. They would have
to work fast.

The tent, flapping in the wind, was large, covering
five thousand square feet. Backed up to one of the
side panels was an eight-wheel truck with the Jahan
logo emblazoned on its side. Bhawan directed the
Dodge around to the other side, where two more mujahideen held open flaps to create an opening for both
the pickup and Hummer.

Inside the tent there were neither film stars nor any
of the amenities they would have likely demanded for
having to endure the discomfort of desert filming. Instead, there were three wooden crates, one packed
with M-60 machine guns, another with shorter-
barreled .50-caliber weapons. The third crate—by far
the longest—contained four Sabre surface-to-air missiles. The Kashmiris who'd opened the tent fold

quickly returned to their task, taking machine guns from the crates and affixing them to their mounts on one of the Desert Patrol Vehicles. Once the attachments were clamped over them, the guns would, like the DPV, look like space props. Hopefully, there would be time to bring the other vehicles in for retrofitting before it was time to launch the missiles.

Bhawan climbed out of the pickup and dropped the tailgate, then crossed over to where the missile launcher was being eased down a loading ramp from the rear of the eight-wheeler.

"Quickly!" he shouted to his fellow mujahideen. "We have only twenty minutes to disguise the launcher and load it. The firing is to begin at 1500 hours sharp!"

Bhawan lent a hand, helping to unfasten the tank casing from the Humvee. He and the others were carrying the shell over to the rocket launcher when they heard, over the loud flapping of the tent's canvas, the sound of an approaching aircraft. Unlike other planes they'd heard on and off the past few hours, this one, like the cargo plane, sounded as if it were flying lower, perhaps even coming in for a landing.

Cursing, Bhawan told the men to set down the shell and grab their weapons. He snatched an M-60 from one of the crates and hurried out of the tent, ready to fend off whoever it was who dared intrude upon their mission. His urgency faded, however, when he recognized Abdul Jahan's private helicopter and, more importantly, the man who was riding in the passenger seat.

"Dehri!" Bhawan set the M-60 aside and rushed

to the chopper as it set down on the hardpan near the white tent.

Neshah climbed out, ducking to avoid the rotors as he jogged away from the chopper, which lifted off and headed toward Jodhpur, where the pilot planned to wait out the storm before returning to Bombay. By some quirk of fate, Neshah let the man live.

"You made it!" Bhawan told Neshah. "How did we fare in Bombay?"

Neshah stared solemnly at Bhawan and shook his head. While in the air, he'd monitored newscasts over the radio and learned of Shili's failure to take out the President and prime minister. Without mentioning the still-present Sabre threat, both leaders had given a brief statement saying that they were going to focus their fullest efforts on eradicating the mujahideen threat in India and getting Pakistan to renounce its ties to the insurgents.

"Our backs are to the wall," Neshah told Bhawan. "We must succeed here or we are finished."

"I understand," Bhawan said. Trying to bolster his leader's spirits, he added, "But if we *do* succeed here, everything will change. We will yet have our chance at glory."

CHAPTER TWENTY-FOUR

Thar Desert, North of Jodhpur

A number of caravan routes fanned out northward from Jodhpur, most of them used by tourists taking day trips into the desert so they could—at least in their own minds—have a taste of what it must have been like to have been Lawrence of Arabia. Only two of the routes continued as far as the movie set; one used by tourists hearty enough for a week-long trek to Jaisalmer, the other part of an ancient trail long used by merchants shuttling their wares from city to city north of the Aravalli Mountain Range.

Mack Bolan, John Kissinger and Jack Grimaldi had decided on the latter route. To any mujahideen lookouts posted along the trail, it would make sense that merchants, rather than tourists, would continue to venture along the trail despite an approaching monsoon that stirred up clouds of dust reducing visibility every bit as much as a snow blizzard in the Himalayas. By the same token, one would expect the camels in a merchant caravan to be loaded with wares. The men could pack their weapons and other munitions without drawing undue notice.

There were forty camels in the procession, trodding across the sand in single file, less than a yard between one and the next. Only thirteen of the humped beasts bore riders; the other twenty-seven were heavily laden with cargo. All in all, it was the same sort of formation that had religiously passed by the film site every day at this time—same number of riders, same amount of cargo, same slow, deliberate pace.

The Stony Man warriors weren't among those astride the camels. Along with a dozen members of the Rajasthan Desert Militia, Bolan, Kissinger and Grimaldi rode alongside the far side of the beasts' humps, each man lying on his side within the webbing of a woven rope cargo sling. There were more comfortable ways to travel, to be sure. With each step the camels took the rope chafed against the men's skin and clothing like a blunt, bristly edged knife. And, too, they were facing the sun, and there was enough of it streaking through the sweeping dust clouds to make the men feel as if they were being roasted on a spit. There was a reason for the ploy, of course. At one point the trail not only wound to within a hundred yards of the film site, but it also passed behind a sand dune fifteen feet high and nearly forty-five yards across. The dune would provide the men the cover behind which they could make their move.

As soon as he heard one of the camel drivers trill on a panpipe, Mack Bolan unsheathed a trench knife and cut through enough of the webbing to free one arm. He reached up over the camel's hump, grabbing hold of a thicker length of rope knotted around the saddle pommel. He quickly untied the knot and yanked on the rope, pulling over a saddlebag weighed down with two twenty-pound sacks of flour. He did the same with one more pouch, then hacked some more at the sling webbing until, like a monarch wriggling from its cocoon, he was able to crawl free. All the while, he continued to hold on to the mesh, however, and it wasn't until he'd dragged over another three saddle packs that he let go, leaving the camel's load properly counterweighted. He stepped back and patted the camel's hindquarters to urge it along, then joined Kissinger, Grimaldi and the RDM soldiers— all of whom had similarly cut themselves loose—and proceeded to the dune.

An RDM sniper quickly broke out a Priva Mechanical Crossbow and began to assemble it. The weapon was similar to the Barnett Commando, which Bolan had used with success on a number of missions, but this was the RDM's turf and he was content to let their man do the honors of taking out the nearest mujahideen sentry. It left him free to see what they were in for should they be able to reach the film site. Grimaldi and Kissinger joined him as he peered over the top of the dune. All three men wore wraparound goggles to keep the stinging sand from their eyes.

"What a goofy-ass batch of spacemen," Grimaldi remarked, catching a glimpse of the costumed extras, who were easy to see through the dust clouds. "They look like rejects from the last Power Rangers movie."

"There are at least forty of them," Bolan said, peering through his binoculars. "Goofy looking or not, if they're all mujahideen we're in for a fight."

"And who knows how many others might be hanging out in the planes," Grimaldi said. "That Guppy especially could hold a good twenty, thirty guys."

"Those space rifles they're carrying look like the real deal," Kissinger observed. "M-50s in sheep's clothing, I think."

"I was wondering about that," Bolan whispered. "Those DPVs coming out from that tent look like they've strapped on some real heat, too."

Bolan was concerned about the sandstorm. Sure, it gave them some extra cover, but it would also hinder the approach of backup forces and possibly work against them if things turned into a firefight; the mujahideen, after all, were more familiar with the film site and could use the knowledge to their favor.

Moments later, the main flaps to the white tent parted and out rolled a futuristic-looking tank, perhaps two-thirds the size of the crimson LVTP-7 AMTRACs. Six men walked out alongside the weapon. Attempting to focus on them through the binoculars was like trying to pull in a television station with a weak signal; the airborne sand obscured everything in sight. Whether it was something about the way the men carried themselves or the fact that none of them wore costumes, Bolan felt in his gut that these were more than mere grips hauling out another prop. One man seemed to be in charge, and he moved about the tank, gesticulating at the others to make sure they positioned it correctly. From this distance and through the sandstorm it was impossible to get a good look at the man's face, but Bolan recognized the hand gestures and gait from video footage he'd studied back at the Farm several days before setting out for India.

"Neshah," he murmured. "Front guy on the right."

"How can you be sure?" Kissinger said.

"It's him," Bolan said.

"In that case," Grimaldi said, "my money says his little space tank is our missing Sabre launcher."

Bolan nodded. "We're in business."

"Should we just rush them?" Kissinger wondered.

Bolan shook his head. "They've got home-court advantage," he said. "We'd only be playing into their hands."

"Well, we can't just inch forward every time we manage to take out a sentry," Grimaldi said. "If they're aiming to get off a few missiles before the storm hits, we need to beat them to the punch."

"Agreed," Bolan said. "But there's got to be a better way than just charging into their guns."

Kissinger patted his knapsack. "I could lob a fireball. If I miss the launcher, I might at least hit the tent, and I'll give you ten-to-one it's not fireproof."

Bolan thought it over. "I like the idea, but I'd rather we got closer so the wind's not working so much against you."

"How about the cargo plane?" Grimaldi ventured, pointing to the aircraft, less than eighty yards to their right on the other side of the dune.

"What about it?" Kissinger said.

Grimaldi quickly laid out the plan he had in mind. When he was finished, Kissinger and Bolan exchanged a look. Then the Executioner told Grimaldi, "It's worth a shot."

"All right!"

"Just wait until the first sentry goes down," Bolan said.

"No problem."

They didn't have long to wait. The RDM sniper had finished assembling his Priva MC. Aside from the actual crossbow, the weapon bore little resemblance to its medieval counterpart. With a full-fledged stock, fore grip, trigger and shoulder stock, it looked more like a submachine gun equipped with handlebars. Once he'd tautened the bowstring and fitted a bolt into the receiver, the sniper lined up his sights and drew a bead on the mujahideen sentry, who had his back to the sandstorm and was hunched over, hands cupped to his face as he tried to light a cigarette. He was still trying moments later when the crossbow shaft suddenly sprouted from his neck, dropping him to the sand.

"All right, let's go!" Bolan hissed.

Along with the RDM, the three Stony Man warriors cleared the rise and charged quietly down the other side of the dune. Grimaldi quickly veered to his right, heading for the cargo plane. Bolan and Kissinger, on the other hand, jogged left, their destination one of the red LVTP-7 AMTRACs parked close by the Guppy.

As HE WATCHED the disguised Sabre system being taken through its prelaunch checks, Dehri Neshah stared out at the film site. If they were actually filming, he mused, the sandstorm would have been a good effect. It gave the set an otherworldly feel and made the costumes and props all look a little less garish.

Ironically, the script—an amateurish student effort Briley had secured for the mujahideen by sleeping with a film-school instructor back in London—had mentioned something about the final conflict taking place in a swirl of mysterious gas emitted by the moon craters. It wasn't the only parallel between the script and the real-life events it had become party to. In the movie, the overmatched moon colonists were on the verge of extermination when they made their final stand against the Martian invaders, triumphing thanks to the so-called trans-quasar recombinant energy cannon the hero had managed to create out of odds and ends scavenged from a lunar scrap yard. While Neshah and the mujahideen had gotten their hands on a prebuilt launcher, coming up with a way to disguise and fire it without enemy detection had required equal cunning. And now, once the countdown was completed and the missiles were launched, their "cannon" would irrevocably turn the tide of battle in their favor. Even if the enemy sent out interceptors, it was unlikely that they would be able to take out more than one or two of the missiles. The others would hit their mark, and the finger-pointing would begin. India and Pakistan would go at each other like rabid dogs. Neshah and the others, meanwhile, would board the cargo plane and fly to Kashmir, where they would patiently await for the forces of New Delhi and Islamabad to neutralize each other. After that, well, they would see.

"How much longer?" he asked Bhawan.

Bhawan conferred with the technician, who was busy establishing trajectory and target coordinates. He turned back to Neshah.

"Two minutes to countdown."

INSIDE THE FRONT cabin of the cargo plane, the pilot smirked as he unscrewed his thermos and refilled his teacup. Through the windshield he could see his fellow workers huddled close, backs to the storm, as they stared out at the film site. How could they, after years of working behind the scenes, still see moviemaking as magical? Didn't they realize that shooting would likely be delayed, if not postponed, because of the weather? And even if the weather had been perfect, they could spend the whole day here without witnessing anything like the final product that wound up on the screen. The war scenes they watched would consist of, at most, a few minutes of filmed action, followed by hours of idle time as sets were moved and the lighting and sound crew moved in to tinker with all their gizmos until the director was satisfied that everything was just right, at which point they'd shoot another fraction of a scene and then begin the process again all over.

Let them suffer, he figured. He'd sit up here in the air-conditioned cockpit and enjoy his tea.

The pilot was adding sugar to his cup when he heard the cabin door open. He hadn't bothered to lock it, figuring there was no reason to. Jack Grimaldi— who'd circled behind the plane and entered by way of the loading ramp—stepped into the cockpit, aiming his Grizzly pistol at the pilot.

"Step aside, Clyde," he told the pilot. "I've always wanted to take one of these babies for a spin."

BOLAN AND Kissinger were halfway to the nearest amphibious tractor when one of the retrofitted DPVs appeared out of the nearest sand cloud and roared to a stop, allowing its tail gunner to take aim with his 7.62 mm machine gun. Both men dived as rounds tore through the sand where they'd been standing.

Lying on the ground, Bolan brought his Desert Eagle into target acquisition and returned fire, sights on the patrol vehicle's driver. One shot found its mark, striking the driver just below the helmet. He died behind the wheel, a hole in his forehead, the bullet burrowed deep inside his skull.

Kissinger, meanwhile, continued rolling as 7.62 mm rounds chased him across the desert floor. When there was a lull in the firing, he bounded to his feet and emptied his Colt at the tail gunner. The mujahideen took a trio of 9 mm slugs across the upper chest and slumped against the roof rack.

Two desert militia soldiers joined in the fray, but their shots were wasted, plowing into men who were already dead. Bolan signaled for them to go ahead and take the DPV, indicating that he and Kissinger wanted dibs on the AMTRAC.

The LVTP-7 was little more than an armor-plated carrier mounted on treads. Unlike a tank, its turret wasn't fitted with a cannon but rather a meager 12.7 mm machine gun, and that gun was absent from

this AMTRAC. Helpful to Bolan and Kissinger, however, was the outer prop shell, which provided them
with a three-foot-high wall behind which to hide.
While Bolan stood watch, Kissinger hurriedly set out
his DHL and began to assemble it. The men thought
the vehicle was unmanned and both were surprised
when the turret's hatch suddenly swung open. Bolan
whirled about and was ready to fire when he saw a
man climb out with his hands held high in surrender.

"Nice call," Bolan held his fire. "Now, if only
your buddies would follow suit."

NESHAH WAS on the alert from the moment he heard
the first gunshots. He shielded the stinging dust from
his face with one hand while he unholstered his pistol
with the other. The shooting was taking place slightly
downhill, beyond the Guppy and the farthest of the
AMTRACs, and there was little he could see but the
clouds of sand. The extras, of course, were either
cowering in the sand or running in all directions like
frightened children, but Neshah's men, he was proud
to see, had responded quickly to the intrusion. He saw
them, blurry silhouettes of red and silver, plodding
through the sandstorm toward the action, firing their
M-60s.

Then, atop the farthest of the tractor tents, Neshah
saw the upper torso of a mujahideen holding his arms
held high in surrender. Enraged, the Kashmiri raised
his weapon, drew aim and fired. Fourteen shells flew
out of the gun's ejection port as he emptied the
weapon at the AMTRAC. The man atop the vehicle

twisted to one side and dangled briefly over the side of the raised wall, then tumbled down to the ground.

"Coward!" Neshah looked around him as he howled to the others, "No retreat! No surrender!"

As he was shouting, Neshah saw movement to his left and turned. The cargo plane had begun to move. Instead of heading down the makeshift runway, the plane turned slightly and began to move toward the set. The cargo's employees, who'd been standing nearby admiring how realistic the action seemed to be, glanced over their shoulders and then scattered as the plane rolled past them.

Neshah realized what was happening and turned to the technicians, commanding them to begin the countdown.

"But we have to finish the prelaunch—"

"Begin the countdown!" Neshah repeated, slamming a fresh magazine into the handle of his Taisho pistol. "Tack on a few seconds if you have to, but move it up! Go!" He turned to Bhawan, now his second in command.

"We have to stop that plane!"

Bhawan nodded. One of the Desert Patrol Vehicles was emerging from the tent, newly outfitted with its decorated machine guns. Bhawan stepped in front of the vehicle and motioned for the driver and tail gunner to get out.

"I'll drive!" Neshah said, giving the driver a hand out of the vehicle and then climbing in. That left Bhawan to take up the rear. He was only halfway into the caged quarters when Neshah put the DPV into gear and pulled away.

Now they began to see some of the enemy approaching. Bhawan stopped a few RDM footsoldiers in their tracks with a burst of rounds. Then, materializing out of the smoke, they saw camels. Their riders, RDM cavalry soldiers no longer masquerading as caravan merchants, had doubled back at the first exchange of gunfire. Armed with MP-5s, they fired down at the costumed mujahideen. One of the camels was hit by return fire and toppled headfirst into the sand, throwing its rider from the saddle. Neshah veered the DPV and passed alongside the fallen militia officer. He slowed long enough to put his gun to the man's head and pull the trigger. In slowing, however, he'd also allowed other RDM troopers to take aim at the patrol vehicle. Gunfire converged on the vehicle from three different directions. Bhawan took the worst of it, dying in the gunner's post with shots through the head and upper torso. Neshah felt a slug lodge in his shoulder but tried to ignore the pain. Hands on the steering wheel, he drove on, heading toward the approaching plane.

As HE SMASHED the cargo plane through a length of cyclone fence and bore down on the missile launcher, Grimaldi kept reminding himself of Kissinger's assurances that the missiles most likely wouldn't detonate if crushed under the moving bulk of the Antonov. Now he wished Cowboy had been a little more specific. What kind of odds did ''most likely'' amount to? Were they ten to one in his favor, five to one? Or was it worse than that? Was there as much as a forty percent chance that tourists a year from now would be flocking here to see Jodhpur Crater, the largest divot on the entire subcontinent?

As if this weren't a troubling enough distraction, Grimaldi now saw a Desert Patrol Vehicle emerging from the storm clouds and bearing down on him. The DPV could never hope to win a head-on collision, but if it managed to clip the Antonov's front wheel at the right angle, Grimaldi knew it could well thwart his chances of reaching the launcher before it fired its missiles.

"This should be interesting," he murmured, holding his course.

BY THE TIME Kissinger had assembled his Dragon's Hairball Launcher, a lull had settled over the film sight. The wind had died down, dropping sand from the air and giving a clear view of the short-term carnage that had been wreaked thus far. There were bodies everywhere. Thankfully, no one had emerged from the Guppy, and the men from Stony Man Farm hoped it stayed that way.

Kissinger was about to draw aim on the missile launcher when he saw Neshah racing toward the cargo plane in the DPV. A stunned extra in a colonist outfit found himself in the vehicle's path and tried to duck away. He chose the wrong direction and the patrol vehicle sent him flying over the hood and up past the gunnery cage, where Bhawan slumped dead behind the 7.62 mm machine gun.

"Can you take him out?" Bolan asked Kissinger.

"Easier said than done," Kissinger responded. He'd never tried firing the DHL at a moving target,

and though the obvious strategy was to shoot ahead
of the DPV in hopes the vehicle would drive into the
path of the incendiary load, if he overfired he stood
a greater chance of hitting the Antonov and turning
Grimaldi into toast.

"Just take your best shot," Bolan urged him.

Kissinger drew in a deep breath and slowly pulled
the trigger. The DHL slammed into his shoulder as it
fired. Both he and Bolan watched the charge converge
on the patrol vehicle. Erring on the side of caution,
Kissinger had aimed short, striking the ground several
yards behind Neshah. However, on impact the resul-
tant fireball rolled forward, carried by momentum,
and fanned out as it engulfed the rear end of the DPV.
All it took was one flicker to the fuel tank and the
patrol vehicle exploded, stopping in its tracks. Neshah
was killed instantly.

As smoke rose from the fiery remains of the DPV,
Bolan and Kissinger watched Grimaldi bear down on
the missile launcher. The countdown was into its final
seconds, and through his binoculars Bolan could see
one of the mujahideen raise his right hand and, one
by one, retract his fingers.

Five, four, three, two...

The counter looked up, eyes widening in terror as
he saw the nose of the Antonov sweep over him.
There was a sickening crunch as he fell under the
cargo plane's wheels, followed by the much louder
crashing of the Antonov's fuselage dragging itself
across the concealed missile launcher. The prop firing
tubes snapped like celery stalks, sending the missiles
sliding their racks into the sand. Kissinger would have

collected in Vegas because, as he'd predicted, none of the warheads detonated, even when the disabled launcher was dragged across them by the cargo plane.

Within seconds after the aircraft came to a halt, the monsoon swept across the film site and the heavens opened up. Rain pounded the sand. Bolan and Kissinger bounded down from the AMTRAC and began helping the desert militia round up the surviving extras and mujahideen. Contrary to their leader's orders, the remaining Kashmiris readily surrendered.

They knew it was over.

EPILOGUE

Stony Man Farm, Virginia

Unlike Ziarat Wal, the men of Stony Man Farm received neither medals nor parades to honor their valor and courage on the field of battle. As they touched down on the Farm's camouflaged runway in the private Cessna that had brought them from Dulles International Airport, the most Mack Bolan, Jack Grimaldi and John Kissinger were hoping for was a decent meal and hopefully a good night's sleep before their next call to arms.

A few farmhands doing chores in the nearby orchard glanced up and offered the men faint nods as they deplaned. Other than that, the only other people who'd come out to welcome them back were Hal Brognola, Aaron Kurtzman and Barbara Price.

After warm, if perfunctory, greetings were exchanged, the six headed on foot toward the main house. Brognola and Kurtzman pigeonholed Grimaldi and Kissinger, pressing them for details about the mission, leaving Bolan and Price to walk alone a few steps behind. As always, in the name of propriety they walked a distance apart from each other; Bolan and

Price both had an unspoken pact not to make a public issue of their relationship. At times like this it wasn't easy, however. Price had anxiously monitored the turmoil the men had faced, and she could see that Bolan had brought back fresh scars from the war zone. There were certain things a woman wanted to do with a man after their separation was marked by a brush with death.

For his part, Bolan, despite his fatigue, felt a familiar stirring at the smell of Price's hair in the late-summer breeze. Sure, he was exhausted, but there would be time for sleep. Later.

"It's Labor Day," Price reminded him as they neared the main building, where she maintained her living quarters.

"Slipped my mind completely," Bolan said.

"I've always been fond of picnics on Labor Day," Price said.

Bolan glanced up at the sky. Dark clouds were gathering; nothing as severe as what he'd seen in India but threatening nonetheless.

"Looks like rain," he said.

Price smiled. "Then I guess we'll just have to do our picnicking indoors."

Bolan glanced at the woman and grinned, telling her, "I like the way you think."

JAMES AXLER

DEATH LANDS®

Breakthrough

Deathlands is a living hell, but there is someplace worse: a parallel Earth where the atomic mega-cull never happened. Now, this otherworld Earth is in its final death throes. Yet, for an elite few, the reality portal offers a new frontier of raw energy, and expendable slaves—a bastion of power for Dredda Otis Trask. Her invasion force has turned the ruins of Salt Lake City into the deadly mining grounds of a grotesque new order—one that lies in wait for Ryan and his companions.

In the Deathlands, danger lurks beyond the imagination.

*Available in March 2002
at your favorite retail outlet.*